DAYS OF UTTER DREAD

Also by Graham Masterton

Horror Standalones
Black Angel
Death Mask
Death Trance
Edgewise
Heirloom
Prey
Ritual
Spirit
Tengu
The Chosen Child
The Sphinx
Unspeakable
Walkers
Manitou Blood
Revenge of the Manitou
Famine
Ikon
Sacrifice
The House of a Hundred Whispers
Plague
The Soul Stealer

THE SCARLET WIDOW SERIES
Scarlet Widow
The Coven

THE KATIE MAGUIRE SERIES
White Bones
Broken Angels
Red Light
Taken for Dead
Blood Sisters
Buried
Living Death
Dead Girls Dancing
Dead Men Whistling
The Last Drop of Blood

THE PATEL & PARDOE SERIES
Ghost Virus
The Children God Forgot
The Shadow People

DAYS OF UTTER DREAD

Graham Masterton
with Dawn G Harris

An Aries Book

First published in the UK in 2022 by Head of Zeus Ltd,
part of Bloomsbury Publishing Plc

Copyright © Graham Masterton and Dawn G Harris, 2022

The moral right of Graham Masterton and Dawn G Harris to be
identified as the authors of this work has been asserted in accordance
with the Copyright, Designs and Patents Act of 1988.

All rights reserved. No part of this publication may be reproduced,
stored in a retrieval system, or transmitted in any form or by any means,
electronic, mechanical, photocopying, recording, or otherwise, without
the prior permission of both the copyright owner
and the above publisher of this book.

This is a work of fiction. All characters, organizations, and events
portrayed in this novel are either products of the author's
imagination or are used fictitiously.

9 7 5 3 1 2 4 6 8

A catalogue record for this book is available from the British Library.

ISBN 9781035905355
ISBN (E): 9781804542194

Cover design: Nina Elstad

Typeset by Siliconchips Services Ltd UK

Printed and bound in Great Britain by
CPI Group (UK) Ltd, Croydon CR0 4YY

Head of Zeus Ltd
First Floor East
5–8 Hardwick Street
London EC1R 4RG

www.headofzeus.com

*In Memory of Friends We Have Lost
James Herbert and Jeff R. Milchard*

'Those are the days when we wake to realise that we are one day closer to the coffin-lid being closed over us, blotting out the light forever.

'Those are the days when we are aware that we are nothing more than a collection of random atoms that have temporarily clotted together to be us.

'Those are the days when we fear how easily we could be ripped apart, long before we have enjoyed the time that should have been ours, causing us terror and agony beyond description.

'Those are the days of utter dread.'

Manfred Waffenmeister, *Das Buch der Angst*, 1934

CONTENT WARNING

This contains extreme adult content and exploration of subjects that will not be suitable to all reading tastes.

CONTENTS

Stranglehold (with Dawn G Harris)
Half-Sick of Shadows
On Gracious Pond
National Balance
Cutting the Mustard (with Dawn G Harris)
A Portrait of Kasia
The Greatest Gift
Epiphany
The Red Butcher of Wrocław
Cheeseboy

STRANGLEHOLD

With Dawn G Harris

'Do you accept clothes from dead people?' the girl asked, peering short-sightedly into the cramped back office of the animal charity shop.

Lillian looked up to see a skinny and nervous-looking young woman, her face half-masked by her long dark hair, her hand quivering as she held out a half-filled bin liner.

'My uncle died. He had a cat. I thought he'd want it all to come here.'

As the girl spoke, Lillian unaccountably felt a shiver run down her back and along her arms, but she gave the girl a quick smile and stood up, and stepped out of her office to take the bag. The girl's hair swung back, and Lillian saw that the left side of her face was twisted and scarred, as if she'd been burned as a child, and that while her right eye was dark brown, her left eye was black and glassy.

'Thank you,' she said. 'I'm sure that whatever is in here will raise some money to help our animals.'

As she took the bag she saw that the girl's hands were dirty, and that there were crescents of mud or dried blood under her fingernails. The bag felt strangely warm, and smelled of dirty clothing, but she said nothing. She had been managing this charity shop for nearly three years now, and she had accepted far more repulsive donations than this. She looked kindly into the girl's good eye and cradled the bag as appreciatively as if it were her uncle's cat itself.

'Please – you *will* take very good care?' said the girl. Her hair fell back to cover the melted side of her face, and then she turned and walked out of the shop.

Lillian carried the bin liner through to the back of the shop and tugged on a pair of blue nitrile gloves. Normally, for health and safety reasons, she would have emptied the contents slowly onto the sorting table, but the eeriness of the girl's appearance and the way she had said 'Please – you *will* take very good care' made her cautious. Once she had untied the bag she lifted it up and tipped all its contents onto the table in a heap.

A few pairs of smelly woollen socks fell out, then a faded blue shirt, an old electric razor, a bent Panama hat, a chunky jumper that was all rolled up, some T-shirts, and lastly a thick, brown, leather belt. The belt was well-worn, and its heavy buckle was shaped like a python's head, so that when it was done up it would appear as if it were swallowing its own tail. On the back of the belt some strange squiggly marks had been burned into the pale brown leather – கழுத்து நெரிக்கும் – which she assumed were some kind of decoration. She started to sort through the items, tossing the socks into the rags bin ready for collection on Tuesday.

She lifted the arms of the jumper and it felt heavy, as if there was something wrapped up inside it. When she picked it right up off the floor, ready to throw it into the rags bin along with the socks, a black cat tumbled out of it. A *dead* black cat, with its yellow eyes staring blindly and its tongue protruding from between its sharp, pointed teeth.

Lillian shrieked and stepped back, horrified that the girl with the melted face could have donated anything so disgusting as a dead cat.

'Oh, God!'

'Whatever is it?' called out Joyce, one of her volunteers. She came hurrying to the door from the shop floor.

'It's a *cat*!' said Lillian. 'Honestly, I thought I'd seen everything working here – dirty underwear, burned-out ironing boards, chamber pots with their handles broken off – but a dead cat! I can't believe it!'

'Black cats – aren't they a symbol of bad luck?' asked Joyce, peering at it over her glasses. 'Or is it good luck? I can never remember. But they're supposed to cross your path, aren't they? Not just lie there, dead.'

The next day, when Lillian opened up the store, she was surprised to see how tidy it looked. Yesterday, when she had left, the rail of newly donated clothing had looked messy and crammed, but now all the coats and dresses were hanging neatly, and all the accessories like ties and scarves and belts were hanging separately. Only one belt remained on the sorting table – the python's-head belt that had been brought in by the girl with the dark hair and the melted face. It was laid out dead straight.

She couldn't remember having tidied the shop up so well, but she had spent nearly twenty minutes on the phone arranging for the council to come and collect the dead cat, and then she had been cashing up the day's takings in her back office, so probably Joyce had been arranging everything while she was busy, and she had been too tired and preoccupied to notice.

She looked at the belt and she had a vision of the young girl's half-scarred face, and heard her voice saying 'you *will* take very good care', and for some reason she left the belt where it was, reluctant to touch it.

As the morning went on, the shop became busier. Several customers were attracted to a grey, striped shirt that had been donated by the young girl. When one woman held it up to show it to her friend, though, her little girl began to cry, and beg, '*Please, Mummy, put it back!*' She was almost screaming.

'Oh, for goodness' sake, what's the matter with you?' her mother snapped, and tugged her, still sobbing, out of the shop.

A middle-aged man with a large stomach and a comb-over had been rooting through the men's accessories but now he came up to Lillian and said, 'Not much of a selection, have you?'

'We can only sell what we're given, I'm afraid,' said Lillian. But then her eye fell on the leather belt with the python buckle. 'Here... how about this charming leather belt? Most unusual.'

She picked it up the belt and dangled it in front of

him. His eyes immediately lit up, and he almost snatched it from her. Then he stared at the python buckle as if he were hypnotised by it, and Lillian was sure that his eyes were gradually becoming bloodshot.

'I'll take it,' and reached into his jacket for his wallet, without once taking his eyes off the belt.

That evening, Lillian decided to cook herself a proper dinner: a roast chicken breast with broccoli and potatoes. She had been eating too many takeaways recently and putting on weight. As she was draining the water out of the potato pan, she glanced across at the small TV in the kitchen and froze. She slammed down the pan on the draining board, tugged off her oven glove and reached for the remote so that she could turn up the volume on the evening news.

'A forty-eight-year-old Banstead man was found dead this afternoon in his kitchen. He was named as Geoffrey Perkins, the owner of Perkins Carpets in the high street. Police have said that he was strangled with an unusual leather belt. His death appears to have been suicide because he was alone and the door to his flat was bolted on the inside, but police said that this is not conclusive since there were one or two unusual circumstances, although at this stage they declined to elaborate. Now for the local weather.'

Lillian switched off the sound. Her skin tingled as if she had suffered an electric shock, and for almost half a minute she stood in the middle of the kitchen just staring at the television screen. They had shown a picture of

Geoffrey Perkins on the news – smiling, standing by the sea somewhere. It was the same man who had bought the python belt, only this morning.

'You *will* take very good care,' the young girl with the melted face had told her. Supposing that had been a warning? After all, why had that little girl burst out crying when her mother had held up that grey striped shirt? What if there was something wrong with *everything* that she had donated from her dead uncle?

She went into the living room and picked up her mobile phone. She called Joyce, but all she heard was her voicemail.

'Joyce? It's me, Lillian. Listen – something awful has happened. First thing tomorrow we need to clear out some of the clothes that were donated yesterday – send them all to rag. Call me back as soon as you get this message.'

She sat down on the sofa. She didn't feel hungry any more. She wondered if she was just being hysterical. But she thought of the feeling that the python belt had given her – her instinctive reluctance to touch it – and the way that Geoffrey Perkins' eyes had appeared to turn red when he stared at it.

For the first time in a long time she wished that she and Jim hadn't broken up. Jim would have laughed and told her not to be so bonkers. But then that was one of the reasons why they had separated. Jim's idea of a supernatural event was West Bromwich Albion winning the FA Cup.

She had just finished the cheese-and-tomato sandwich that she had made for her lunch when the shop doorbell jangled.

It was the girl with the melted face again, carrying a plastic shopping bag. Her hair was windblown and she was out of breath, but Lillian noticed that she was wearing high-heeled black suede boots, so it was unlikely that she had been running.

'Got more for us, have you, love?' said Joyce, who was busy arranging the shelf of dog-eared, second-hand books, but the girl ignored her and weaved her way between the coat-rails and came straight up to Lillian.

'I was *sure* I'd given you this,' she said, holding up the shopping bag. 'I don't know… somehow I must have dropped it. I found it lying on my front garden path this morning.'

Lillian cautiously took the bag and looked inside. Curled up at the bottom of it was the leather belt with the python's head. She tipped it out with a clatter onto the sorting table, and there was no question that it was the same belt. She recognised the squiggly marks on it.

At first she couldn't think what to say. She felt as if she must still be asleep in bed, and this was nothing but a dream.

'You *did* give it to me,' she said, at last. 'You gave it to me, and we sold it.'

The girl stared at her with her single dark brown eye. 'Oh, Jesus,' she said. 'Are you sure?'

'Of course I'm sure. I can show you the receipt. We sold it to a man called Geoffrey Perkins. But haven't you seen the news this morning? He was found dead – strangled. They couldn't tell if it was suicide or not, but they said he was strangled by an "unusual leather belt". I was sure they must have meant this one.'

The girl said nothing but continued to stare at her. She didn't look down once at the belt, which had been slowly uncurling by itself and was now lying almost flat.

Lillian said, 'I don't see how it could have been, though, do you? Not if you found it on your garden path this morning. I mean, the police would have taken it away as evidence, wouldn't they?'

'If it had been a normal belt,' the girl said, her voice so quiet and husky that Lillian could hardly hear her over the shop's background music... Julie Bright singing '*I'm Not An Angel*.'. 'But it's not.'

'What do you mean? And – by the way – there's something else I have to ask you about. There was a dead cat among the clothes that you gave us. I very much hope that you didn't put it in that bag on purpose. I had to ring the council to take it away.'

'Ördög.'

'Sorry?'

'Ördög. That was the cat's name. He was my uncle's cat. In Hungarian *Ördög* means "devil." My uncle was half Hungarian. No, of course I didn't put Ördög in the bag. He must have crept in by himself, to follow my uncle's scent. He was devoted to my uncle and when my uncle died Ördög refused to eat. Perhaps he just died of hunger.'

'So what's not normal about this belt?'

The girl hesitated for a moment, looking around. Then she said, 'Is there somewhere we can talk in private?'

'Yes. Come into my office at the back. Joyce! Can you look after the shop for a while?'

She led the girl into the cramped office at the back. They

sat down at her desk, which was heaped with paperwork and cluttered with empty coffee mugs and pens and buttons and elastic bands and two pricing guns.

'I've told only one person this before,' said the girl. 'That was my teacher at school because I thought I could trust her, but I don't think she believed me because she never did anything about it.'

'Before you start, why don't you tell me your name?' said Lillian.

'Grace. My mother named me after Grace Kelly because she thought she was so beautiful. At least that was what my aunt told me. My mother and father both died in a car accident when I was three and I had to go and live with my aunt and my uncle.'

'I'm sorry.'

'Well, Grace Kelly died in a car accident, too, didn't she? Anyway, my aunt was very kind to me because she was my mother's sister, but my uncle resented that he had to take care of me. He was always shouting at me and slapping me. One night soon after I went to live with them, I had a dream that my mother and father were still alive and when I woke up and realised that they were both gone, I started to cry and cry and cry.

'My uncle came into my bedroom and shouted at me to shut up, but I was so sad that I couldn't. So he came back with a kettle full of boiling water and poured it over my head.'

'Oh, my God, Grace. But why were you allowed to stay with them, after that?'

'My uncle told the doctors that I had gone into the kitchen

and tipped the kettle over myself, and my aunt never said anything, so I can only imagine that he threatened to hurt her if she ever told anyone what had really happened.'

Grace turned around and looked behind her before she carried on, as if she were anxious that somebody else might be listening. Then she said, 'My uncle never showed any remorse. He always treated me as if it had been my fault that I was scalded. He was always brutal to me and I was bullied at school, too. The other kids used to call me Disgrace Face.

'When I turned thirteen my uncle started to abuse me, too. Or try to. He was always coming into the bathroom when I was having a bath, or asking me personal questions and touching me. I ran away twice but I had nowhere else to go and I was found both times and brought back.

'Then one day on my way back from school I went into that little shop at the end of the High Street – Magic Mirror.'

'I know it,' said Lillian. 'They sell all kinds of charms and amulets and Tarot cards and crystal balls and stuff like that, don't they?'

'I wanted to buy a bead bracelet because everybody at school had loads of them. But while I was looking at them the woman in the shop started talking to me. Right out of the blue she asked me if somebody was hurting me. I don't know how she guessed, but I said yes, even though I didn't tell her about my uncle. I was too scared to.'

Grace's eye began to glisten, and a single tear slid down her cheek.

'The woman went to the back of the shop and came

back with the belt. She said that I could borrow it, because nobody could ever own it, but I could keep it for as long as I needed it. She said it came from Sri Lanka, where they called it a *Kaluttu Nerikkum*. That's what's written on it, in Tamil. It means "stranglehold".'

'Go on,' said Lillian. She was beginning to feel distinctly apprehensive now, and she leaned sideways so that she could make sure that the belt was still lying on the sorting table.

'The woman said that so long as I had the belt in my possession, it would always protect me, and if anybody tried to hurt me, it would make sure that they never tried again. I didn't believe her, to tell you the truth, and I didn't want to take it, but in the end she insisted, especially when she offered to give me two bead bracelets for free. I kept the belt in the bottom of my wardrobe, and never really thought about it much. My aunt was ill then with leukaemia and my uncle was too busy taking care of her to bother about me.'

Grace wiped her eye with a crumpled tissue, and then continued.

'Two months ago, though, my aunt passed away. My uncle didn't come near me or say much to me for a while, but then two weeks ago he came into my bedroom in the middle of the night, naked and drunk. He got into my bed. I was struggling to push him off me when he suddenly started to make these choking sounds. He fell off the bed and onto the floor and when I switched on the light I saw that the wardrobe door was open and the belt was wrapped tight around his neck. He was staring at me and his face was purple.

'I confess that I didn't try to pull the belt off him. Perhaps I should have done, but in any case I don't think I would have been strong enough. I just sat there and watched him being strangled. When he stopped breathing I called for an ambulance, and soon after the ambulance arrived, the police came, too.'

'Why didn't the police take the belt away then?'

'Because it had gone.'

'I don't understand.'

'The paramedics managed to unwind it and take it off him, and they put it down on the floor next to the bed. But by the time the police came it had disappeared. The police looked everywhere for it, but they couldn't find it.'

'Didn't the police ask you what had happened? I mean, there was your uncle, in your bedroom, with no clothes on, and strangled to death.'

'I told them that he had tried to rape me, and I think they thought that he had wound the belt round his neck himself. You know, some people do that, don't they, half-choke themselves when they have sex?'

Lillian sat there for almost half a minute, saying nothing. Why in the world had Grace brought her uncle's old clothes here, let alone his dead cat and her python-buckled belt?

'Thank you so much for listening,' said Grace, as if she could read Lillian's mind. 'I came into the shop last week and I heard you talking to an old lady and I thought you'd be the kind of person who could understand, and just, well, listen without judging me.'

'Grace – I'm really sorry for what's happened to you

– but I really don't want your uncle's old clothes. I have no idea why but nobody wants to buy them. And most of all I don't want your belt. I don't believe in black magic but it almost seems like it's alive. And if it strangled poor Geoffrey Perkins, who's to say it's not going to strangle the next person who buys it?'

'But you *have* to take it. I'm giving it to you. Don't you see? I'll bet you anything the reason it strangled him was because it wanted to get back to me. It has such power, though, and if you're a vulnerable person it can make you feel so safe. He probably tried to stop it from getting away.'

'Grace, I don't want it. Take it out of my shop and get rid of it some other way. Chop it up. Burn it. Throw it down a drain. I don't care. And take the rest of your uncle's things back, too.'

Grace stood up. 'Too late,' she said. She pointed at Lillian and said, '*Kaluttu Nerikkum*, it's yours now. *Unakku en paricu*. The lady in the Magic Mirror told me to say those words when I found somebody to pass it on to. They mean: "It's my gift to you."'

'Grace—' Lillian protested, and stood up, too. But Grace turned around and walked quickly towards the shop door.

'Joyce – stop her!' Lillian shouted. Joyce dropped the CDs she was stacking and tried to seize Grace's sleeve, but Grace pushed her so hard that she lost her balance and fell backwards into a rack of overcoats. Before she could regain her balance, Grace had disappeared out of the door and into the street.

Lillian ran outside, but the pavement was too crowded with afternoon shoppers for her to see where Grace had gone.

She went slowly back into the shop. If Grace hadn't wanted to get rid of the belt, then she would have to. Maybe the lady at Magic Mirror would take it back. If not, she would have to cut it up herself.

'What was that all about?' asked Joyce, looking flushed.

Lillian didn't answer her but went over to the sorting table. The belt was gone. She wondered if she ought to be alarmed or relieved. She bent down and looked under the table, and under all the clothing racks and shelves, but there was no sign of it.

What were the words for passing the belt on to somebody else? *Unakku en paricu.* She would have to remember those, just in case.

Lillian had to finish the week's accounts that evening, so she stayed in the shop until late. Joyce had gone home by the time she closed her ledger, and it was dark outside. The street was deserted except for passing traffic.

She switched off the lights and set the alarm, taking a last look around. Then she went outside, closed the shop door and locked it top and bottom.

As she turned around, a bulky, shaven-headed man in a black Puffa jacket rammed himself into her, and pushed her so hard against the door that she heard the glass crack. She couldn't see his face clearly because the streetlight was behind him, but she could see his glistening eyes and she could smell the beer and stale cigarettes on his breath.

'*Get off me!*' she screamed at him, and beat at his jacket with her fists. But he clamped his left hand over her mouth, forcing his fingers between her lips and right up against her teeth, and with his right hand he tore open the front of her coat. She tried to drop to her knees but as she did so he pulled up the hem of her woollen dress and clawed at the waistband of her tights.

She bit his fingers and he growled, '*Bitch!*' and banged her head against the door, which almost concussed her.

'Just shut up and think yourself lucky!' he said, spitting in her face. He managed to drag one leg of her tights halfway down her thigh, and as he did so he pressed himself harder up against her and gave her a slobbery, stubble-prickled kiss on the cheek.

Suddenly, though, he gave a seismic shudder, as if he were having an epileptic fit. For a split second he went totally rigid, from head to foot, and let out a phlegm-thickened cough. Then, stiffly, he dragged his fingers out of her mouth, released his grip on her tights and drew his hand out from under her dress. With a gargling sound in the back of his throat, he staggered two steps backwards.

Lillian immediately ducked out of the doorway, but the man didn't try to stop her. He was standing with both hands held up to his neck and his gargling had turned into a series of thin rasping noises, like a locksmith filing a key. His white-coated tongue was hanging out, and his eyes were bulging out of their sockets as if they were going to pop.

Although she was backing away from him, Lillian saw the glint of silver around his neck. It was the python buckle. He was being strangled by the belt, the *Kaluttu Nerikkum*.

He pitched sideways with a thump and lay with his heels kicking against the pavement. Some teenagers on the opposite side of the road could see him, but they only jeered, because they probably assumed that he was drunk.

He lifted one hand towards Lillian and managed to choke out, '*Help me! Please! Help me!*'

Lillian stayed where she was, about five metres away from him. Now she knew what Grace must have felt as she watched her uncle being strangled. Cold, and unforgiving. She had never felt like this before, and she was shocked by her own heartlessness.

The man gave one last wheeze, and then his head fell back, and his arms dropped to his sides, and it was obvious that he had died.

Lillian took out her iPhone, thinking that she should call 999. But as she stood there, the belt unwound itself from the man's neck and started to slide across the pavement towards her.

'*So long as I had the belt in my possession, it would always protect me, and if anybody tried to hurt me, it would make sure that they never tried again.*'

It slid right up to her, and its python head touched her shoe. She hesitated for a moment, and then she bent down and picked it up. It had a tensile strength of its own, just like picking up a snake.

She opened her coat and buckled the belt around her

waist, the python head swallowing its own tail. She was still trembling from being attacked so violently, and her head throbbed where she had hit it against the door, but the belt made her feel strong, and peaceful, as if nothing bad could ever happen to her again. She dropped her phone back into her pocket.

'*One day I'll be an angel, wait and see!*' she sang softly to herself, as she walked to the station to catch the late train home. '*But now I'm still alive and fancy free!*'

HALF-SICK OF SHADOWS

He stood well back from the window, waiting for the wintry sun to sink behind the leafless poplar trees and bite into the edge of the roof. The paved courtyard between the apartment buildings filled up with shadow, and one by one the lights came on, and the evening's performances began.

In one fourth-storey window, high up to his left, he could see a Hispanic woman in a bright-red, sleeveless sweater, reaching up to her kitchen cupboard with tattooed arms, and bringing down a large casserole dish. In the next window, he could just make out the top of her husband's high black pompadour, as he slouched in his armchair watching television. The light from the television flickered and jerked, so that the interior of the apartment looked like an auto-repair shop.

Below him, to his right, an elderly woman in a grubby pink housecoat was bending over to feed her cats. Next door, two young children were sitting at their kitchen table, laboriously writing in their homework books. Immediately above them, a bald bespectacled man was sitting with a cello in between his knees, not playing, just staring into space as if he had forgotten all the music that he had ever learned.

When he had first moved here to Van Cortlandt Apartments, Jimmy had felt guilty about watching his neighbours as they went about living their daily lives. He had closed his blinds and tried to concentrate on writing his articles for *Manhattan Living*, *Architectural Review* and *Realty Weekly*. But again and again he had been drawn to close his laptop, switch off the lights in his living room, and pull up the blinds again. Each window on the opposite side of the courtyard was a miniature theatre, and every evening he had over twenty different dramas to choose from.

The drama that he had been following most attentively was the continuing battle between a heavily built, middle-aged man and his much younger wife, a dark-haired woman who habitually wore far too much make-up. Jimmy had seen her sitting at her dressing table, peering into the mirror with utter self-absorption as she applied her thick scarlet lipstick. Then her husband would come in, and an argument would start. Jimmy could tell that the man was shouting because of the way he kept banging his right fist into the palm of his left hand. Sometimes he would storm out and slam the door behind him. Other times he would grab hold of his wife by the arms, shake her violently, and throw her onto the bed.

Jimmy had christened the couple Punch and Judy. In fact he had given names to all of the residents on the opposite side of the courtyard. The Huxtables – they were a black family, always smartly dressed, whom he had named after the characters in *The Cosby Show*. Then there were Milly, Molly and Mandy – three girls who shared one chaotically messy apartment. Milly and Molly were American Airlines flight attendants, and were always bringing different men home. They seemed to spend most of their evenings in their underwear, or their boyfriends' shirts and nothing else.

Most colourful of all were the Flying Burrito Family, an argumentative crowd of Mexicans, who he had named after the rock band. They were constantly rushing from room to room in brightly coloured T-shirts, squabbling and gesticulating.

The sad, bald cellist Jimmy had named Donald, after the late Donald Pleasence. Donald always wore brown.

On the second floor, between Punch and Judy and the Flying Burrito Family, there was an empty apartment with blacked-out windows. It had been empty ever since Jimmy moved in. But this evening, the lights were switched on, and a woman in a blue dress walked into the living room. She crossed over to the windows and Jimmy instinctively stepped back even further, in case she looked up to the third floor and saw him staring down at her. But without any hesitation. she reached up and drew the purple, loose-weave drapes across the window, and tugged them to make sure that they were tightly closed.

So – a new drama was beginning. A new soap opera to add to his evening entertainment. Even if she kept her drapes drawn together, he could see the woman's shadow crossing and recrossing the living room, like a figure in a Burmese puppet theatre.

She seemed to be alone. At least, hers was the only shadow he could see. Several times she walked through to the bedroom. She didn't switch on the bedroom light, but she didn't close the drapes, and enough light was falling across the corridor from the living room for him to see her lift a suitcase onto the bed, and start to unpack it. She had coppery, shoulder-length hair, which hid her face from him, but he could tell from her bearing that she was probably in her late twenties or early thirties. Tallish – maybe five-seven or five-eight even – and very large-breasted. So large-breasted that after a few minutes he went across to his bureau, opened the top drawer, and lifted out his racing binoculars.

Jimmy was always extremely cautious about using his binoculars, in case the lenses caught the light, and one of his neighbours realised that he was spying on them. He thought that if he ever got caught for peeping, he would probably die from humiliation. But he was fascinated by the way that all of these different lives unfolded in front of him, evening by evening. He had grown almost to love his neighbours, as if they were part of his extended family – even Punch and Judy and the lugubrious, bald-headed Donald. He felt that he was doing more than watching them – he was watching over them.

All the same, the woman in the blue dress had a spectacular figure. She was wide-shouldered, but she had narrow hips and endlessly long legs. He focused his binoculars on her, ready to put them down instantly if she came closer to the window. She leaned over her suitcase, and he could see deep into her cleavage, where a glittering gold star dangled.

Lucky star, he thought. *I bet it's warm where you are, star, and fragrant with perfume. Chanel, probably.*

He watched the woman for over an hour, although she spent most of that time in the living room and the kitchen, and so she appeared as nothing more than a provocative silhouette. He wondered what her name was, what she did for a living, and why she was alone. Maybe she was a divorcee, or had recently separated from her boyfriend. Maybe she was a call girl. Maybe she didn't like men at all, or maybe she preferred to live on her own. He decided to call her Annie, after Little Orphan Annie, because she had red hair, and she was alone.

At about 11:00 pm Annie switched off her living-room lights. She drew her bedroom drapes together, but only a little more than halfway, and he could see her staring down at the courtyard. Her bedroom was too shadowy for him to be able to make out her face in any detail, but she was very pale, as if she were the ghost of a woman who had lived there when she was a child, and was trying to remember what it had been like to be young, and alive.

Eventually she turned away, and he presumed that she had gone to bed. He stayed watching for a while, but then he went back to his couch and opened up his laptop. He had outstanding emails from South Korea and Australia, and one from the Colegio de Arquitectos de Chile, inviting him to give a talk in Ritoque, all expenses paid.

He was in the middle of writing back, accepting the Chileans' offer, when something made him stop, with his fingers poised over the keyboard. He sat there for a while, frowning, and then he laid down his PC, and returned to the window. On his stereo, Barbra Streisand was singing about love being evergreen.

Annie had switched on her bedside lamps, although she had left the drapes as they had been before, halfway apart. Inside, her bedroom looked inviting and warm, with a pale green patterned comforter diagonally pulled back across the bed, and dark green cushions and carpet. Annie was standing naked with her back to the window, her coppery hair spread out over her dead-white shoulders. But even though she had her back to him, there was a tall mirror on the opposite side of the bedroom, and he could see her full-frontal reflection with startling clarity.

He turned his head away. He didn't really know what to do. This was hard-core slot-machine-style Peeping Tomism. His decency told him to draw down his blinds and go back to his laptop and finish his reply to the Chileans. '*Gracias por su invitación buena. Me plazco decir "si"!*'

'Oh Jimmy-Jimmy-Jimmy,' he breathed. He was supposed to watch over these people. He was supposed to take care of them; or at least make sure that no great harm befell them. If Punch had started to beat up on his wife – like, seriously beat up on her, knocking her teeth out and blacking her eyes – Jimmy would have been round to their apartment so fast, hammering on the door. Or at least he would have dialled 911.

If the elderly lady in the grubby pink housecoat had taken a tumble while she was feeding her cat, Jimmy would have phoned for a paramedic. Or if he had seen any of those Mexican kids being mistreated, he would have informed children's services. They were totally unaware of it, the people who lived in Van Cortlandt Apartments, but Jimmy was their protector – their unseen, all-seeing, guardian angel.

Yet here he was, peering secretively into Annie's bedroom. And here was Annie's full-length full-frontal reflection, and she was wearing nothing at all, except for that glittery gold star.. What was he supposed to do? Turn away? Close his eyes and pray for redemption? She was standing completely still, her arms by her sides, staring at herself, and she had the faintest smile on her face.

If she moves, thought Jimmy, *then I'll stop looking. I'll go back to my laptop and finish my emails. If she moves, or if she starts to fondle herself, or anything like that, then I'll respect her privacy. Everybody is entitled to their privacy, even if they leave their bedroom drapes open and stand in front of a full-length mirror with the lights on.*

But Annie didn't move. She stayed motionless, still smiling at herself, as if she were hypnotised by her own flawlessness.

Jimmy felt hot. He wiped the perspiration from his forehead with the back of his hand and then he wiped his hands on his shirt. Goddamned heat in these apartments was always too high. Sometimes it made him feel as if he were suffocating. He glanced across at the binoculars on top of the bureau. *No*. That would be much too intrusive. It was obvious that Annie didn't realise that anybody was watching her. To stare at her through binoculars would be a breach of trust. A lack of human respect. Or something.

All the same, it wasn't as if he was going to rape her or anything. He wasn't even going to touch her, and what she didn't know couldn't hurt her, could it? And from the way she was admiring herself so intently, it was obvious that she was more than proud of her nudity. *I'll bet she's even modelled for* Playboy, *and if several million* Playboy *readers can ogle her in the nude, why shouldn't I?*

Jimmy propped his elbows on the windowsill so that he could focus the binoculars to pin-sharp detail. God, she was beautiful. Her red hair was soft and shining. Her eyes were as green as a cat's. She had high cheekbones and a tilted nose and lips that looked as if she had just finished kissing.

'Annie,' whispered Jimmy. 'You really are something.'

Although they were so big, her breasts were high and rounded, with the palest pink nipples. Her waist was narrow, and there was an emerald set in her navel to match her eyes. She held her hands together between her thighs in a pose that was modest and yet highly provocative, as if at any moment she might slyly choose to expose herself.

Jimmy stared and stared for almost a minute and then he deliberately fell back on the carpet and lay there, staring up at the ceiling tiles. He felt stunned. A goddess, he thought. A goddamned goddess, sent by God. Without any question Annie was the most beautiful girl that he had ever seen in his life. Even more beautiful than Evaline Chatwin, with whom he had fallen in love at Barnard College, when he was studying architecture, but who had always laughed at him and called him Frank Lloyd Wrong.

He sat up again, but while he had been lying on the floor Annie had switched off her lights. She still hadn't drawn her drapes, but her bedroom was too dark for him to see anything except shadows.

It took him a long time to go to sleep that night. When he did, he dreamed that he was crossing the courtyard in between the apartment blocks and entering the lobby on the opposite side. There was a thick rushing noise in his ears, like water running. He pressed the button for the elevator, but its door refused to open. He pressed it again and again, but still nothing happened. There was a small window in the door, however, and when he looked through it he could see Annie standing naked inside the elevator car, under a single bare lightbulb. She was trying to say something to him, but he couldn't hear her. When he shook his head to show her that he didn't understand, she came right up to the window and shouted at him. He thought she was shouting, '*You can't come in here! You mustn't!*'

The following evening, Jimmy had to attend a promotional party for *US Design* magazine at their glossy offices on Madison Avenue. It was the usual crowd of preening interior decorators in black shirts and arrogant celebrity architects with grey, swept-back hair and all of the scruffy bespectacled oddballs who designed peripherals such as bathroom faucets and light switches and kitchen cutlery drawers.

As he circled around the room, with a glass of warm red wine in one hand and a prawn canapé in the other, he saw several people he recognised, but he didn't feel very sociable tonight – at least, not to the extent of shouting about armchair designs for half an hour with perspiring men in overtight bow ties.

He went to the window and looked down over Madison Avenue. It was raining, and the glass was beaded with glittering droplets. He could see his reflection in the window, and he wondered if Annie was home yet, and whether she was standing in front of her mirror, admiring her nakedness.

He was still standing there, watching the endless stream of traffic below him, when he felt a tap on his shoulder. In the window, he saw a woman's face, and for one ridiculous second he thought it was her, but when he turned around it was a plumpish woman with a short black bob, with wide blue eyes and bright crimson lipstick. She was wearing a tight, brown, velvet dress with a plunging cleavage, which made her look like a burst-open bratwurst at a neighbourhood barbecue.

'Jimmy Lightoller!' she said, in a breathless little scream. Jimmy blinked at her. 'Heidi?' he ventured. 'Heidi Branning?'

She gave another little scream and flung her arms around him and gave him a sticky kiss directly on the lips. 'It's so good to see you! How long has it been? Look at you! You haven't changed one bit!'

'I don't know if that's a compliment or not,' he told her. 'You always used to say I was "visually unstimulating". Those were your exact words.'

'Oh, come on! It was only the way you dressed! Everybody else was walking around the campus like Goths, or punks, and you were dressed like a bank manager!'

'Well, *you've* sure changed,' he acknowledged. When he had known her at Barnard, she must have weighed at least 165 pounds. She had always worn black lipstick and her hair had reached down to her waist. They had slept together only once, after a very drunken party at a friend's loft in the East Village, but they had remained friends until they graduated.

'I'm working for Bloomingdale's now,' she told him. 'Interior design consultancy for people with more money than taste. How about you?'

'This and that. Writing articles, mostly, and lecturing. I worked for Minoru Yamasaki for a while – you know, the guy who designed the World Trade Center. But all I got to design was a glass-covered wheelchair ramp at Bellevue Psychiatric Unit.'

'You married?'

Jimmy shook his head. 'How about you?'

'No, me neither,' she said, and he could tell by the tone of her voice that there must have been somebody once, but she had lost him.

Jimmy looked around. 'How about splitting this place?' he suggested. 'I think I've had it up to here with posers. And all this boasting is giving me a migraine.'

'Okay, sure. Where do you want to go?'

'How about you come back to my place?'

He hesitated, wondering if he was making a ridiculous mistake. But he couldn't keep Annie to himself much longer. Somebody else had to see her. Somebody else had to know what he was feeling about her. And who better than Heidi, who had always understood him better than most?

In the taxi on the way to Van Cortlandt Apartments, Heidi reached across and held his hand, just the way she used to when they were students together. When Evaline Chatwin had knocked him back, she had hugged him tight and made him feel that she would always be there to comfort him, no matter what. He supposed, in a way, that he had loved her, and that she had loved him, but it had never been a passionate love. No fire, no danger, no excitement. Only a deep mutual affection, and a pleasure in each other's company.

'When we get to my apartment,' he said, 'there's something I have to show you.'

'You want me to see your etchings?'

He gave her the briefest of smiles. 'Actually, it's a person, rather than a thing.'

'A person? You have a partner? Are you gay?'

'No, no. Nothing like that. You'll just have to see for yourself.'

He opened a bottle of shiraz cabernet and they stood side by side in the darkness looking at all the apartment windows on the opposite side of the courtyard.

'This is just like *Rear Window*,' said Heidi. 'Did you see anybody murdered yet?'

'To tell you the truth, it makes me feel more than a little guilty. But it's not like I wish them any harm. I just like to watch them living out their lives.'

'Who's the guy on the exercise walker? The one with the muscles and the khaki T-shirt?'

'Him? I call him Punch. And the woman he lives with, I call her Judy. She's not home yet, by the look of it. But you wait. As soon as she comes in the door, they'll start arguing. Then he'll hit her. Then she'll laugh at him. Then he'll hit her again, until she stops laughing.'

'My parents were like that. Makes you wonder why they go on living together.'

Jimmy looked at her. 'I guess everybody needs somebody, when it comes down to it.'

Annie didn't come home until well past 10:00 pm, when they were already on their third glass of wine. By now, Jimmy had introduced Heidi to almost all of his ongoing soap operas – Punch and Judy; the Huxtables; the Flying

Burrito Family; Milly, Molly and Mandy; and Donald. But suddenly, Annie's living-room light was switched on, followed almost immediately by her bedroom light.

'She's back,' said Jimmy.

Heidi glanced across at him but said nothing.

After about ten minutes, Annie switched off the living-room light and appeared in the bedroom. She was wearing a dark-red dress, which she unzipped at the back, and stepped out of. Underneath she was wearing a red bra and a red thong.

Heidi cleared her throat. 'I think this is making me feel a little uncomfortable.'

'It's okay,' said Jimmy. 'We're not touching her. We're not doing her any harm.'

'You really have a *thing* for her, don't you?'

Jimmy continued to stare at Annie's bedroom window. She reached behind her to unfasten her bra, and then she sat down on the end of the bed to take off her thong. He could only see her back, however, because the full-length mirror was covered with a dark green sheet.

'I just wanted somebody else to see her,' said Jimmy. 'Somebody else apart from me.'

'Why?' She smiled. 'So that you wouldn't feel like such a pervert?'

'I don't know. If you could see a really handsome naked guy out of your window, waving his dick around, wouldn't you look?'

Heidi thought about it, and then she said, 'I guess I would, yes.' She paused. 'But not if he was a redhead.'

Annie went through to the bathroom. She stayed there for at least ten minutes, and Heidi started to grow fidgety.

'Maybe I should call it a night. This is all a little too weird for my taste.'

'Please,' said Jimmy. 'She shouldn't be long now.'

Annie came out of the bathroom with a towel around her waist, but almost immediately she took it off and threw it onto the chair beside the bed. Then she went up to the full-length mirror and stood in front of it, but she didn't pull the sheet off. She just stood there, almost as if she were tantalising herself with the anticipation of her own nakedness.

Heidi put down her wine glass and came up close to Jimmy, putting her arm around his waist. He looked down at her, and she looked up at him. He kissed her on the forehead, and then her lips. They were only quick kisses, but then she reached up and touched his cheek and kissed him back – and this time the kiss was long, and exploratory, and she closed her eyes.

'Heidi—' he said. But she raised her fingertip to her lips and said, '*Ssh.*' They both knew that what they were doing was strange, and maybe a little depraved, too, but this was one of those moments when the normal rules of morality were suspended. Annie would never know, and neither would anybody else.

They looked back to Annie's bedroom window. She had pulled the sheet away from the mirror now, and was standing in front of it, quite still.

Jimmy said nothing, but looked at Heidi to see what her reaction was.

'She's stunning,' said Heidi. 'I have to admit it. Even as a woman.'

She stared at Annie's reflection for a long time, and then

she turned around to face Jimmy. She kissed him, and kissed him again, and then she reached down and grasped the front of his pants.

'She turns you on, doesn't she?' she said. 'She really turns you on.'

'Heidi—'

'What? Maybe she turns *me* on, too.'

She kept her mouth pressed against his while she located his zipper and tugged it downward with three insistent jerks. Then her hand burrowed inside his boxers until she found his gradually stiffening erection. She pulled it out, quite roughly, and started to pump it, until it reared up hard and curved as a rhino horn.

She pushed him, two or three awkward steps, until he was stopped by the back of the couch. He perched himself on the edge of it, while Heidi dragged up her dress to her waist. Her thighs were big and white and soft, and she was wearing a tiny pair of black lace panties. She didn't take her panties off: she pulled them to one side so that her bulging bare lips were exposed.

She climbed onto him, panting with effort, lifting one heavy leg over the back of the couch and then the other. Then, awkwardly, she guided him inside her. She was very warm and very slippery.

'I should use a condom,' he said.

'No, you shouldn't,' she told him, burying her head in his chest. 'This isn't *me* you're making love to. It's her.'

'What?'

'Don't look at me. No – *don't look at me!* Look at *her*!'

Jimmy stared out of the window at Annie's naked reflection in her bedroom mirror, while Heidi rode up and down him, grunting and gasping. Annie's face was so calm and beautiful; her breasts so full; her legs so long. As Heidi bounced up and down in his lap, he wished only that Annie would take her hands away and expose herself, but she remained in that same self-protective pose.

For a split second, he really imagined that he was making love to Annie. He could feel her, he could smell her – that foxy smell of redheaded women when they become sexually aroused. He came, in three distinct jolts, and with each jolt he felt as if his back was breaking. Heidi gave a breathy shout, and then the two of them toppled off the back of the couch and onto the cushions.

They lay there, all tangled together, breathless, and they both started laughing. Then they both stopped laughing, and Jimmy kissed her, and they held each other like Hansel and Gretel, brother and sister, when they got lost in the forest and the robins covered them with leaves.

'You know something?' said Jimmy, as they disentangled themselves. 'I think you must be my best friend ever.'

'We should have married,' said Heidi. 'We could both have had affairs, to keep it spicy.'

Jimmy zippered himself up. 'How about another glass of wine? Are you hungry?'

Heidi pulled her dress down. 'I should go, really. What's the time?'

'Come on, have another glass of wine and a pastrami sandwich.'

'Well… okay. If you insist.'

He went into the kitchen, while Heidi went to the window and stared at Annie.

'It's very odd,' she said, after a while. 'But she looks kind of familiar, don't you think?'

'She reminds you of someone?'

'Yes, very much. But I can't think who.'

'There's a pair of binoculars on the side there. Just make sure you don't stand too close to the window with them.'

Heidi picked up the binoculars and focused on Annie's bedroom window.

'*My God*,' she said.

Jimmy paused in his sandwich-making and came to the kitchen door. 'What is it?' he asked her.

'It's Nadine Frost.'

'You're kidding me.'

'No, I'm not. I'm sure of it. It's Nadine Frost.'

Jimmy came over and took the binoculars from her. He trained them on the reflection's face, and Heidi was right. It *was* Nadine Frost.

'But she disappeared, didn't she?' said Jimmy. 'Her agent said that she never wanted to make another movie.'

'*Valley of Dreams*, that was her last picture,' said Heidi. 'I thought it was easily her best movie ever. I cried all the way through.'

Jimmy focused on Annie's reflection again. 'You're absolutely right, though. It's Nadine Frost. Nadine Frost with nothing on. But what the hell is she doing, living here? She must be worth millions.'

'Maybe she just wants to be left alone. You know, like Greta Garbo. She was the same.'

'I doubt if Greta Garbo stood stark naked in front of her bedroom window every evening, looking at herself in the mirror.'

As soon as he said that, Annie's bedroom light was switched off. Jimmy waited for a moment, to see if she would switch it on again, but it looked as if that was the end of their voyeurism for tonight.

They sat together, drinking wine and eating sandwiches. Jimmy found it hard to believe that only a short time ago they had been perched precariously on the back of the couch, having sex.

Heidi said, 'You should introduce yourself.'

'Excuse me?'

'You should go round to Nadine Frost's apartment and introduce yourself.'

'And say what? "I've been watching you take your clothes off for the past few nights, and I've been drooling so much that my living-room rug is totally soaked through."'

'No, stupid. Just politely say that you've recognised her, and that you loved all of her pictures, and if there's anything she needs at any time, all she has to do is ask you.'

'And what if she tells me to go take a running jump?'

Heidi swallowed, wiped her mouth, and then kissed him. 'What do you have to lose?'

Jimmy sat and thought for almost half a minute. Then he said, 'Why?'

'Why what?'

'Why would you want me to?'

'Because it would make you happy. I'm your friend, aren't I? And that's what friends do – they make each other happy.'

'I think you're kinkier than I am.'

She kissed him again. 'Thanks for the compliment.'

Late that night, he googled Nadine Frost and looked up her career in the movies. Nadine Frost, real name Zsuzanna Erdélyi, was born in a suburb of Budapest, Hungary, in February 1973. Her father was an electronics engineer, and the family moved to Los Angeles California in 1982 so that he could work for Modex, Inc.

Zsuzanna excelled at school, both in sport and drama, and when she was fifteen she was offered a part in the family TV drama *The Lovehearts*. After that, she appeared in seven more movies, and was nominated for an Oscar for her supporting role in *Thunder Bay*.

A month after the release of her last movie, however, she disappeared from public view, and her agent Cy Willard made a statement that she had given up her acting career and was looking for 'seclusion and spiritual solace'. Despite the efforts of the media, her whereabouts were never discovered.

Until now, when she had unexpectedly appeared in one of Jimmy's nightly dramas, in the Van Cortlandt Apartment block, in Manhattan.

He didn't have enough nerve to go around to Nadine Frost's apartment until two evenings later. On the first evening, he stood and watched her for over twenty minutes as she stood naked in front of her mirror. Now that he knew who she was, he found himself asking even more questions about her. Did she regret giving up her movie career? Was that why she stood in front of her mirror night after night, admiring her body? Or was she looking for something beyond her physical beauty – maybe that 'spiritual solace' that her agent had mentioned?

Early on the second evening, Heidi called him.

'Did you go to see her yet?'

'Not yet.'

'Be brave. Go. Like I told you, what do you have to lose?'

'I don't know. My self-esteem?'

'Go. Go now.'

'I don't know what number her apartment is.'

'You can *count*, can't you? Go.'

Reluctantly, he left his apartment, went down in the elevator and crossed the courtyard. An elderly man was sitting on one of the benches, underneath a leafless aspen. He was wearing a hat, a heavy tweed overcoat, and a scarf.

'Evening,' he said, as Jimmy walked by.

'Pretty chilly out here,' said Jimmy.

'Oh, I'm just giving myself a little quiet time. Sometimes a body needs a little quiet time.'

'I guess so. Me, I think I get too much of it.'

The elderly man adjusted his hat. 'In that case, you need to find yourself a companion. Everybody should have a companion. Road of life, it's too damn long and too damn empty to walk along it all on your ownsome.'

If Jimmy had been thinking of turning back, the elderly man's words gave him fresh resolve to go on. He went into the lobby of the apartment block opposite, and pressed the button for the elevator. When it arrived, he looked into the window but there was nobody inside it. No naked Nadine Frost, screaming '*You mustn't!*'

He went up to the fourth floor, and walked along the corridor to the fourth door on the right. The corridor was dimly lit, with a faded, royal-blue carpet. From all sides he could hear televisions and music and people talking. He came to the fourth door and stood in front of it, with his finger poised an inch away from the buzzer.

This was madness. He knew it was madness. She would simply tell him to go away and leave her alone. Yet he kept thinking of her reflection in the mirror, and the way that his back had almost cracked when he had made love to it.

He pressed the buzzer. Out here in the corridor, it was scarcely audible, like a blowfly in a sealed bottle. He waited, but there was no response. He knew that she was home because he had seen her switch on her living-room lights. Maybe she had taken a taken a squint at him through her peephole and decided that he looked too visually unstimulating.

He pressed the buzzer again. After a long pause, a muffled woman's voice said, 'Who is it?'

'Ah – my name's Jimmy, Ms Frost. Jimmy Lightoller. I live right opposite. I saw you move in and I wondered if you needed any help.'

An even longer pause. Then: 'You know who I am?'

'Couldn't mistake you, Ms Frost. I'm one of your biggest fans. I was really sorry when you gave up making pictures. Me and about fifty million other fans.'

'What do you *really* want?'

'Truthfully? Just to be friends. There are one million six hundred thousand people in Manhattan, but that doesn't mean you can't be lonely.'

The next pause was so long that Jimmy thought she had

lost interest, and he was almost ready to go back to his apartment.

But then she said, 'What makes you think that *I* need a friend?'

'I don't know, Ms Frost. Just trying to be sociable, that's all.'

Without warning, the apartment door clicked open, and stayed a few inches ajar.

'Come on in, Jimmy,' said Nadine Frost, although he still couldn't see her.

'You're sure about this?'

'I'm sure.'

'I don't like to impose or anything. It's just that I'm such a great fan.'

'Come on in. Don't be shy.'

Jimmy stepped into the apartment. As he did so, he saw Nadine Frost disappearing through the living room, heading towards the bedroom. She was wearing a long white satin robe, with a hood, so that she looked like a ghost.

'I'll – ah – I'll close the door, shall I?' Jimmy called out.

'Of course,' she called back.

He closed the door and walked into the middle of the living room. It was plainly furnished with dull Swedish-style furniture – oatmeal-coloured chairs and a pine coffee table, and a pottery jar with dried bulrushes in it. On one side of the room hung a large multiple portrait of Nadine Frost in all of the major roles she had played – as the heiress to a cotton plantation, as an Egyptian queen, as a female aviator, as a frontierswoman, as a prostitute with a heart of gold.

'Fantastic picture,' he said, loudly.

'You like it?'

'Fantastic. If you don't mind my saying so, you really look terrific.'

'Only "terrific"?'

'Well… beautiful. You really look beautiful.'

He waited. He wondered what she was doing in the bedroom, and whether he ought to sit down and make himself at home.

'So, you think I'm beautiful?' she said.

'No other word for it.'

Another pause. Then: 'I've seen you watching me, Jimmy. It *was* you, wasn't it?'

'Excuse me?'

'Oh, don't try to pretend. I saw you watching the very first night I moved in. That's why I put on my little show for you.'

'I don't know what you mean. I really don't.'

'Oh, come on, Jimmy. You don't have to pretend. You stood in your window and you watched me for hours.'

Jimmy felt himself flushing hot with embarrassment. 'Look,' he said, 'maybe this wasn't such a good idea after all. Maybe I'd better leave.'

'No, Jimmy, don't do that. Come into the bedroom and see me as I really am.'

'Listen, please. I'm sorry if you thought I was spying on you. I really wasn't. It's just that I saw you in your mirror – only a few seconds' glimpse – and – well, you're beautiful. That's all I can say, except that I'm sorry.'

'You saw me in my mirror?'

'Only a few seconds' glimpse, I swear it.'

'You saw me in my *mirror*?'

'Yes.'

'Come into the bedroom, Jimmy.'

Jimmy hesitated, and then he walked out of the living room and into the corridor. The bedroom door was half-open, and up against the left-hand wall he could see the full-length mirror, framed in gilt. And there was the image of Nadine Frost, utterly naked, smiling.

Except that the full-length mirror wasn't a mirror at all. It was a full-length painting, in oils. Meticulously detailed, highly realistic, but only a painting.

'Come on in,' Nadine Frost repeated. 'Come and see me as I really am.'

It was only now that Jimmy noticed a curious whistling sound in her voice, followed by the soft cackle of phlegm at the end of every phrase.

'I think I've made a mistake,' he said. 'I think it's probably better if I go.'

'No, Jimmy. I wouldn't go, not if I were you. You wouldn't want me to cause a fuss, would you? A peeping Tom who forced his way into my apartment, and tried to assault me?'

'I'll just go,' said Jimmy, his voice rising in panic.

'Don't you want to take advantage of me first?'

'What?'

'It's been a long time since a man took advantage of me. Not once in seven years, ever since my accident. Come on, Jimmy. Think of what we could do together. Deep throat, with a woman with no face. You could actually watch it as it disappeared.'

The bedroom door opened wider. Nadine Frost was standing in front of him now, in her white hooded robe.

Inside the hood, he could see her eyes glittering, but underneath her eyes there was nothing but shadows.

'Oh, God,' he said, and sank to his knees, his head bowed.

Nadine Frost came up to him and rested her hands lightly on his shoulders. 'Come on, Jimmy,' she said. 'You and I are going to be wonderful together.'

She twisted her shoulders so that her satin robe whispered to the floor. Jimmy raised his head and her plume of russet hair was right in front of him.

Then he looked up.

ON GRACIOUS POND

'They took them for a walk, Hetty and Emily and Charlotte,' said Louisa, 'but they never came back.'

'Who took them for a walk?' Charles asked her, looking up from his pencil drawing of a fat, grumpy queen. The late summer sunlight was slanting in through the window behind Louisa, so that it looked as if her plaits were on fire.

'Sir Walter What's-his-name and that funny Mr Sawyer.'

'Oh, you mean Sir Walter Warboys. But what's funny about Mr Sawyer?'

'I don't know. He's always sniffing. Sniff, sniff, sniff, as if he's got a cold, although he hasn't. And he speaks like a puppy whining. And he smells.'

'What of?'

Louisa thought for a moment, wrinkling up her nose as if she were trying to recreate Mr Sawyer's smell.

'Like sardines,' she said, at last.

Charles shaded in the queen's gown, and drew pointy black arrows on its ermine lining.

'And when was this?' he asked. 'I'm sure saw all three girls the last time I came to visit, and that was only last Monday.'

'Wednesday, I think. Yes, Wednesday.'

'Did you ask where they'd gone?'

'Yes. I asked Mrs Silver, but all she said was they'd been adopted.'

'Perhaps they had.'

'But they hadn't even come back from their walk. When one of us gets adopted, their new parents usually come here to help them to pack up all their belongings, and they always say a proper goodbye to everybody.'

'Perhaps they had arranged to meet their new parents elsewhere.'

'Well, yes, I suppose they might. But they didn't take their clothes or anything else. All their belongings were still there the next morning. Even Emily's ballerina doll, and she never went to bed without her ballerina doll. It was nearly bedtime on Thursday before anybody came to take away their dresses and their nightgowns and their shoes and everything else. Netty and Wilhelmina stuffed them all into the same hamper willy-nilly and carried them off, and that was that.'

Charles put down his pencil. 'I'm not sure I like the sound of this. I think I might have a word with Mrs Silver myself.'

'She was jolly cross when I asked her. She said that I should learn to mind my own beeswax.'

'Well, I'm sure she won't say the same to me. Look – here's the Queen of Hearts I've drawn for you. She's very grumpy because her gardeners have painted her roses all the wrong colour. She says, "Off with their heads!"'

'I know, because I've read it,' said Louisa. 'We weren't supposed to but Caroline borrowed a copy from the bookshop in town. Well, stole it actually, but she's going to sneak it back. Mrs Silver says she doesn't approve of nonsensical stories. The only book she allows us to read is the Bible.'

Charles handed Louisa the drawing and tucked his pencil into his waistcoat pocket.

'I'll see you next week,' he told her. 'I'm staying with my sisters until the end of the month, but then I have to go back to Oxford.'

Louisa held up the drawing and stared at it for a long time. She was painfully thin, and pale, and although she was thirteen years old, she was small for her age, like most of the orphans at The Beeches. All the same, Charles thought she had a strange dark-eyed beauty about her, like a nymph that you might find bathing in a forest pool. He decided to bring his camera with him next week, and take some photographs of her in the orphanage garden.

As he reached the door, Louisa said, 'May I ask you a question? I hope you won't think that I'm being impertinent.'

She wasn't looking at him. She was still staring at his drawing.

'Of course you may,' he replied. 'You can be as impertinent as you like. The queen won't be cross. She's two-dimensional, and made of graphite, nothing more.'

'Well, my question is – what's it like inside your head?'

Charles stood with his hand against the doorframe, feeling unexpectedly sad. He thought for a while, and then he said, 'It's like a seashore. A seashore with the gulls crying and the tide endlessly lapping and the sun shining on the waves. Not a cloud in the sky, and nobody there but me.'

'Not even a fishing boat?'

'Not even a fishing boat.'

Louisa turned now and looked at him, and the expression on her face was extraordinary for a girl so young, and from a background of such abuse and deprivation. It was one of pity, but of understanding, too, as if she knew exactly what he was talking about. Almost as if she had stood on that seashore herself, once upon a time, her plain brown dress flapping in the wind, feeling as lost as he did.

Charles gave her a quick non-committal smile. He really had no idea what to say to her. He went down the creaking mahogany stairs to the ground floor and then along the corridor to Mrs Silver's drawing room. Its door was open, and he could see Mrs Silver at her desk, writing a letter. Her lips were pinched as if she were sucking a lemon drop, so that her words would come out as acidic as possible. Her iron-grey hair was wrapped up tightly in a bun, with two long hairpins sticking through it, and her pince-nez were perched on the very tip of her nose.

She looked up as Charles appeared in her doorway, but he knocked all the same.

'You're leaving so soon, Reverend Dodgson?' she asked him. 'Have you had enough of my girls already? I thought you might stay for luncheon. Cook is baking a mutton pie today.'

'I have to take my sister Henrietta to the doctor's, Mrs Silver, although it's nothing serious. But I'll be back next Thursday, if that's convenient. I'll have some new stories I can read to the girls.'

'So long as they're none of your usual gammon and spinach. Talking playing cards and such piffle.'

Charles cleared his throat. 'I didn't see Charlotte today. Or Emily, or Hetty. Apparently they were taken for a walk by Sir Walter Warboys and his companion Mr Sawyer but never returned.'

'Who told you that?'

'I don't think it really matters who told me. I was simply wondering what had become of them.'

Mrs Silver took off her pince-nez. Charles thought that he had never seen eyes so grey and expressionless. They were more like pebbles from his lonely seashore than eyes.

'The three of them were all adopted,' said Mrs Silver. She had retained her Mancunian accent, speaking in a Northern monotone that betrayed no emotion whatsoever. 'Sir Walter and Mr Sawyer took them up to London to meet their new parents.'

'Really? So why did they leave all their clothes and their belongings behind? Even a favourite doll, from what I was told? They didn't even say goodbye to all of their friends here.'

'They had no need to take their things, Reverend Dodgson. Their new parents are all very well-heeled and will buy them all the dresses and dolls they require, and much more. They didn't say goodbye to their friends here at The Beeches because they believed it would be too upsetting.'

'Their friends are more upset that they vanished without a word.'

Mrs Silver stood up and walked around her desk. She came up close to Charles and stared up at him. He was over six feet tall, and she was a foot shorter, but in spite of that he felt menaced.

'You're a good man, with good intentions – I'll grant you that. When you visit you bring the girls laughter and amusement and you also give them a glimmer of hope for their futures. But you're a weaver of fantastical tales, and you shouldn't start to weave fantastical tales about the way this orphanage is managed, and how we handle the girls' adoptions. In other words, Reverend, I'm politely asking that you keep your nose out.'

There was a moment of tension between them that almost creaked, like a harness under strain. Charles thought of so many ways that he could respond to her, from straightforward contempt to some whimsical nonsense about noses that refused to behave themselves. But he was afraid that he would stammer, which he often did when he lost his temper, although he lost his temper very rarely. He also knew that if he upset Mrs Silver she might never allow him to visit The Beeches again. Apart from the friendships that he had developed with many of the twenty-seven girls here, he was still anxious to find out exactly what had happened to Hetty, Emily and Charlotte.

Perhaps Mrs Silver was telling him the truth, and they really had been adopted by wealthy parents. But why had it been given to Sir Walter Warboys and Mr Sawyer to take them away? Charles knew Sir Walter by sight: a big stout man, a Surrey magistrate with a wave of white hair and a grey walrus moustache and crimson cheeks that looked as if they had been roughed up with sandpaper. Charles had seen him in the estate agent's office in Guildford when he was arranging the lease on his sisters' house, and he had been struck by his shouty voice and the way that he was almost bursting out of his soup-stained waistcoat. The estate agent had raised one laconic eyebrow and that had told Charles all that he needed to know.

He decided that it would be wiser to say nothing more about the missing girls. Not yet, anyway. Not until he was sure what had become of them.

'I'll bid you good afternoon, then,' he told Mrs Silver. 'I look forward to seeing you next week, God willing.'

It was almost three o'clock in the afternoon before he arrived at the orphanage the following Thursday. His sister Mary had announced that morning that she had been asked for her hand in marriage by the Reverend Collingwood, and so he had stayed for lunch in order to celebrate with her. Fanny had roasted two ducks, and they had toasted Mary's engagement with glasses of sherry.

It was a ten-minute walk from his sisters' house to The Beeches. The day was sunny and warm, but a blustery wind was blowing, so that the poplar trees were thrashing as if they wanted to uproot themselves.

When he arrived, he saw that a black, four-wheeled brougham was drawn up by the stable at the side of the house, with its shiny chestnut horse feeding from a nosebag. He knocked at the front door, and Netty the maid let him in. She was skinny and pasty-faced, but her eyes were needle-bright and she was giving him a cheeky grin.

'Something amusing you, Netty?' he asked her.

'Your titfer, Reverend. I loves 'ow you've gone and decorated it.'

Charles took off his wide-brimmed hat and saw that there were seven or eight prickly burdock burs clinging to the crown. There were three more stuck to the back of his coat, all of which must have been blown there by the wind.

'You know what they say about burdock burs, don't you, Reverend?' said Netty. She took his coat, hung it up in the hallway and picked off the burs.

'I'm afraid not. What *do* they say about burdock burs?'

'"Miss or madam, master or sir, be you wary of the burdock bur. The day she sticks, so small and brown, she'll turn your whole life upside down."'

'Well, I can't say I've ever heard that before. But if there is any truth to it, I shall proceed with the utmost caution – not that my life isn't upside down already. Perhaps they're telling me that it's about to be turned the right way up again.'

As she followed him along the corridor, Netty said, 'Sir Walter Warboys is in with Mrs Silver at the moment, Reverend, along with that Mr Sawyer.'

With that, she pinched her nose and flapped one hand as if she had suddenly caught the whiff of something unpleasant.

Charles couldn't help smiling. 'Yes. I am reliably told that he has the redolence of sardines about him.'

'Sardines? More like whales, if you ask me. And *dead* whales at that, long gone mouldy.'

Mrs Silver's door was closed, and so he knocked, and

when Mrs Silver called out, 'Come!' he turned to Netty and winked at her and then he went in.

Mrs Silver was seated at her desk, while Sir Walter Warboys was standing by the window, blocking out half the light, and Mr Sawyer was wedged into a small tight armchair in the right-hand corner, next to Mrs Silver's bookshelf.

'Aha! The famous spinner of silly stories!' cried Sir Walter. 'I'm sure you know who I am – Walter Warboys – and this is my aide-de-camp Jack Sawyer. How do you care to be addressed, sir – as Mr Carroll, is it? I must say that you are good deal less extravagant in your dress and your appearance than I expected. I thought you might at least be wearing a topper with a ten-and-sixpenny price ticket in it.'

Jack Sawyer let out a cackling laugh, and kicked his boots on the carpet like a galloping pony.

'Thank you all the same, Councillor,' said Charles. 'I am flattered that you appear to have read my book, or perused the illustrations at the very least. But I would be quite content if you called me Reverend Dodgson.'

'Hoity-toity.' Jack Sawyer grinned, baring his tobacco-stained teeth, with the front two missing. Charles took a breath to restrain himself from answering back, and he could definitely smell fish of some kind. Perhaps Jack Sawyer existed on a diet of mackerel and coley, and it seeped out through his pores when he perspired.

'Your girls are waiting for you in the summer room, Reverend,' said Mrs Silver. 'They have plenty of sewing to keep them occupied while you amuse them with your latest stories.'

'What will you be telling them, Reverend?' asked Sir Walter. 'Some twaddle about smoking caterpillars?'

'Actually, no, I have a story based on Jesus feeding the five thousand, told from a young child's point of view. Mrs Silver is not enthusiastic about absurdity.'

Sir Walter grunted. The longcase clock in the hallway struck half past one and he took out his pocket watch and flipped open its lid to check that it was keeping good time.

Charles cleared his throat and said, 'Before I go upstairs, Sir Walter, I have a question for you, if I may.'

'Hmm, yes? And what would that be?'

'I was wondering about the parents who adopted Charlotte, Hetty and Emily – what manner of people they might be. I became quite close to those girls while they were here at The Beeches and I would be reassured to know that they had all been found good homes. Perhaps it might even be possible for you to inform me of their new addresses, so that I may visit them on occasion.'

Sir Walter glanced at Mrs Silver with what Charles took to be a look of some concern, but Mrs Silver slammed shut the desk drawer in which she had been rummaging, tented her fingers, and snapped, 'Not possible, Reverend, I regret. The law is adamant that when one of our charges is adopted, her adoptive parentage must remain confidential. And I believe that we discussed those three girls last week, did we not?'

Charles looked down at Jack Sawyer, who was still giving him a gappy grin, as if he were really relishing his discomfort.

'Very well,' said Charles. 'I will see you before I leave. Sir Walter – Mr Sawyer – I'll bid you good afternoon.'

Sir Walter bowed his head and Jack Sawyer gave him a salute. Both appeared to be mocking him.

He left Mrs Silver's office, went along the corridor and started to climb the stairs. He was less than halfway up when three girls came scampering down, all of them wearing coats and bonnets and gloves, their boots clattering loudly on the uncarpeted treads.

Charles recognised all of them: Fiona, a skinny-wristed blonde of about eleven years old; Hilda, a freckly redhead who had just celebrated her twelfth birthday; and fourteen-year-old Mavis, a serious brunette with a bun and circular glasses.

'Careful, young ladies!' he cautioned them, raising both hands. 'Remember the nanny who rushed down to the hall, only to stumble and only to fall. Why are you in such a hurry?'

'Sir Walter Warboys is taking us out for a picnic!' said Fiona.

'That should be pleasant. It's a nice sunny afternoon, if a little fresh. Did he say where he was taking you?'

'Gracious Pond,' put in Mavis. 'He said it's private, and quiet, and we can sing and dance and make as much noise as we like.'

'He's not taking you off to be adopted, then?'

'Oh, *no*!' said Hilda. 'He said that we'll have venison pies and raspberry tarts and sillybub!'

'Oh, you mean "syllabub". Well, that sounds very tempting indeed. I hope you have a splendid time!'

The girls carried on hurrying down to the hallway. Charles stayed where he was, halfway up the stairs, one hand resting on the banister rail. He heard the door to Mrs Silver's study open, and Sir Walter shouting out, 'Wonderful! There you are, my little treats. All ready to go, are we?'

As Sir Walter and Jack Sawyer and the girls made their way along the hallway to the front door, another girl leaned over the banisters from the landing and called out, 'Can I come?'

Charles recognised her as Lizzie, a half-caste girl of about fifteen years old, who had been rescued by Dr Barnardo six months ago from a brothel in Stepney.

Sir Walter stopped and called back, 'Who is that?'

'Lizzie! Lizzie Ruffles!'

'Perhaps next time, Lizzie! We came today in my brougham, which has but two seats and two more small seats that tip down. I'm afraid that we have only one place for each!'

'Next time, then, if you'd be so good, sir!'

'We shall see, Lizzie! I cannot make promises!'

With that, Sir Walter stepped out of the front door and Netty closed it behind him. Charles looked up at Lizzie and she shrugged and smiled and said, 'Come to tell us more Bible stories, have you, Reverend?'

Charles hesitated, but at that moment he heard a knock at the front door, and Netty opened it again. When he looked down to the hallway, Charles saw a hansom cab driver standing outside in the porch. He handed Netty a small wicker hamper with a label tied onto it, and Netty closed the door and took it into Mrs Silver's study.

Charles hesitated for three seconds more, but then he turned around and galloped back down the stairs. He ran along the corridor and burst out of the front door just as the hansom cab driver was snapping his whip to start his horse moving.

'Wait! Please wait!' Charles cried out.

'Requiring transportation, are we, guvnor?' said the cabbie, pulling back on his reins.

Charles could see Sir Walter's brougham disappearing around the corner at the end of the lane.

'Do you know happen to know Gracious Pond?'

'Yes, by Chobham Common that is. You thinking of going fishing, might I ask?'

'Can you take me there, but discreetly, so that we are not spotted by the driver of that brougham who has just left here?'

'It's a fair way, guvnor, Gracious Pond. Fifteen miles or more.'

'That doesn't matter. Would half a crown cover it?'

'An alderman? Whoa! I'll need to make my back here to Guildford, won't I? If you can make it two more deaners.'

'How about three-and-six? I'll have to make the return journey myself, somehow.'

'Fair enough, guvnor. Hop in.'

Charles opened the folding doors at the front of the hansom cab and climbed up into the seat. The cabbie snapped his whip again and they rattled off down the lane.

As they crossed Whitmoor Common, Charles began to wonder if it was madness, following Sir Walter Warboys and Mr Sawyer to spy on their picnic. What was he really going to do – hide in the bushes to watch them eating venison pies and raspberry tarts and syllabub and singing 'The Man On The Flying Trapeze'? And how was he going to make his way back to his sisters' house once they had finished their picnic and packed up?

He could have told the cabbie to turn around, but he had a burning feeling that he was on a mission to protect those three girls – Fiona, Hilda and Mavis – even if he did nothing more than watch over them while they ate their picnic and played. He believed deep in his heart that his ordination as an Anglican deacon had not been in name only. He was sure that God had forgiven him his past errors so that he would carry out His chosen will.

The cabbie opened up the hatch in the hansom's roof. 'I spy your fellow up ahead, guvnor. Don't you worry none, though. I'll stay well back, so he doesn't twig that we're tailing 'im.'

And so they rattled on, through Mayford and Hook Heath and Horsell, between trees that waved in the wind as if they were frantically warning Charles not to go any further. After nearly an hour they saw the brougham turn into Gracious Pond Road, and disappear amongst the dense bushes that surrounded it. The cabbie drew his hansom to a halt.

'This do you, guvnor?'

Charles counted three shillings and sixpence out of his waistcoat pocket and handed it up to the driver.

'Thank you, yes, this will do perfectly.'

'Begging your pardon, but these coves we've been following after, they're not busters of any kind? They've not half-inched nothing of yours, or nothing like that, 'ave they? You need to be well wary if they have.'

'I am hoping against hope that they are men of virtue. However, one can never be too certain. Appearances can be deceptive. As can smells.'

The cabbie stared at him, not knowing how to reply to that. Then he wheeled his cab around and snapped his whip and headed off back to Guildford.

Charles cautiously made his way along the rutted path that led to the pond. It was more of a lake than a pond, covering more than an acre and a half, and surrounded on all sides by bushes and birch trees. It reflected the clouds that were sailing across the blue August sky as perfectly as a mirror. Charles thought it could have been a wonderland like Alice's, only upside down, and he remembered what Netty had warned him about the burdock burs.

Jack Sawyer had driven the brougham into a small clearing about fifty yards away from the pond and tied up the horse. Charles could faintly hear the girls' voices, chattering and laughing, but he approached the pond very cautiously, in case he was spotted. He wished he had been wearing his dark-green jacket today instead of his light-caramel suit, and he also wished that he had thought to put on his overcoat. Although the sun was shining, the breeze was brisk, and in two or three hours the temperature would start to drop.

He struggled his way through the bushes on the northern side of the pond, following the sound of the girls' voices but keeping himself as well hidden as he could. Soon he saw grey smoke rising from a clearing by the water's edge, and he approached it as near as he dared without being seen.

Jack Sawyer had stacked up birch branches into a pyramid and set them alight, while Sir Walter was sitting on one of two tartan blankets, cross-legged like a Buddha, humming to himself and lifting pies and cheeses and bottles out of a hamper. The girls had taken off their coats and were sitting on the other blanket, laughing and playing some game that involved clapping their hands together.

Charles sat down behind the nearest tree and tried to make himself comfortable. His pocket watch told him that it was nearly half past two. He was thinking again that this might have been a foolhardy expedition, and wondering how he was going to be able to get back to Guildford. Perhaps he should have asked the cabbie to wait for him. He might be short of cash now, but he could have paid him on his return to The Chestnuts.

Still, Chobham village was only about two miles away. He could walk there, and with any luck he might find somebody there to drive him to Guildford, if he offered them enough.

'Why on earth didn't you think this through?' he berated himself. 'You're a logician, a mathematician. But as soon as young girls come dancing into your life, you become as mad as a hatter.'

He heard Sir Walter calling out, 'Cheers! Good health, and may we all have a hearty appetite!' Jack Sawyer and the girls echoed, 'Cheers!' and this was followed by the clinking of glasses.

Jack Sawyer started to sing 'Three Jolly Butchers' in his

high, nasal voice, and when Charles carefully peered around the side of the tree, he saw that the girls had taken off their boots and stockings and were skipping in the shallows of the pond. Fiona staggered and almost fell over, but Mavis managed to grab her arm. All three girls started laughing so much that they had to splash out of the water and drop back down onto their blanket.

Charles heard 'Cheers!' again, and more clinking of glasses. Then, less than five minutes later, 'Cheers!' yet again.

Another quarter of an hour passed by. The girls stopped giggling and Jack Sawyer stopped singing in mid-verse. Soon the only sounds that Charles could hear were the crackling of the fire and the rustling of the wind in the trees. He looked around the side of the tree once more, and saw that all three girls were lying on their backs on their blanket with their eyes closed, as if they were sleeping. Sir Walter heaved himself onto his feet and turned around in Charles's direction, so he quickly ducked his head back.

He waited for a while, holding his breath, but after about a minute he heard Jack Sawyer cackling like a chicken, and so he took a chance and looked around the tree yet again. Both Sir Walter and Jack Sawyer were standing up now, bending over the girls, and at first he couldn't understand what they were doing. But then Jack Sawyer triumphantly lifted up a white broderie anglaise petticoat, flapped it around his head and shouted out, '*Ta-daah!*' Charles realised that the girls weren't sleeping at all, but were drunk or drugged, and that Sir Walter and Jack Sawyer were stripping their clothes off them.

He sprang to his feet and stormed out from behind the

tree. '*Stop that!*' he roared, almost screaming. Striding around the fire, he went up to the two men, his fist lifted as if he were ready to hit them. 'What in the name of *God* do you think you're doing?'

Sir Walter had rolled Hilda onto her side, so that he could unbutton her dark red dress. He let her drop onto her back again and stood up straight, wuffling in indignation.

'Well, I'll be *damned* and double-damned! The Reverend Dodgson! Where the infernal hell did you spring from?'

'That's of no consequence. What matters is what bestial acts you're intending to commit with these innocent young girls!'

'Innocent? Pah! These girls are about as innocent as Oholah and Oholibah. I presume you know your Bible, Reverend Dodgson? The two whores of Egypt.'

'I am warning you, sir, not to lay one more finger on them. What have you given them to make them fall unconscious? Drink, was it, or some kind of sleeping draught?'

'None of your affair, as it happens. Mrs Silver told us that you've been poking your proboscis in where it's not wanted.'

'I am doing nothing more than protecting these young girls from the depredations of two loathsome lechers. You will allow them to recover and then you will return them to The Beeches. In any event, I intend to report you to the Clerk of the Peace, so that he can decide what action to take against you. If there's one thing you can be sure of, Sir Walter, you will never again find yourself presiding over the quarter sessions!'

Charles managed to say all of this without a single stammer. His chest had tightened up, but he was so fired up with righteous rage that he felt all-powerful, as if God were right behind him.

Sir Walter, however, seemed to be utterly unimpressed.

'I'm afraid you're deluding yourself, Reverend Dodgson. You still seem to be living in that topsy-turvy world you wrote about in that fantastical book of yours. Well, let me tell you this: this is the real world, and it isn't ruled by rabbits, or smiling cats, or playing cards pretending to be kings and queens. This world is ruled by gentlemen like myself. It is up to *us* to judge what is moral, and what is not. We are the ones who will decide if a fellow is to be given an award for his service to the community, for instance, or if he is to be jailed for some petty misdemeanour.

'These girls are nothing. Nothing but sluts, and thieves, and a needless drain on the public purse. The fate they will meet here this afternoon is in the common interest, and if they happen to afford us a little pleasure and a little nourishment as their miserable lives draw to a close, at least they will have made some contribution to this world before they leave it. Isn't that so, Jack?'

'Just so, Sir Walter,' said Jack, and gave a rattling sniff.

Charles was aghast. 'You intended to *murder* them? Rape them, and then *murder* them?'

'Oh, come now, Reverend Dodgson. Congress with whores has never been rape, whether they're awake or asleep, willing or unwilling. And sending a worthless soul to heaven can hardly be classified as murder.'

'You are not to touch a single hair on these girls' heads,' Charles warned him. 'Otherwise, believe you me, you will suffer the con – suffer the con—'

'Spit it out, Reverend D!' Jack said with a laugh.

Sir Walter stalked up to Charles, so that his swollen waistcoat was almost touching him. His breath smelled brown, tainted with brandy, cigars and dental caries.

'I have never tolerated threats of any kind from anybody, ever,' Sir Walter told him, and Charles could hear his lungs wheezing in and out like leather bellows. 'You are making such a damned nuisance of yourself that I am tempted to dispatch you, too, here and now. Unfortunately you are too damned celebrated, because of that ludicrous book of yours, and if you were to vanish, the whole damned country would be gibbering to know where you'd been spirited off to.'

'True, Sir Walter, too true,' Jack put in, with a solemn sniff. 'And think about it. There might well be a witness to his whereabouts already. He couldn't have *run* here after us, could he? He must have followed us by cab or carriage, and if he didn't drive it himself, somebody must have driven him.'

'I'm not concerned too much about that,' said Sir Walter. 'You can induce most witnesses to suffer selective amnesia, if you reward them sufficiently. But we don't know who else the reverend might have told where he was going.'

'You can't poh – you can't possibly expect to get away with this,' said Charles. 'You can't rape and murder three young orphans and then sail through the rest of your life as if you had done nothing wrong.

He paused, and looked down at the three girls sprawled on the blanket, their petticoats lifted, their dresses half-unbuttoned, and their eyes still closed. 'Or perhaps you can. What *did* happen to Hetty, Charlotte and Emily? Were they really adopted, or was that a fiction to cover up the fact that you raped and murdered them too?'

Sir Walter looked at Charles with his eyes narrowed, stroking his moustache over and over in the same way that he might have stroked a cat on his lap.

'Jack,' he said.

That was all he needed to say. Jack immediately took three quick steps forward and punched Charles hard on the left side of his head. He was wearing two heavy signet rings, and so his blow burst open Charles' earlobe, and blood spattered over the shoulder of his jacket. Charles staggered sideways, stunned, and then dropped onto his knees.

Sir Walter went up to him and pushed him, so that he fell backwards amongst the dead leaves that carpeted the ground.

'No threat from nobody, mister airy-fairy storyteller, that's what I said, and that includes you.'

Charles dabbed his blood-wet earlobe with his fingertips. 'You're a villain, Sir Walter. A villain of the darkest dye. I shall see you justly punished for this.'

'Jack, strap him up,' said Sir Walter.

Jack dragged off his thin leather belt. Charles tried to sit up, but Sir Walter kicked him in the ribs and then kicked him in the head, hard, so that his patent toecap caught him right on his bleeding ear. For a few seconds, Charles blacked out, and while he was unconscious, Jack pushed him onto his side, twisted his arms behind his back, and used his belt to lash his wrists together in a tight and complicated handcuff knot.

When Charles opened his eyes, his head was banging and his vision was blurry. Jack may have looked skinny and spidery, but he was deceptively strong, and he humped Charles backwards across the dry leaves until they reached the tree where he had been hiding. There, he propped him up in a sitting position with his back against the trunk.

'There, Reverend.' He grinned. 'Now you have a seat in the front stalls. I trust you enjoy the show!'

'The Lord will strike you down for this!' Charles raged at him, although his voice was so hoarse that it was barely more than a squeak. His chest felt as if it had wide steel bands wrapped around it, and with every second they were being screwed tighter and tighter. He prayed that he wasn't going to suffer an asthma attack. He didn't want to die, gasping for breath by Gracious Pond.

'Do you *truly* believe the Lord is watching us?' called out Sir Walter. He had already pushed Hilda onto her side again, and was twisting open the remaining buttons of her dress. 'Contrary to what you holy men purport, the Lord cannot keep his eye on all of us, every minute of every day. The population of the world now exceeds twelve hundred million of various colours, so it's estimated. I think you'd agree that it must be impossible for Him to surveille us individually, even if He has eyes in the back of his head.'

'I shall call on Him!' Charles shouted back. 'I shall cry out for His help, and He will hear me!'

'Oh no, you bloody well shan't!' said Sir Walter. Now he was tugging Hilda's dress up over her floppy arms. 'Gag him, Jack! We don't want him attracting anybody's attention, temporal or spiritual!'

Jack pulled a grimy grey handkerchief out of his trouser pocket. He forced it between Charles' teeth, almost choking him, and then he knotted it tightly at the back of his neck. Whatever Jack had been wiping with it, the handkerchief tasted sour, like vinegar and stale perspiration.

He had to watch, dumbly, while Sir Walter and Jack wrenched off all the girls' clothes and left them naked and white-skinned. Both men then unfastened their britches and dropped them down to their ankles, although Jack left his collarless shirt on, and Sir Walter retained his shirt, his bow tie, his waistcoat and his tan tweed jacket.

They knelt down in the leaves and parted the girls' legs, but after that Charles closed his eyes tightly shut. He could guess what repulsive acts they were about to commit, and the last thing he wanted was to be a witness. His mouth was flooded with bile, partly because of the stinking handkerchief that Jack had used to gag him, and partly because he felt so helpless to protect the girls from rape. He was unable to spit the bile out, so he had to swallow it, and that made him retch.

Although he could keep his eyes tightly closed, he was unable to stick his fingers in his ears, so he had to listen to the two men grunting and shuffling in the leaves. This went on for over a quarter of an hour, and then he heard a trickling sound as if they were urinating.

After that, there was silence for a minute or two, followed by a clanking sound. He opened his eyes to see Sir Walter buttoning up his britches and Jack setting up some kind of iron framework over the fire. The girls were still lying naked and unconscious on the ground, with crimson bruises on their thighs and breasts and their hair bedraggled.

Jack took hold of Fiona by her ankles and dragged her over to the fire. Then, to Charles' utter horror, he took out a butcher's cleaver and with three hard blows he hacked off her head. Blood pumped out of her severed neck and was instantly soaked up by the peaty ground.

Charles managed a throaty roar of protest behind his gag, and kicked his heels, but both Jack and Sir Walter ignored him. Jack nonchalantly slung Fiona's head to one side so that it rolled off into the leaves. Following that, he briskly chopped off both of her arms, and then he picked up a carving knife and proceeded to cut out her ribcage. Her intestines poured out in a wriggling mass on either side of her body, and the wind blew dead leaves that stuck to them like butterflies.

Jack whistled and sang 'Three Jolly Butchers' as he worried her ribs away from her spine. He looked as if he were wearing glossy red gauntlets.

He finished up by cutting thick slices from her thighs, right down to her knees, and draping these slices over the framework that he had constructed over the fire. The fire itself had died down now to an orange glow, but its heat was intense, so that the air above it wavered like a gathering of ghosts, and Fiona's flesh crackled and spat as it was roasted.

Charles had no choice but to watch as Sir Walter and Jack sat down by the fire and cooked the pieces of flesh that Jack had cut from Fiona's body. Sir Walter took cutlery and plates out of the picnic hamper, as well as bread rolls and a ceramic butter dish. When the flesh was well browned, he forked it off the fire and laid it out as if it were slices of roast beef, with pickles and baby beetroots. Charles could smell it, and he couldn't stop himself from retching again, and yet again.

Sir Walter and Jack took their time eating. The sun sank down behind the trees and the pond gradually grew dark, punctuated only by occasional bubbles as carp and tench came to the surface. The breeze became chillier, and stirred the dried leaves that lay on the ground so that it sounded as if an invisible crowd were rushing through the bushes.

Sir Walter and Jack spoke very little, although Charles heard Jack complain that Sir Walter had spread the butter on his bread too thickly.

The other two girls, Hilda and Mavis, remained where they were, naked, either unconscious or dead. Charles felt exhausted, physically and morally, and his chin dropped down onto his chest. He wished he could sleep. He wished he could die. But he could do neither. All he could do was listen to Sir Walter and Jack eating their grisly picnic, and occasionally making random remarks, or laughing.

At last they finished, and started to pack up. Jack dragged Hilda and Mavis into the woods, one after the other, and then he came back for Fiona's remains, and dragged them off, too. Charles could hear the chopping sound of a spade, and he presumed that Jack had previously dug a hole in the ground somewhere in the woods, so that he could bury the bodies.

He came back after about ten minutes to dismantle the framework over the fire, and kick what was left of the ashes into the pond. Meanwhile Sir Walter folded up the blankets and stowed the plates and cutlery and other food into the picnic basket. By the time they had finished, there was hardly any trace of what they had done here, except for a grey burned patch on the ground.

Eventually, the two men came over to Charles. Jack untied his gag and unfastened the leather belt that was binding his wrists together.

'You're monsters,' said Charles, rubbing his wrists. 'I swear to God that you will be punished for what you have done here today.'

'Oh, I think not, Reverend Dodgson,' said Sir Walter. He was picking a shred of flesh from between his teeth with his thumbnail. 'There are no witnesses, apart from your good self, and I am quite confident that you will not be speaking out. Not to the Clerk of the Peace, and not to the Surrey constabulary, neither.'

'And what will stop me?' Charles demanded. He started to get to his feet but Jack pushed him back down.

'Your own good sense,' said Sir Walter. 'You have seven sisters, do you not, who live halfway up Castle Hill in Guildford, in a house called The Chestnuts? It would be such a pity if any harm were to come to your sisters. If the house were consumed by fire, for example, in the middle of the night, and all your sisters were to be cremated alive? Or if their water were to be mysteriously contaminated with strychnine, so that all of them were poisoned and died in agony?'

'You wouldn't dare!' Charles challenged him.

'Reverend Dodgson, we dare to eat orphans. Don't think we wouldn't dare to dispose of your beloved sisters.'

There was a long moment of silence. Sir Walter stared down at Charles, smiling, and Jack was shuffling his feet and grinning, too.

'Now we'll bid you good day,' said Sir Walter. 'You made your own way here to Gracious Pond. I am sure you will be able to find your own way back.'

With that, Jack went over to pick up the hamper and the blankets, and the two of them walked off, leaving Charles sitting against the tree.

He rarely wept, but he felt so helpless and so devastated by what he had been forced to witness that he started to weep now, his shoulders shaking and the tears streaming down his cheeks.

He kept his silence, and told nobody about the horrendous crimes that Sir Walter and Jack Sawyer had committed in front of his eyes – not the Surrey constabulary, nor the court of sessions, nor the press. He stayed with his sisters for a week longer than he had originally intended, in case Sir Walter took it into his head to harm them, by way of a warning. He sent a letter to Christ Church college in Oxford to inform them that he would be delayed out of concern for his sisters' health. It was the nearest he could bring himself to telling a lie.

The following Thursday, though, he walked to The Beeches to inform Mrs Silver that he would no longer be visiting the orphanage to tell the girls stories. A fine soft rain started to fall when he was halfway there, so he was glad he had taken his umbrella. When he arrived, he was relieved to see that there was no sign of Sir Walter's brougham.

Mrs Silver had the first signs of a cold, and kept coughing and blowing her nose on a lacy handkerchief and folding it smaller and smaller.

'Well, the girls will sorely miss you, Reverend Dodgson. You always amused them, and your Bible stories were most improving. May I ask if there is any particular reason why you no longer intend to visit us?'

'My publishers are pressing me to write a sequel to *Alice*, but I will continue to have my duties lecturing in mathematics at Christ Church, so my days will be far too crowded to spend any time here. It's a matter of great regret, but there are only so many hours between rising and retiring.'

'You're sure that's the only reason? We haven't offended you in any way?'

Charles didn't answer that, but gave Mrs Silver an ambiguous smile.

'Goodbye, Mrs Silver, and thank you for allowing me to visit. May God be with you.'

As Netty opened the front door for him, Louisa came running down the stairs.

'Reverend Dodgson! Reverend Dodgson! Aren't you coming upstairs to tell us a story?'

Charles hesitated. It was still raining on the shingle driveway outside, although he could see that the clouds were clearing from the west.

'Very well, Louisa. I think I may have time for just one.'

He followed her upstairs to the sewing room. Lizzie and Caroline and half a dozen other girls were there, too, embroidering and darning stockings.

Charles sat down in the spoonback armchair by the window and said, 'You may find this story strange, but in common with Alice's adventures in Wonderland, and some of the stranger stories in the Bible, there is a grain of truth in it, and a moral.'

'I love the Cheshire cat,' said Caroline. 'The way it disappears, leaving nothing behind but its grin. Is there a cat in this story?'

'No, but there is a walrus. A walrus, and his friend, who happens to be a carpenter. I know that is rather odd that the two of them should be companions, but there you are. One day they decided to talk a walk by the seashore. Actually it was one night, but it had been cloudy all day, much like today, and the sun was not yet tired, so it had decided to stay up for a few hours longer – much to the irritation of the moon!

'Anyway, the walrus and the carpenter were strolling along the sand when they decided that they should like some company. They called on the oysters who lived in the shallows and invited them to join them on a pleasurable walk. The oysters were extremely bored, as you might expect, with nothing to amuse them but the tide coming in and going out again, and so they eagerly agreed to accompany them.'

'But oysters can't walk,' put in Lizzie. 'They haven't any feet.'

'You're perfectly correct, of course,' said Charles. 'I hadn't thought of that. But never mind… they came hopping along regardless. At first the walrus told them that they could take no more than four, so that they could hold their hands, and Lizzie – please don't tell me that oysters haven't any hands! However, more oysters wanted to come for the walk, and they ended up with scores of them, all walking along the beach together. A whole crowd of oysters!'

'And then what did they do?' asked Caroline.

'They sat down on some rocks, and the walrus suggested that they have a picnic. But the eldest oyster said, "How can we have a picnic, when you've brought but a single loaf?" The walrus smiled, and it was then that the oysters realised that he and the carpenter had brought plenty to eat, and it was them, the oysters themselves.'

'Oh, no!' cried one of the girls, putting down her embroidery. 'Don't say that they ate all the oysters! What a rotten trick!'

'I'm afraid they did,' said Charles. 'With bread and butter, and pepper and salt, and vinegar.'

Louisa was looking at Charles keenly. He could see in her periwinkle-blue eyes that she half-understood what he was trying to tell them.

'Is that the end of the story?' she asked him.

'Yes, my dear, I'm afraid it is. After they had finished, there was nothing left on the beach but empty shells.'

'So what is the moral?'

'I suppose the moral is, beware of walruses and carpenters who promise pleasurable walks. The only people who will derive any pleasure from such outings will be them.'

The sewing room was silent. Charles had never told the girls a story like this before, with such a depressing denouement.

'I must go now,' he said, standing up. 'But please don't forget about the walrus and the carpenter. Life is hard enough as it is, especially for orphans like you, without such characters sweet-talking you into giving them much more than you ever intended.'

DAYS OF UTTER DREAD

★★★

Twenty-seven years passed, yet Charles stayed at Christ Church, lecturing in mathematics and helping to run the library, and he continued to visit his sisters regularly at The Chestnuts.

Alice Through the Looking-Glass was published two days after Christmas in 1871, and became a great success, although it was universally thought to be a darker story than *Alice in Wonderland*. Some thought that this must have been the result of the depression that he suffered following the death of his father in 1868.

Two weeks before Christmas in 1897, when the county of Surrey was thickly blanketed in snow, Charles arranged to meet his boyhood friend Harold Chimes at the Kings Head pub in Quarry Street, since it was less than a five-minute walk downhill from his sisters' house.

They sat by the fire in the oak-beamed bar and exchanged reminiscences about their days as boys at Rugby School, where Charles had used his fists on several occasions to protect Harold from bullies.

'I believe that was the most miserable time of my entire life,' said Charles. 'If ever I was inspired to write a book about what it would be like to be condemned to hell, I would have only to describe my three years at Rugby.'

They were eating a lunch of lamb chops and mashed turnips when a woman in a dark blue coat excused herself from her companions, who were just about to leave the pub, and came over to their table. She was pale-faced but attractive, with her dark hair tucked under a cloven-crowned hat.

'It's the Reverend Dodgson, unless I'm mistaken. Do you not remember me? Louisa, from The Beeches.'

Charles tugged his napkin out from his collar and stood up.

'My goodness, Louisa! After all these years! I trust you've been keeping well?'

'My husband and I have just celebrated our twenty-first wedding anniversary. We have had the happiest life that I could possibly have wished for, with three beautiful children.'

'Well, it's wonderful to see you. This is my friend Harold. We were at school together – not the happiest time for us!'

Louisa looked serious. 'There is one question I must ask you, Reverend Dodgson. It has troubled me ever since I last saw you, when you told us the story about the walrus and the carpenter. I bought your book, of course, and I read it to my children when they were little. You told the same story in that, as a poem.'

'So what is your question?'

'It was not really about a walrus and a carpenter at all, was it? It was about Sir Walter Warboys and Jack Sawyer, the one who smelled like sardines? It was about what happened to Hetty, Emily and Charlotte, and all those other girls they took to Gracious Pond. All those girls they took out for walks and who never came back.

'Mrs Silver would never tell us where they'd gone, but I'm guessing that *you* knew, didn't you? And that is what your poem is all about. *The Walrus and the Carpenter*.'

Charles glanced over at Harold, and then looked over

Louisa's shoulder at her husband and her friends, who were waiting for her impatiently by the door.

'Sir Walter Warboys is still alive, Louisa. He might be an old man now, but it would not be safe for me to tell you, even today.'

'You have to tell me. *Please*, Reverend Dodgson. It has been nagging me for all these years. What did they do to those girls?'

'Do you live far from here?' Charles asked her.

'Just across the river, on The Mount.'

'Then please, meet me here tomorrow, at noon, say, if you can, and I will tell you everything.'

Louisa re-joined her husband and they left the pub. Charles sat down and stared at his lamb chops, and all he could think of was the smell of the birch sticks burning at Gracious Pond, and Fiona's ribcage.

'Lost your appetite, Charles?' Harold asked him.

'Yes,' said Charles. 'I think I lost it a long time ago.'

The next day it was snowing heavily, and the town of Guildford was eerily silent. Charles made his way down to the Kings Head, slipping several times on the icy pavement. He found Louisa waiting for him at a corner table, accompanied by a young man with a neatly clipped moustache.

'This is my eldest son, Gordon,' she said.

'It's an honour to meet you, sir,' said Gordon. 'I was brought up in Looking-Glass Land.'

Gordon left Charles and Louisa and went to sit at the

bar to have a beer and talk to the landlord. Charles bought himself a glass of port wine and sipped it in silence while he summoned up the courage to tell Louisa what atrocities Sir Walter Warboys and Jack Sawyer had committed at Gracious Pond. She waited for him patiently. She had already waited twenty-seven years to find out what had happened to her orphanage friends when they had been taken for a walk. A few more minutes would make no difference.

At last, Charles said, 'In my poem, the walrus and the carpenter took the oysters for a walk along the seashore. I thought of setting it by the seashore because of the name, The Beeches. And of course Sir Walter was the inspiration for the walrus, because of his name, and because of his appearance, and Jack Sawyer was the carpenter.

He paused, and took another sip of port. 'The oysters, of course, were the unsuspecting girls they took to Gracious Pond. I never found out for certain what became of Emily and Hetty and Charlotte, but I witnessed for myself what those two monsters did to Fiona, Mavis and Hilda. You see – I recall all their names, even after so many years.

'They removed all their clothes and ravished them. Then they decapitated Fiona, and dissected her, and like the oysters, they ate her.'

Louisa's mouth slowly dropped open in horror. 'They *ate* her?'

Charles nodded. 'After they had gorged themselves, they took away all three girls and buried them in the woods. I am still not sure to this day if Mavis and Hilda were buried alive.'

'And you never told anybody about this? You never reported Sir Walter and Jack Sawyer to the police?'

'To my eternal shame, no. You are the first person to

whom I have ever disclosed it. Sir Walter threatened to have my seven sisters murdered if I so much as breathed a word about it.'

Louisa sat back. 'I hardly know what to say, Reverend Dodgson. I have always assumed that those poor girls were taken off to meet a bad end, but I never imagined that it was anything worse than being forced into prostitution. They killed them and *ate* them? Dear God, I feel as if I might faint.'

Charles reached across the table and held her hand. He felt huge relief at having at last told somebody about the nightmare that he had experienced at Gracious Pond, but at the same time he wondered if he had been reckless, and had been selfish to use Louisa to share his guilt. Now she too would have to bear the burden of knowing who the walrus and the carpenter really were, and what they had done.

Gordon came back to their table and sat down.

'Mama, you're looking dreadfully pale. Are you sure you're quite all right?'

'I'm afraid I have given your mother some bad news,' said Charles.

'Is it anything that I can help with?'

'I regret not. It all happened long ago, and is far beyond anybody's help.'

By the middle of January, the snow had mostly cleared, but a biting cold north-east wind persisted every day, and whistled softly and ominously through the ill-fitting windows of his sisters' house.

Charles had finished his breakfast of boiled eggs and was putting on his coat so that he could visit St Saviours Church, which was being built in the Gothic style on Woodbridge Road, and was almost completed.

He was winding his scarf around his neck when there was a heavy knocking at the front door.

'Who is that?' called out Margaret, from the kitchen. 'None of us are expecting any visitors, are we?'

'Not me!' said Aunt Lucy, from the drawing room.

'I'll get it,' said Charles, and opened the front door.

Standing outside was Sir Walter Warboys. He was top-hatted, and bundled up in a thick black coat with an astrakhan collar. Age had shrunk him, and he was round-shouldered now, and wearing spectacles, but behind the lenses his eyes still gleamed with the same watery arrogance, like freshly opened oysters.

Jack Sawyer was close behind him in an ankle-length Ulster coat and a bowler hat. His face was shrivelled and his cheeks were drawn in, so that his nose looked as pointed as a dagger.

'Reverend Dodgson,' said Sir Walter. His voice was thin now, as if he were being strangled. 'After all these years.'

'What do you want?' Charles challenged him. 'I thought you would have realised that you two monsters would be the last people I would ever wish to meet again, for as long as I lived.'

'Believe me, Reverend, the feeling was mutual. But I thought I had made it patently clear that you were never to speak of those events to which you were a witness at Gracious Pond.'

'I never did, although there were many times when I

wished that I had been brave enough. I will go to my grave regretting that I failed to report you.'

'I'm afraid that you are being mendacious,' said Sir Walter. 'You recently described what you saw that day to a woman by the name of Louisa Mellors. Apparently you had been acquainted with her when she was housed as an orphaned girl at The Beeches. Mrs Mellors passed on what you had told her to the deputy chief constable, Henry Carstairs, who happens to be a friend of her husband at the same Masonic lodge.'

'Then I am surprised he didn't take steps to arrest you,' said Charles.

'Well, he didn't. Partly because those events occurred so very long ago, and you are the only person who alleges to have witnessed them. And partly because Deputy Chief Constable Carstairs also happens to be married to my only daughter, Olive.'

'In that case, you have little to fear, do you? More's the pity.'

'Reverend Dodgson, if you have informed on us once, there is every likelihood that you will be tempted to inform on us again.'

'Why should I, when it appears to be fruitless?'

'All the same, I have a considerable reputation in this county, and I have no wish to risk having that reputation sullied by a spinner of fantastical stories, no matter how celebrated he may happen to be. You may not inform on me now, while I remain alive, but you may very well find the courage to do so when I have passed away.'

'You will be in hell then, Sir Walter, you can be sure of that, and that will be punishment enough. Having your reputation besmirched will be nothing in comparison to the eternal fires that you will have to endure.'

Sir Walter grunted, although Charles was unable to tell if it was in amusement or annoyance. 'Nonetheless, Reverend, we would like you to come along with us.'

'Certainly not! What for?'

'"A pleasant walk, a pleasant talk." Oh yes, I read your poem, and I knew at once what you were really saying.'

'As far as I am concerned, you are welcome to go to hell now. I'll bid you good day.'

Charles was about to close the front door when Jack Sawyer produced a long-barrelled revolver from the folds of his coat, cocked it, and pointed it at him.

'Let me repeat myself, Reverend,' said Sir Walter. 'We would like you to come along with us. In fact, we insist on it. I am sure you would not wish to distress your sisters by being shot dead on their doorstep.'

'Why *should* I come with you? For what ur – for what ur – for what earthly purpose?'

'All will soon become clear, Reverend Dodgson, I promise you. Now, shall we go?'

Charles was tempted for a split second to slam the front door in their faces, but if Jack were to fire his revolver at him, it was likely that the bullet would penetrate the panelling and hit him square in the chest. He was not a coward. His time protecting Harold at Rugby had proved that. But he had no wish to die yet, and he could imagine how distraught his sisters would be.

'Margaret!' he called out. 'I am going out now! I am not sure how long I shall be!'

With that, he closed the door behind him and followed

Sir Walter out of The Chestnuts' front garden and down Castle Hill. Jack stayed close behind him, his revolver concealed in the flaps of his coat, although the street was deserted.

A black, four-wheeled clarence was parked at the bottom of the hill, and a young boy in a cloth cap was holding on to the reins of its two grey horses. Sir Walter gave the boy sixpence and patted him on the cap. Then Jack opened the clarence's door and Charles and Sir Walter climbed in.

They went rattling off through Guildford's cobbled streets, and then turned due north. Charles and Sir Walter said nothing to each other as they headed up through Whitmoor Common, so that the only sound was the clopping of the two horses, the grinding of the wheels, and the intermittent creaking of the clarence's springs.

By the time they had reached Hook Heath, the cold east wind was blowing even harder, and black clouds began to roll in over the waving trees, so that the landscape gradually turned as dark as night. When they arrived at the woods around Gracious Pond, it started to snow.

'We thought you'd enjoy a trip down memory lane, Reverend Dodgson,' Sir Walter wheezed, as Jack helped him to lower his foot down onto the clarence's step. 'A reminder of what you should have learned to forget.'

'What I witnessed here I could never forget,' Charles retorted. 'There are some events that are far too terrible ever to erase from one's mem – one's mem—'

'Yes, Reverend, we get the point,' said Jack. 'Now shift your rear end out of there now, and let's get a move on before this snow starts coming down any worse.'

Jack tied up the horses to a tree and then the three of them made their way along the leaf-crusted path towards Gracious Pond. The snowflakes settled on their shoulders, and on their hats, and up ahead they were falling so thickly that they were floating on the surface of the water.

They skirted the pond and Sir Walter led them into the woods, until they reached a clearing surrounded on all sides by birch trees. The wood was utterly silent except for the faintest plipping of the snow dropping through the branches.

'So what now?' Charles demanded. 'This is where you brought those unfortunate young girls, is it not?'

'Quite right,' said Sir Walter. His spectacles were misted up, and so he took them off and polished them on his scarf. 'And since you showed them such concern, those girls, we decided that it would be appropriate for you to join them. Then you will be able to rest together in peace and quiet, without any further threat to my good standing in the Surrey community.

He turned to Jack and inclined his head. 'Jack, whenever you're ready.'

Jack walked up to Charles until he was less than six feet away. Then he took out his revolver, holding it in both hands, and pointed it directly at Charles' face. He cocked back the hammer and sniffed.

'Do you wish to say a valedictory prayer?' asked Sir Walter. 'I think we can allow you to do that, even though you will be meeting your Maker face to face in a few moments, and you can chat with Him in person.'

Charles clasped his hands together. His weak chest had made him feel sometimes as if he were just about to breathe his last, but he never thought that his life would be ended like this, in a wood, far from Oxford, with his brains blown into the snow.

As he tried to think of a prayer, he heard a shuffling sound. The shuffling grew louder, as if somebody were raking leaves.

Sir Walter said, 'What – what in the name of God – Jack! What in the name of God is that?'

Charles turned around and saw that fibrous lumps of peat were being torn up, as if a mole were digging them up from under last autumn's leaves.

To his horror, a human head slowly rose out of the ground. A girl's head, with damp dark hair sticking to her scalp. Her eyes were black as jets, and glittery, and her face was dead white, although her lips were tinged pale green.

She rose higher and higher, as if she were being lifted on a stage trapdoor. She was wearing a red dress stained with mud, and drooping grey stockings.

'Go away!' screamed Sir Walter, in his high whistly voice. 'You're not real! You're an apparition! Go away!'

He started to back towards the trees, but stumbled down onto one knee.

'Jack!' he wailed. 'Shoot it, Jack! Shoot it! It's an apparition! Shoot it!' That was all he could manage to say before he collapsed into a fit of coughing.

Jack pointed his revolver at the girl, but she pointed back at him with the finger of her right hand. Charles could see that he was struggling to hold the pistol straight. He was gritting his teeth and trying to keep it steady with both hands, but then the girl opened her mouth and let out the weirdest shriek that Charles had ever heard. It was like a hundred fingernails being scratched down a hundred blackboards. The revolver flew out of Jack's hand and spun off into the trees.

Jack staggered around and tried to run after it, but the girl shrieked again. He dropped face-down onto the leaves and lay there, trembling, while the snowflakes continued to gather on his back.

Now more lumps of peat were starting to be forced up from under the ground. Another girl's head appeared, as white and as ghastly as the first, with greenish blonde curls that were stuck to her head like seaweed. Then another, and another, and then a girl who had no head at all, but only the stump of her neck. When she rose up to her full height, Charles saw that she was naked and that her stomach was split apart, so that her intestines hung down to her knees, speckled with peat and leaf mould.

'Fiona,' he whispered to himself. 'Oh dearest Lord. It's Fiona.'

Within the space of a few minutes, eleven girls were resurrected from the ground, most of them naked, some of them terribly mutilated, so that their bones and their muscles and their sinews were exposed. They stood in a group together, white and silent as statues, while Sir Walter knelt in the falling snow, coughing and sobbing and helplessly waving his arms, and Jack muttered prayers to the leaves that were pressed against his nose.

The girl in the red dress screamed again, a scream that went on and on, and the girls started to walk forward, although some of them were limping, and there was one girl whose legs were both severed from the knees downward, who had to swing herself along with her arms, like an ape.

'No!' coughed Sir Walter. 'No, please, no! You're not real! I beg of you! I beg of you!'

But four of those girls who still had arms and legs took hold of his astrakhan coat and began to drag him along the ground. Three more girls seized the tails of Jack's long Ulster and pulled him along behind them.

They ignored Charles completely, as if he wasn't even there. But Charles followed behind them as they dragged Sir Walter and Jack through the trees, until they reached the muddy edge of Gracious Pond.

The girl in the red dress continued to scream, on and on, like an unbearable attack of tinnitus.

When they reached the water, the girls didn't stop. They started to wade into the water, up to their knees first of all, and then up to their waists, even Fiona, who was headless. They pulled Sir Walter after them, even though he was thrashing his arms and kicking his legs and shouting out in terror. In contrast, Jack was strangely limp and unprotesting as they dragged him further and deeper into the middle of the pond. As he stood at the water's edge watching them, Charles could only think that Jack must be accepting God's punishment for what he had done.

The girls' heads disappeared under the surface, one after the other. There was a brief flurry of splashing as Sir Walter was pulled under, but then the pond was still, with only the snowflakes floating on it, like fairies, or confetti.

Charles waited by the pond for more than half an hour,

but neither the girls nor the two drowned men reappeared. He wondered if he ought to have made some attempt to save Sir Walter and Jack, but he had been too stunned by the girls' reappearance from their grave. He found it almost impossible to believe that it had really happened, and yet here he was, by Gracious Pond, on a bitter January day, alone and miles away from Guildford.

Eventually he walked back down the path to the clearing where Jack had tied up the clarence. He unfastened the horses' reins and climbed awkwardly up onto the driving seat. He had driven a carriage only three times before, but after he had clicked his tongue and tugged at their horses' bridles they started off, and he managed to turn the clarence around and steer it back to the road.

The journey back to Guildford was like some appalling nightmare. The wind was so cold that Charles started to shudder uncontrollably, and his hands were so numb that he could barely hold the reins. Apart from that, the snow was whirling down so furiously that he missed several signposts and drove west to Lightwater, which added another five miles to his journey.

By the time he managed to return to Guildford and unlock the front door of his sisters' house, he was gasping for breath and he fell into the hallway on his knees.

Henrietta and Caroline came rushing down the stairs with bustling dresses to help him up.

'Charles! What's happened to you? Where in the world have you been? We've been so worried about you!'

'They came back,' he whispered.

'Who? Who came back?'

'Hilda – and Hetty – and Mavis – and Fuh—'

★★★

The Reverend Charles Lutwidge Dodgson succumbed to the flu after his journey back from Gracious Pond, and because of the weakness of his lungs, it developed within only a few days into pneumonia.

He died in his bed at The Chestnuts on January 14, 1898, at the age of sixty-five, two weeks shy of his sixty-sixth birthday, and is buried in The Mount Cemetery in Guildford.

The clarence belonging to Sir Walter Warboys was found tied up outside Castle Arch, at the bottom of Castle Hill, with nobody in it and its horses cold and hungry and in need of watering. No trace of Sir Walter Warboys or his companion Jack Sawyer was ever found.

NATIONAL BALANCE

Michael was stirring aspidistra soup in the kitchen of his restaurant when two officials from the Home Office came in to tell him that his wife had ceased to exist.

One of the officials was short and podgy, with a thinning comb-over and a scarlet face that looked as if it had been sand-blasted. The other was tall and lugubrious and kept swaying like a poplar tree in a morning breeze. Both wore bronze Puffa jackets that were still sparkling from the rain outside.

'What the hell are you talking about?'

'You are Mr Michael Chandler, of The Dentures, Boxtree Road, Streatham SW16?'

Michael turned off the gas. 'Yes.'

'And your former wife was Susan Chandler, of the same address?'

'What do you mean – *former* wife? She is my wife.'

The short podgy official took out an identity card and held it up in front of Michael's face. 'I assume you know about the National Balance Act?'

Michael's assistant Hamid stopped slicing the badger steaks that he was preparing for tonight's special. He came around the counter and stood beside Michael, with his arms folded. Although he reached only up to Michael's shoulder, he was broad-shouldered and muscular. His hair was twisted up into a black man-bun and his nose was broken from elbow-boxing.

'I heard of this,' he said, with a hint of aggression in his voice. 'But it is not law – only talk.'

'Well, I'm afraid that it *is* law now,' said the short podgy official. 'It was ratified three weeks ago although it wasn't publicised for the sake of public order.'

'What do you mean – "ceased to exist"?' Michael demanded. 'That's my wife. She can't "cease to exist". We've been married for eleven years and she's perfectly healthy.'

'That's as may be, Mr Chandler, but she was on the list, and if you're on the list, there's nothing that anybody can do it. There's no appeal. An individual who doesn't exist doesn't exist, so they can't lodge an appeal.'

Michael wrenched off his apron. 'Where is she? What have you done with her? If you've hurt her in any way at all—'

'She wasn't hurt, I can promise you that. But I can't tell you where she is because there's no such person.'

'Are you out of your mind? If you don't tell me what you've done with her and where she is, I'm calling the police right now.'

'You still don't understand, Mr Chandler. The police won't be able to help you because they can't go looking for somebody who never was. We're extremely thorough, I have to tell you that. You won't be able to find a birth certificate in your non-existent wife's name. Neither will you be able to locate any school reports, employment records, tax details, bank accounts, or credit card statements. Nothing.'

'I have our marriage certificate. I have letters from her. I have Valentine cards. I have photographs. Hundreds of photographs. Look – I have pictures of her on my phone.'

Shaking with anger, Michael tugged out his phone and prodded the app for his photo albums. As he swiped through them, though, he couldn't find a single picture of Susan. There were twenty or thirty pictures of their holiday last September in Barbados, but in every picture he was standing alone. Sunbathing by himself on the sand; lifting a bright crimson cocktail; sitting on the hotel terrace, smiling. But always alone.

'You've hacked my phone. You've photoshopped her out of every picture. You bastards. This is insane.'

He flicked across to WhatsApp. There was no trace of Susan's address, and no email address for her, either, on Hotmail.

He stood staring at the two Home Office officials, so bewildered and shocked that for a few seconds he was unable to speak.

Then he said, 'Get out. Get out, both of you. I'm going to report you for this. I'm going to have your guts for garters. Just get out.'

'Very well,' said the short podgy official, completely unruffled. 'We're quite used to a response of this nature, Mr Chandler. There's only one thing I have to do before we leave, though, and that is to formally remind you of the terms of the National Balance Act. In order to alleviate the pressure on the population and the public services of the United Kingdom, for every immigrant granted asylum from another country, one member of the British public will cease to exist, thereby maintaining the population at a constant level. Particular consideration is of course being given to improving the diversity of the population, so priority will be given to immigrants of varying ethnic origins, non-Christian faith, and differing sexual identity.'

The officials turned around and left, talking to each other as they made their way through the restaurant. Michael said, 'Hamid – I'm closing down for today. I have to go home right now and find out what's happened to Susan. This is lunacy. It must be some kind of a practical joke.'

'If it is a joke, Mr Candlemaker, then it is a joke in the worst of taste,' said Hamid. Whatever anybody's name was, Hamid would always translate it into its historical origin. 'He who laughs hysterically at the desperation of others will surely have his sides split when it comes to the day of ultimate reckoning.'

Michael drove home to Boxtree Road and parked his Ford Rocket outside their large semi-detached house. As he was making his way up the crazy-paving path to the front door, his neighbour Major Broughton came past, in his usual brown herringbone overcoat. His Afghan hound lifted its leg against Michael's gatepost and doused it with a copious stream of urine.

'You're home early, old chap!'

'Yes, John. Bit of a crisis. Sorry, can't talk.'

'Totally understand. It's nothing but one crisis after

another these days. The shortages! The power cuts! Did you see the news this morning? The lorries are tailing back all the way from Dover to Hemel Hempstead! And do you think that Tesco had any dandelion cheese left?'

Michael unlocked his front door and went inside. The hallway was chilly and smelled of dust and dry rot. The whole house was silent, which it had never been when Susan was at home, because she liked to keep the television muttering away in the background.

'Susan?' he said, softly, although he knew that he wouldn't get an answer.

He went into the living room first. It was furnished with a bulky three-piece suite, in beige corduroy, and the walls were crowded with framed family photographs. Through the French windows Michael could see the York stone patio and the birdbath, but there was no sign of the Gro-bags in which Susan was cultivating edamame beans, and beside the white cast-iron table there was only one chair.

He went over to the beige-tiled fireplace. His reflection approached him in the mirror over the mantelpiece, and its expression was so emotionless that it could have been another man approaching him from another room. He stood and stared at himself for a moment, breathing slow and deep, summoning up the courage to look at the family photographs.

The largest was their wedding photograph, taken on that gusty March day when they had emerged together from St Tofu's church, Michael holding on to his fedora and Susan trying to stop her veil from flying upward. The photograph was still there, and all the guests were just as Michael remembered them, and Michael was there, too.

Standing arm in arm with him, though, with one eye closed against the wind, was the lady vicar, the Reverend Willifred Uterus. There was no sign of Susan, not even in the background.

Every photograph in which Susan had appeared was the same. She had been completely erased from all of them, and in her place there was either another person, or a tree, or an animal.

Michael trudged upstairs. He knew now what he was going to find but he still had to look to see if there was any trace that Susan had existed. In the bedroom, when he slid open the wardrobe doors, he saw that his own clothes hadn't been touched, but that all of Susan's dresses and jackets and skirts had disappeared. Even her quilted hangers had been taken.

The drawers of her dressing table were empty, too, and the indelible pink stain where she had spilled her foundation had miraculously vanished.

He drew back the green candlewick bedspread and buried his face in her pillow. She had always sprayed on essence of traveller's joy before she went to bed, but now her pillow had absolutely no perfume at all. Somehow, they had eradicated even the smell of her.

He checked the bathroom and the two smaller bedrooms, as well as the lavatory and the airing cupboard. Everything of Susan's had gone – her towels, her toothbrush, her razor, her yak-fat body lotion. He could find nothing that proved she had once been living here, and that she had once been his wife.

He sat at the top of the stairs with his hands cupped over his face. He didn't want to see any more. He didn't want to know any more. Without Susan, he felt as if the Home Office had emptied not only her wardrobe but his whole world, too. He wasn't even a widower, because widowers have graves to visit, or ashes, or recordings of long-ago laughter, and widowers always have pictures.

His front doorbell chimed. At first he ignored it, but it chimed again, and then again, and after the fifth chime he climbed slowly down to the hallway and opened the door. It was Hamid, wearing a tight, navy, duffel coat. He was holding up a paper bag from Ethnic Wines & Spirits.

'I have brought you a bottle of gin, Mr Candlemaker, in order to mitigate the pain of your loss.'

'Come in, Hamid. That's very thoughtful of you, but I'm numb enough already.'

He led Hamid through to the living room and they sat on the corduroy sofa together. They said nothing at first, but after a minute or two Michael stood up and went to the kitchen and came back with two glasses. He opened the bottle of Saintly Gin and poured them each a large measure.

'Here's to non-existence,' he said. The gin smelled of wet laundry.

'I am thinking, Mr Candlemaker, that whatever the efforts of the Home Office, your wife can never be utterly eradicated. She exists still in your memory, which they cannot erase.'

'Don't count on it, Hamid. They'll probably come sneaking into the house when I'm asleep and give me a lobotomy.'

'If you are devoutly religious, you will believe that she

survives in heaven, or some other hereafter. Or that she has been reincarnated as a vixen, or a cormorant.'

Michael shook his head. 'I was brought up a Christian, but then my twin sister was killed. A window frame fell onto her in Oxford Street. I turned to the Bible for consolation and it was only then that I realised what a collection of poisonous, ignorant, primitive rubbish it actually is.'

Hamid laid his hand on Michael's arm. 'Ah yes, but even if you are not religious, and you do not believe in heaven, it is scientific fact that no matter what happens to us, our atoms survive. Our atoms are constantly streaming from place to place, and they come together only momentarily to make you, or Susan, or me. The *me* that you see sitting beside you this afternoon, Mr Candlemaker, is not the same me who was born and educated in Pakistan. It is not even the same me who first came and applied to you two years ago for work in your kitchen at the Deluded Brill. The atoms that made *those* Hamids have all flowed away, and the same has happened to your wife's atoms. In order to delete her existence completely, the Home Office would have had to track down every single one of the atoms and split them. You cannot obliterate even one human being totally without setting off the biggest nuclear explosion that ever was.'

Michael stared at him. 'How do you know all this?'

Hamid gave a coy, sideways smile. 'Before I decided to become a chef, I was trained in the Pakistani nuclear programme. I was taught how to destroy the world. But I decided that I would rather feed the world than destroy it. Even if some maniac does choose one day to unleash

Armageddon, at least I would have given a reasonable number of people a tasty last supper.'

Michael sat and thought for a while, taking occasional swallows of gin.

'It's no good, though, is it?' he said at last. 'The Home Office may not have been able to find every one of Susan's atoms, but there's no way that I can, either. How can you find something you can't even see?'

'That is not what I am suggesting, Mr Candlemaker. All I am saying is that somewhere on the wind, your Susan still exists. You may not be able to hold her in your arms again, but you will be breathing her in through your nose, and who can get closer than that?'

Michael's eyelashes were crowded with tears, and his lips puckered. Hamid laid his hand on his shoulder.

'Every living creature has a different reality. For all it knows, the wasp that is drowning in your washbasin could be drowning in the Atlantic. Does that make its death any less dramatic?'

A month went by. There were days when Michael felt like closing down the Deluded Brill and driving far away and never coming back. Somewhere like the Aran Islands, where he could sit alone on a rock and watch the Atlantic rolling in, with or without wasps.

However he found it easier to cope with his grief if he continued to work, and invent new dishes. It was much more difficult to think about Susan when he was blending a mixture for a yew and hamster sauce, or making sure that his kestrel's-beak soufflés didn't fall flat. Every night he would return home to The Dentures exhausted and half-drunk. Once he had climbed into bed he would put on headphones so that he could listen yet again to Bizet's Creaking Door Chorus, which made it impossible for him to wish for anything, except for it to end.

On the first day of March, though, his next-door neighbour Bill Twill came into the restaurant. Bill was about forty-five, bald except for some wildly straying blond strands. He had been a goat juggler until the Vegan Performance Act had been passed, but now he paid his mortgage by doing odd jobs, such as painting soffits and sculpting butter, because he had always been artistic.

He knocked on the open kitchen door. 'Michael? Haven't caught you at a bad moment?'

Michael was flambéing a panful of chopped pony livers but as soon as the flames had died down he beckoned Bill to come into the kitchen. Bill came and stood close to his shoulder as he carefully tipped the livers into a trayful of vol-au-vents.

'I love watching a skilled man at work,' he said. 'I don't care what they're doing. Plastering a ceiling. Draining a pustule. It's pottery in motion.'

Hamid was grating horseradish. 'It is *poetry*!' He laughed.

'I agree,' said Bill, gravely. Then he said, 'Michael... I've seen something and I didn't know if I ought to tell you about it, but in the end I decided I would because to be frank with you, I found it extremely disturbing.'

'What is it, Bill? Don't tell me my overflow's leaking again.'

'No, nothing to do with your house. But this morning I went to the Tate to see that new exhibition of circus paintings. Bit of nostalgia, I suppose, for the old goat-juggling days. While I was there I went and took a shufti at that Derby Day painting. Do you know the one? Derby Day in eighteen fifty-six by William Powell Frith. One of my favourites. That's when painting was painting and not your splodges.'

'Can't say that I know it, Bill. Mind out, this pan's hot.'

'It's a magnificent painting. Huge. Hundreds of people in it – you know, spectators, entertainers, bookies, gypsies. But here's the thing: there's a very posh-looking woman sitting in a carriage underneath her parasol, on the right-hand side of the painting, and I don't exactly know how to put this.'

Michael stopped beating eggs and put down his whisk.

'Go on, Bill. What are you trying to tell me?'

'It's Susan, Michael. She's the absolute spit of Susan. I know that sounds bonkers, but I stared at it and stared at it and there's no doubt in my mind whatsoever.'

'Bill – she may look like Susan – but when did you say that was painted? Eighteen fifty something?'

Bill reached into his anorak pocket and pulled out his phone. He jabbed at it five or six times and then he handed it to Michael.

Michael wiped his hands, took it, and held it up. The picture showed a young woman in a white-and-yellow dress, sitting in a shiny black landau under a small white parasol. She was studiously ignoring a leathery-faced old gypsy woman in scarlet, who was leaning into the landau, holding out her hand for money. The young woman had rouge-red cheeks, which Susan had never had, but the resemblance was so extraordinary that Michael felt as if a torrent of ice-cold woodlice were running down his back inside his shirt.

'It's a coincidence, Bill. It has to be.'

'Ah, that's what I thought at first,' Bill told him. But he reached out and took his phone back, and then he jabbed at it again.

'That picture you've just seen… that's the one I took. But when I got home I looked up the painting on your Google, to make a comparison. Here.'

Michael's mouth felt dry. Hamid could see that he was upset, and came across the kitchen, frowning, still holding his cleaver.

The Google version of the Derby Day painting was identical to the photograph of it that Bill had taken, except that the young woman in the landau didn't look like Susan at all. The shape of her face was oval, with a receding chin; her eyebrows were thicker; and she had a more prominent nose, with a slight bump in it.

Michael showed the two pictures to Hamid.

'I don't understand this,' he said. 'How could this possibly happen?'

Hamid shook his head. 'I have to agree that the woman in this picture does look so much like your wife, Mr Candlemaker. And it is not as if you are hallucinating. I see it, too. You remember what we were speaking about, how nobody can ever be rubbed out of existence? Somehow your dear wife's likeness has appeared in this painting. I once saw my late grandfather's face in a rock when I was walking in the Margalla Hills near Islamabad. Perhaps this is how all of us reappear, after death. Perhaps we should look for the features of our deceased loved ones in wallpaper, in the bark of trees, in paving stones.'

Michael said, 'This *is* Susan. This is one hundred per cent Susan. Somebody has tampered with this painting and changed this woman's face to look exactly like her, and I want to know who did it and I want to know *how* they did it. I'm going to the Tate right now, Hamid. Can you manage on your own? I can ring Josh and get him in to help you.'

'Are you sure this is wise? Will you not be causing yourself even more grief than you are suffering already? If a man hits his thumb with a hammer, he does not ease the agony by throwing himself into a blackberry bush.'

'Hamid, I have to see this for myself. You can take the stag's-antler pâté off the menu if you like – that will give you more time. I don't think our working-class customers were ever very comfortable with it, anyway.'

It was raining hard when Michael arrived at the Tate, so that the Thames was shrouded in a light grey mist. He could hardly see the shoals of orange rented pedalos, although he could distinctly hear the frantic shouts of their pedallers, as they tried to avoid bumping into each other.

Once inside the gallery, he made his way stiff-legged to the room where the Derby Day painting was hanging. There was nobody else in the room except for an elderly Japanese couple who were peering intently at a tiny still-life of cucumbers and discussing it in breathy Japanese.

'*Kyūridesu ka, soretomo gākindesu ka? Wakari nikuidesu.*'

Michael approached the Frith painting slowly, his attention already focused on the woman in the white-and-yellow dress sitting in her landau. Even from halfway across the room, he could see that she was Susan, and when he came right up to the canvas he was sure of it. The likeness was so overwhelming that it could have been a photograph.

'Susan,' he said, under his breath. 'Susan, can you see me? Can you hear me, Susan? Please… give me a sign, my darling. Anything. A wave. A nod. A smile. A blink of your eyes. You don't know much I miss you, Susan. *Please*.'

The Japanese couple turned and stared at him.

'*Watashi wa kare ga kyōjindenakereba naranai to omou*,' said the husband. He took hold of his wife's arm and shuffled her out of the room.

Michael stood in front of the painting for more than ten minutes, occasionally moving from side to side to see if Susan's eyes were following him. She gave him no response whatsoever, any more than she was giving to the scarlet-dressed gypsy woman who was accosting her for change. All around her, the Downs were crowded with race-going punters all dressed in their finery, as well as acrobats and pie sellers and assorted Epsom riff-raff. In the distance, the grandstand was filled with hundreds of spectators, and beyond that, Michael could see as far as Cobham and Painshill.

'Susan – I'm going to stay here all afternoon if I have to – *please*, Susan, just let me know that you're still alive.'

He waited for nearly a quarter of an hour longer, silently mouthing her name over and over, pleading with her. A gallery attendant appeared in the doorway and stared at him for a while, but then he obviously decided that he was harmless, and strolled away.

He was about to give up when Susan dropped her white glove out of the landau onto the ground. He saw it actually fall, and his heart almost stopped. A painted glove fell out of her painted hand and down to the painted grass. And what had Susan always done, at a drinks party or a dinner or a local preservation society get-together, when she was bored? She would never say a word, or even look at him and raise her eyebrows. She would drop her handkerchief. Dropping her handkerchief meant *get me out of here, as quickly as you decently can.*

'Oh, Susan. Oh, my God. You *are* alive. Don't worry, my darling. I'm not leaving you here in this painting, my darling. I'm taking you with me.'

He looked over his shoulder to make sure that the room was deserted, and that nobody could see him from the next room, either. Then he took a snap-off craft knife out of his raincoat pocket and carefully positioned the point above Susan's parasol. He was just about to cut into the canvas when he heard the squeaking of crêpe-soled shoes on the parquet floor behind him. A husky voice called out, 'Hey! You there! What do you think you're up to?'

Michael quickly pushed the craft knife back into his pocket, slicing the tip of his index finger as he did so. A bulky man in a beige corduroy jacket almost the same colour and texture as Michael's sofa came striding up to him. He had black, thick-rimmed spectacles, a mess of tangled grey hair, and a bulbous, bifurcated nose.

'I hope I didn't see you trying to vandalise that picture,

did I?' he said, coming up to Michael and standing uncomfortably close. His breath smelled of walnuts.

'No, of course not, why would I? I was admiring it, that's all.'

'What's that in your pocket? I saw you put something in your pocket.'

'Nothing,' said Michael. He took his hand out of his pocket and held it up, but his finger was smothered in blood.

'You were going to vandalise it, weren't you? Right – I'm calling for security. And don't try to deny it, because they'll have you on CCTV.'

'I wasn't going to vandalise it. I just wanted to cut that one woman out of it.'

'Oh, I see. And you don't call that vandalism?'

'She's my wife. I know you'll probably think I've gone mad but she's my wife. They took her away five weeks ago under the National Balance Act. They told me she'd ceased to exist but she's here, in this painting. That's her.'

'You expect me to believe that?'

'Like I said, you'll probably think that I've totally lost my marbles, but it is her. She doesn't even look like the woman in the original painting. I can prove it to you.'

'I believe you.'

Michael stared up at him. His glutinous brown eyes were hugely magnified by his glasses and the hairs in his nostrils looked as if spiders were hiding up his nose.

'You believe me? Really?'

'Yes. I believe you. And the reason that I believe you is because I'm responsible.'

'I don't understand.'

'Well, that doesn't surprise me. The emulsification of atoms is not the easiest of scientific procedures to get your head round. But I can assure you that I was I who prepared your wife for inclusion in this painting, and your wife is not the only one. Eleven other characters that you can see here are people who have been atomised under the National Balance Act, and there will be more. It was chosen as the ideal painting because of the number of people in the crowd and because Frith was such a representational painter. One could hardly hope to hide anybody's face in Picasso's *Guernica*, for example.'

'I think I'm dreaming this. Are you honestly telling me that you can put real living people into paintings? That you put my wife into this painting?'

The messy-haired man sniffed and nodded and turned towards the picture. 'There,' he said, 'that fellow in the smock, I did him. That woman next to him, in the orange. And that fellow in the red coat, waving his arm. They're all National Balancers. And him with his back to us, in the maroon coat and the top hat. He's one, too.'

Michael said, 'I'm not sure I can take this.' He went over to the seats in the centre of the room and sat down, and the messy-haired man came and stood next to him.

'As I told you, it's a process called atomic emulsification. It's done with a Sanford-Bugle nuclear disperser. Usually this will disassemble the atoms of any solid objects, or in this case human beings, and allow them simply to fly away randomly into the atmosphere. But my speciality is to blend those dispersed atoms with other media, such as liquid alabaster, or molten bronze, or oil paint. This means that all the atoms of the original object, or in this case human being, are retained in their entirety, but in a malleable form.

'The process is even named after me – the Leonard Homefyre Process.'

Michael nodded towards the Derby Day painting. 'So she's there, my wife – all of her. All of her atoms, anyway?'

'Indeed. And there she will remain. A most attractive young woman, if I may say so.'

'Can she feel anything? Is she conscious at all? She's not in any pain, is she?'

'This is still questionable. There's no reason for me to believe that National Balancers suffer any physical trauma. But there is some evidence that they might retain at least a modicum of their senses, once emulsified. That's something I'm still working on.'

'Is it reversible? I mean – could you bring her back to life, the way she was before you mixed her up with oil paint?'

'Oh, yes. I'm not saying it's easy, and the result is not always one hundred per cent satisfactory. But, yes, it can be done.'

'So you've done it before?'

'Yes. Three times. The first one was what you might call a bit of a mix-up, but the other two were reconstituted quite well.'

'Then if you can reverse the process, do it for Susan. Do it for my wife. I can pay you. I can pay you whatever you want.'

Leonard Homefyre sucked in his breath through gappy brown teeth.

'I'm deeply sorry, Mr – Chandler, isn't it? I remember from your wife. I was instructed to emulsify her by a Home

Office directive. If I were to reconstitute her… well, it would be more than my career's worth. If some of the stories that I've been hearing are true, it would be more than my life's worth.'

'I'm sitting here begging you. I won't say a word to anyone. I mean, who's going to know? There'll still be that woman in the painting, won't there, and Susan and I could move to another part of the country, or even abroad.'

'I feel for you, Mr Chandler, I really do. But the Home Office… they have their agents everywhere.'

Michael thought for a moment. Then he stood up and walked over to the painting. The glove was still in the grass.

'What if you did the same to me, so that I could join her?'

'You mean, emulsify *you*? Are you serious?'

Looking at Susan sitting in the landau, Michael's throat tightened up so much that he could barely speak. 'I love her, Mr Homefyre. She's my life.'

When Hamid arrived at the Deluded Brill the next morning, he was surprised to find that the front door was still locked and the blinds were still drawn down from yesterday evening. He had his own keys and so he let himself in and walked through the gloomy restaurant to the kitchen. It was chilly in there, and it smelled of yesterday's onions.

There was a large envelope propped up on the counter. He took off his brown bobble hat and opened it. Inside was a handwritten letter and Michael's snap-off craft knife.

My loyal friend Hamid,
 I have chosen to join Susan in the painting of Derby

Day. I won't explain to you how this was done, but trust me when I tell you that it's true. All I ask is that you visit the Tate gallery in a week from today, and recognise me in the painting. If I give you the slightest sign that I am stressed or unhappy, take this knife and cut both of us out of the painting. After that, contact Mr Leonard Homefyre at the address below and tell him what you have done. Ask him to reconstitute us. He will know what you mean. If he refuses, then burn us. We would rather die together than live apart. In that event, our house and this restaurant are both yours.

Gratefully and sadly, Michael

Hamid pressed the letter against his heart. 'Oh, Michael. Even when a man or a woman is reduced to clouds of smoke, they can never escape this earth.'

On his third night inside the painting, Michael began to feel that he was losing his mind. He was standing in an open carriage, wearing a top hat and a tight grey waistcoat, peering through a pair of binoculars. Through his binoculars he could see only the empty room in the Tate gallery, even though in real life he would have been focusing on the horses racing around Tattenham Corner.

He could hear, and he could see, but he was unable to move. Out of the corner of his eye he could see Susan's landau in front of him, but Susan was hidden by her parasol, and even though he had tried calling out to her, she hadn't and probably couldn't turn around – even at night, when the gallery was empty, and there was nobody to see her.

In the painting, it never grew dark, and the wind never stopped blowing across the Downs, and the roaring of the crowd never died down. He would never die, either. He could be standing in this carriage for hundreds of years to come, driven mad by the thudding of racehorses' hooves and the endless cries of "*eather! Lucky 'eather!*'

On the seventh day, Hamid appeared in front of the painting. He was wearing a long black coat and he looked sad and worn out. Michael wondered if he had closed the Deluded Brill or tried to continue running it on his own.

Hamid frowned closely at the painting and said, 'Michael? Are you in there? I can see Susan but which one is you?'

It was then that Michael realised that, with his binoculars in front of his face, Hamid couldn't recognise him. He gritted his teeth and strained, and strained, but he couldn't release his grip on the binoculars.

'I can't see you, Michael, even if you're in there. I'm sorry.'

Hamid had already started to turn away when Michael jolted his head back, so that his top hat dropped off. Hamid turned back, his mouth open in shock.

'Michael? Is that you?'

Hamid looked around the room, and then he took out the craft knife and approached the painting with it lifted high, breathing as if he had been running.

'I will save you, my friend! You and your Susan! I will save you!'

He was about to stab the point into the painting close to Michael's shoulder when – through the distorted vision of his binoculars – Michael saw two gallery attendants running into the room. Without a word they seized Hamid's arms and dragged him away.

'I have to save my friends!' shouted Hamid. 'I implore you! I have to save my friends!'

Susan was woken by the doorbell chiming. She sat up and looked around the bedroom, unsure of where she was or what time it was – and where was Michael? The doorbell chimed again, and again, so she climbed out of bed and went over to the window. When she drew back the curtains, she saw two men in Puffa jackets standing outside the porch, one short and one tall, and they had the look of men who were going to stay there until she opened the door.

She put on her dressing gown and went barefoot down to the hallway.

'Who is it?' she called out.

'Home Office, Ms Brightwell.'

She opened the door. It was chilly and grey outside, and dry leaves were rattling across the crazy paving.

'What do you want?'

'We've come to fetch you these, Ms Brightwell. Your birth certificate, your school reports, everything that was confiscated when you temporarily ceased to exist.'

The podgy man handed her a large blue plastic folder.

'You were lucky, there,' he told her. 'That chap Hamid Bukhari who worked at your restaurant, he was deported, so that made room for you again. National Balance, that's what it was, Ms Brightwell. National Balance.'

'My name's not Brightwell any more. It's Chandler. I'm Mrs Chandler.'

'I don't think so, Ms Brightwell.'

'Ask my husband, Michael Chandler.'

'Sorry. There's no such person. Not any more, anyway. He's ceased to exist.'

With that, the two officials walked off, talking to each other. When they reached the front gate, the tall one laughed.

CUTTING THE MUSTARD

with Dawn G Harris

The library door flew open with a bang and a chilly gust of wind blew in, so that the leaflets on the librarian's counter were blown up into the air like a flock of seagulls and were scattered all over the floor.

Terrance Colman looked up from his computer as Mrs Parker stamped over to slam the door shut again. That was the second time this afternoon that it had swung open by itself, and the second time that Mrs Parker had been obliged to bend over, puffing in annoyance, to scoop up all of her leaflets.

Terrance hadn't gone across to help her. As far as he was concerned, he was in charge of the non-fiction section of Broadbent Community Library and his responsibilities were clearly demarcated. He kept a running inventory of all the non-fiction titles and their condition and ordered more when requested. Fiction, children's books, CDs and library administration – none of those were Terrance's department. As far as he was concerned, shutting the door and picking up scattered leaflets would come under 'library administration'.

Apart from his computer, its screen clustered all around with Post-it notes, there was nothing on Terrance's desk apart from a well-chewed ballpen, a notepad, and a half-eaten ham roll. There wasn't a photo of a loved one; there wasn't even a lucky mascot.

Terrance typed in: *The History of Double-Enveloping Worm Gears* by B.M. Truscott, B.Eng, B.Sc. The library needed a new copy because somebody had inexplicably stolen the last one, or forgotten to bring it back.

A noisy group of about fifteen schoolchildren passed his aisle, as they did almost every day at 3:40 pm after they had finished their reading circle, and almost every day they would poke fun at him. It was mostly because of his name, which was displayed in a plastic holder on his desk, but maybe it was the way he looked, too, with his gingery-grey hair that stuck up like a worn-out scrubbing brush.

'Colman's must-*ard*! Colman's must-*ard*!' they would chant at him. But today one girl of about twelve or thirteen came right up close to his desk and whispered, '*Terrance Colman doesn't cut the mustard!*'

He stared back at her, and she gave him an extraordinary smile, a *knowing* smile, as if she were privy to all of his innermost secrets. She had blonde hair plaited into a tight coronet and limpid blue eyes, and for a girl of her age she was almost unnervingly pretty.

'What?' he said.

'Terrance Colman doesn't cut the mustard!' she repeated, but this time she shrieked it at the top of her voice, and all her schoolfriends laughed and jeered and made raspberry noises.

'Doesn't cut the mustard!' they chanted. 'Doesn't cut the mustard!'

They were still chanting it as they pushed their way out of the library, leaving the door open behind them. At the open door, the blonde girl with the blue eyes paused for a moment and turned around to look at Terrance and smile, and as she did so another cold gust of wind blew in, so that her dress flapped. Then she was gone, and more leaflets flew onto the floor.

Terrance sat unresponsive and stared at the computer screen in front of him. He was used to this daily taunting, even though it made him feel even more unworthy at work than he did at home, all alone without even a fish to care for. Today, though, that girl had unsettled him more than anybody had for a long time, and he didn't understand why.

'You still here? Doesn't your shift end at four?' said a sudden deep voice behind him. Terrance turned slowly to see a man in a black gaberdine jacket staring directly at him. He looked back at his keyboard before answering.

'What do you want, Inspector Riley? Come to see what I'm up to, have you?'

'Whatever would give you *that* idea, Mr Colman?' replied the man, lifting himself slightly onto his toes in what was almost a parody of a police officer. 'Working in a library, teenagers around, ex-school teacher – is there something I *need* to worry about? I can see I don't need to worry about your *dress* sense. No, no – benefit of the doubt, I always said that I'd give you. Benefit of the doubt.'

'If you must know I'm awaiting information on the new book *For the Sake of Reptiles*, Inspector. I'm the head of non-fiction as you well know and we have a customer order request.'

'Reptiles? Ah, you mean like *snakes*? Deal with snakes too, do you, Mr Colman? Consider yourself something of a snake yourself, do you? Always thought you were a bit on the slithery side.'

Terrance took in a deep breath and closed his eyes. *I wish he would leave me alone.*

'I'm simply misunderstood, Inspector,' he replied. His patience was beginning to wear thin. 'I'm no more of a snake than the next single middle-aged man. Just because I live on my own and like to keep myself to myself.'

'If only I could believe that, Mr Colman. But – well – the jury believed it, didn't they, and I suppose that's all that matters as far as you're concerned.'

The afternoon sun suddenly shone through the narrow library windows and lit up the dust particles that were floating above Terrance's desk. Strangely, they seemed to be drifting towards his blank computer screen, and as they reached it, it looked as if they were disappearing into the blackness like a swarm of tiny fireflies being drawn into a long dark tunnel. But then the sun went in again, and they vanished. Terrance ran his fingertips across the screen, but there was no dust on it.

'I'll leave you be, Mr Colman,' said Inspector Riley. 'The wife's cooking bangers and mash tonight and I love a bit of mustard with my bangers and mash, so I might well be eating your namesake. Be good, won't you, Mr Colman? Keep yourself to yourself.'

He patted Terence on the shoulder and walked off. Terrance was so agitated that he slammed his fists down onto the desk, breaking the pencil that he was holding. *Why? Why me? I never hurt them – none of them. Some of them even called me Uncle Terrance. Some of them even came back for more.*

It was dark by the time he left the library. He walked along the high street to the bus stop so that he could catch the 57 to take him home. A strong headwind made the tails of his raincoat billow and snap and he gripped his lapels tightly together because it was so cold. He felt almost as if the wind was trying to blow him back towards the library.

At least a dozen people were already waiting at the bus stop, and he joined the end of the queue. He stood there shivering and stamping his feet to keep warm, cupping one hand over his left ear to stop the wind blowing into it and giving him earache, and still clutching his lapels together. This morning's weather bulletin had said that it was going to be chilly, but he didn't remember a warning of strong winds. The Met Office never seemed to get their forecasts right.

After only a minute or two he noticed something that puzzled him. The woman in front of him in the queue was wearing a broad-brimmed brown hat with a beige ostrich feather stuck in the hatband, but the feather wasn't ruffled by the wind at all.

Frowning, he looked further up the queue and saw that a man was reading the *Evening Standard*, holding it wide open. The pages of his newspaper weren't flapping, as he would have expected. And near the front of the queue, two young men were smoking. The smoke from their cigarettes drifted away across the road, but lazily, and in the opposite direction from the way the wind was blowing.

Terrance looked around. Sweet wrappers and discarded plastic bottles were lying in the gutter and cluttering a nearby shop doorway, but none of this rubbish was stirring, even though he would have expected the wind to be scattering it everywhere. The wind seemed to be blowing only for him.

When the bus arrived, he struggled to make his way to the doors, and the driver gave him a curious look as he clung onto the rail and held on to his hat at the same time. It was only when he managed to stumble inside the bus and the doors closed behind him that the wind stopped blowing.

'Hey, man,' he said, as Terrance started to climb the stairs to the upper deck. 'You isn't *drunk*, is you? I can't let you on the bus if you're drunk.'

'Do I *look* drunk?' Terrance retorted. 'Do I smell of alcohol? Do you want to smell my breath?'

'No, you're all right, man. You was so unsteady on your feet, that's all.'

The only seat left on the upper deck was right at the back, next to a skinny schoolgirl in a green gingham dress. She shifted uncomfortably away from Terrance when he sat down. He gave her a smile and said, 'Hey... I like your friendship bracelets.'

The girl stared at him, frowning, as if he had spoken to her in a foreign language.

'I said – I like your friendship bracelets.'

'Oh, do you? But I don't want one from *you*, thanks, if that's what you're thinking.' The girl spoke in a lisping voice, because she was missing her top two front teeth. 'You don't cut the mustard.'

Terrance stared back at her, feeling as if his entire insides were draining away, like bathwater. 'What did you say?'

'You heard,' said the girl, and turned away to look out of the window.

'Do you *know* me?' Terrance insisted. 'Have you seen me in the library?'

'No, and no,' the girl replied. 'And I don't *want* to know you, either.'

Terrance hesitated for a moment, and then he stood up and rang the bell for the next request stop. He got off the bus even though he was still at least a mile and a half away from his home. He started to walk along Streatham High Road, past Pakistani newsagents and brightly lit launderettes and Chinese supermarkets. At first he felt only the softest of breezes, but the further he walked, the stronger the wind started to blow. By the time he reached the Savada Bhojana Restaurant, the wind was so strong that he was leaning forward against it, and passers-by were staring at him as if he were some kind of street magician.

He pushed open the restaurant door and stumbled inside, and immediately the wind dropped. He stood there for a few moments, his mouth tightly closed, holding his breath, because he couldn't stand the smell of curry.

The door had a bell attached to it, which jangled loudly every time a customer went in or out, and it jangled now, and seemed to go on jangling for longer than usual. He could hear that jangle from his bedsit upstairs and every time he heard it he sucked in saliva between his teeth in futile annoyance. Upstairs he could also smell fenugreek from the restaurant: it seemed to permeate everything from his clothes to his mattress. He could even smell it in his nostrils when he was sitting in the library, although that may have been imaginary.

If he could afforded more than £125 a week, he would have moved tomorrow. He sorely missed the large ground-floor flat where he used to live in Polworth Road, when he was head of physics at St Martin's Secondary School. He missed it to the point of grief. He missed the silence and the high ceilings and the morning sun that shone through the living-room windows. He missed the finches that flustered around the bird table.

The children had loved finches, too, and Terrance used to give them a box of Trill so that he could watch them fill up the bird table and throw it around the patio calling out 'birdies! birdies!'

Terrance weaved his way between the restaurant tables to the door that led upstairs. The restaurant was wallpapered in dark crimson with bronze statuettes of Shiva on either side. It was early in the evening but two couples were already eating. Even the sound of them laughing and snapping poppadoms irritated him, and he was sure when he died the pathologist would find that the fumes from bhuna gosht and chicken dupiaza had stained his airways irrevocably orange, like nicotine.

He tried to keep holding his breath but Ghulam the owner saluted him from behind the bar and called out, '*Roz bākhair*, Mr Mustard-sir! A very good evening! How are you?' and he had to wave back half-heartedly and say, 'Fine, thanks!'

As he opened the door to go up to his bedsit, Ghulam came around the bar and said, 'You had a caller, Mr Mustard-sir.'

'A caller? What do you mean? Who was it? Not the Sky technician? I told him not to come till after seven-thirty.'

Ghulam was stocky, with wavy grey hair and a grey moustache like a dirty nailbrush. His eyes always twinkled in a way that made Terrance feel that he might know more about him than he was letting on. He wore a brocade waistcoat the same crimson as the walls, with spatters of dried curry sauce on it.

'It was soon after we opened. A young girl. She asked if you had been able to come back from work. When I said no, not yet, she said, do not be surprised if he does not come back at all.'

'Really? Did she explain what she meant by that?'

Ghulam shook his head. 'No. But she said that if you *did* come back, I was to tell you a special word.'

'Which was what?'

'I don't have a good memory, Mr Mustard-sir, except for what my customers order. But here... I have written it down.'

He went over to the till, picked up an order-pad, and tore off the top page. He handed it to Terrance and said, 'This was all she said. But she gave me a big, big smile, as if she was happy about something. Pretty young girl. Very pretty. Perhaps your niece? She seemed to know you very well.'

Terrance took the page from the order-pad. He stared

at it for nearly a quarter of a minute, feeling as if a Tupperware box full of woodlice had been emptied down his back, inside his shirt. Normally he opened and closed the door that led to his bedsit as quickly as he could, to stop the smell rising upstairs, but this time he left it half-open. He held up the page with his hand trembling and he opened and closed his mouth several times before he was able to speak.

Scrawled across the page, almost illegibly, was *ushabati53Y*.

'Are you sure this what she said?' he asked Ghulam, at last.

'That is it exactly, Mr Mustard-sir. She even spelled out the letters for me, one by one. *You-ess-aitch* – and so forth.'

Terrance said nothing more, not even 'thank you', but climbed the steep hessian-carpeted stairs to his bedsit, closing the door behind him. It was too late, though. The strong smell of jalfrezi had already risen to the landing and he knew that it would have leaked under his door.

He had intended to heat up the fish pie that he had bought yesterday from Lidl, but now he had no appetite at all. He could do nothing but sit on his sofa bed with his head bowed and his hands clenched together. His room was bare. There were no pictures on the walls, no ornaments, only a dead cactus in a pot on the windowsill and an empty budgerigar cage. The inside of his brain felt like a blizzard – not of snowflakes, but of ripped-up photographs, thousands of ripped-up photographs, each of them featuring a leg or an arm or a bare shoulder or a wide-eyed pleading face.

He should have deleted them. He knew he should have deleted them. He should have used that software that blanks out pictures with zeroes, so that they can never be recovered from any hard drive or data bank or iCloud, ever. But they were so precious to him. They meant so much. Every one of them told a story of gentle coaxing and soft encouragement; of laughter and tears and promises of Ferrero Rochers; of kisses on lips that had never been kissed before. Softness, darkness, muted sobbing. For Terrance, those pictures were a record of everything that had given his life meaning – the only times that he had ever experienced anything that approximated love.

He poured out the rest of the can of Carlsberg that he had opened last night. It was flat, but that suited his mood completely. Who in the name of God could have found out the password to his work computer? He had never told anyone what it was and he had never written it down. Who could have guessed that he had used the name of Ushabati Ghosh, the child bride of the 1920s Indian physicist Satyendra Nath Bose, who had married her when he was twenty and she was only eleven?

He didn't pull out his bed that night. The restaurant's doorbell kept on jangling, and the smell of curry seemed to be stronger than ever. He lay sideways on the sofa and dropped off to sleep at about two o'clock. He dreamed that he could hear the wind whistling sarcastically and children's voices taunting him.

'Cut the mustard!' they were singing. 'Cut the mustard! You can't – cu-hut – the mustard!'

At about five in the morning he was woken up by a refuse lorry banging and crashing in the street outside. He sat up, confused, and found that his trousers were soaking.

When he arrived at the library the next morning he found a stack of books waiting for him on his desk – seven or eight of them, even though he had ordered only *For the Sake of Reptiles* and *The History of Double-Enveloping Worm Gears*. His name *Terrance Colman* was scribbled on a Post-it note and stuck to the top book.

He laid his ham roll down beside his notebook and peered at the titles of the books with growing bewilderment. This was the non-fiction section but these books all appeared to be fiction, or poetry. *The Dance of the Nymphs. Children of the Lost Forest. The Day My Youth Was Stolen. Lolita.*

Terrance looked around, feeling increasingly unsettled. The library was deserted, except for Mrs Parker and an elderly man sitting in the corner leafing through an encyclopaedia and systematically wiping his nose with a large white handkerchief. There were no schoolchildren, teasing him about his name: too early for that. No Inspector Riley, standing behind him like Moros, the legendary Greek messenger of impending doom.

He turned back to his desk but even before he had reached forward to switch on his computer, he heard the library door swing open behind him, and a soft, fluffing sound. He paused, not turning around, but alert and listening. The fluffing grew louder, and he heard a leaflet flutter from Mrs Parker's counter and onto the floor. It was that wind again, he was sure of it, that wind that had blown only for him. The titles of those books should have told him that this was something sinister. More sinister than a knock on the window on a dark night; or the scratching sound of steel in a bleak winter storm.

He didn't dare to look behind him, but as he sat there, a small figure glided to stand close beside him, on his left-hand side. He slowly turned his head, his heart beating so hard that it hurt his ribs. The figure was only two metres away, and yet it was in shadow, as if it were standing against the sun.

He leaned forward and adjusted his glasses, trying to see the figure's face. It was a girl – he could see that by her long hair, which was stirred by the rising wind. But he couldn't make out what she looked like, or if he knew her.

'Who are you?' he demanded, trying to sound authoritative, as he did in school. 'What do you want? This is a public library – I hope you know that! We don't allow any nonsense in here, I'm afraid!'

Without warning, his computer monitor flicked on, fuzzed and settled. Words started to appear on the screen, typing quickly from line to line with the keyboard keys denting in accordingly, even though Terrance wasn't touching them. He shoved his chair away from his desk, a blinding pain swelling in his head.

'Who are you? Get away! Get away from me!' he shouted at the girl. He scrambled across his desk for his phone and frantically pressed Mrs Parker's extension number on the front counter.

The girl came closer, although her face remained in darkness.

'Read the words, Terrance,' she told him, pointing to his computer screen. 'Read the words and weep.'

'Audrey? Audrey you must help me – something's happening! I... I can't explain – but it's happening now! Please come!' and with that he slammed the phone down. He looked back to the monitor. The lines of words were still climbing up the screen. There were hundreds of them, thousands, even. At first he found it impossible to focus on them, but then they stopped.

'Read them, Terrance,' the girl repeated, and as she did so her face was gradually lit up, so that he realised it was the same girl who had challenged him yesterday.

Terrance squinted at the monitor. As far as he could make out, the words were all a list of names, and dates, and places. *Sandra Livingstone, 14th May, Tooting Graveney Common. Jessie Wilson, 18th June, Norwood Grove Recreation Ground. Asha Mabela, 12th August, Brockwell Park.*

He read the last lines aloud, but in a whisper. '*You must come in and talk to us, Terrance. You must come in and pay the price for what you did. You think you're special, Terrance? You think you can win? We will show you. We will show you your darkest thoughts, and make you live them for us, the way that you made us live them for you.*'

He turned back to the girl and said, 'I don't understand.'

She gave him a knowing smile, but she didn't answer. Instead, she raised both of her hands, and the library doors swung open again. A wild gust of wind blew in, almost like a hurricane, so that the pages of books flipped furiously back and forth with a sound like hundreds of people clapping. The girl paused beside Terrance for a few moments more, her hair whipping across her face. Then she glided away, towards the door, with books flying off the shelves on either side of her.

'Terrance!' shrieked Audrey. 'Terrance, what's happening?' She was struggling against the wind as she came around her counter and started to clamber over the fallen books towards his desk. More books tumbled off the shelves and a heavy dictionary hit her on the shoulder. '*Terrance!*'

Gradually, though, the wind began to die down, and by the time she reached his desk the library was silent again, and still. A last book dropped off a shelf, like the last lump of ice after a thaw.

'Terrance?' said Audrey, cautiously. 'Terrance, where are you? Terrance?'

There was no sign of Terrance anywhere. His corduroy jacket was still hanging over the back of his chair. His ham roll, wrapped in cellophane, was still lying on his desk. His computer was still switched on but the screen was blank. Audrey went to the back of the non-fiction section, wondering if he had sheltered from the wind in the U-shaped recess of the geography section, but he wasn't there, either.

She walked slowly all around the library, picking up fallen books as she went. She even half-opened the door to the gents' toilet, and called out, 'Terrance?'

There was no reply. Terrance had disappeared. She could only imagine that he had been frightened by the wind and run out of the library, although she was sure that she would have seen him as he came past her counter. Perhaps he had simply had enough of being a librarian and walked out without giving her any notice. He had always been taciturn and never exchanged pleasantries, not even 'good morning,' or 'miserable weather, isn't it?' or 'did you see *Strictly Come Dancing* last night?'

But if he had simply had enough and quit, why had he left his jacket behind, and not taken his lunch? Perhaps he would come back, and explain where he had been. Meanwhile, she switched off his computer.

The hours went past, however, and borrowers came and borrowers went. Books were taken out and books were returned. The school reading circle came in, laughing and jostling as usual, and they seemed to be disappointed that Terrance wasn't there to be jeered at.

'Where's old mustard, then? Hasn't cut it today! That's it! Hasn't cut the mustard!'

That evening, two hours after the library had closed, the sound of shrill singing echoed through its corridors. It was Mavis the cleaner, singing to her heart's content, accompanied by the discordant squeak of trolley wheels. Her trolley was crowded with dusters, disinfectant sprays, a sponge mop and a plastic bucket, as well as a fluffy blue mascot of a bear that her granddaughter had given her.

She swept the floor past the library doors and into the non-fiction section. As she entered it, a chilly draught blew around her ankles and fluttered her pinafore. She looked to see if any of the windows had been left open, but as far as she could make out they were all closed. She carried on warbling, '*You were such a fool to leave me – but the rain keeps singing its song!*'

She pushed her trolley to the middle of the room and then approached Terrance's desk, duster in one hand and Mr Sheen furniture polish in the other. But then she stopped, and saw that Terrance's jacket was still draped over the back of his chair.

She looked at her watch, and said, 'That's weird.' It was past seven o'clock and the library closed at five. As scruffy as he was, she couldn't imagine Terrance leaving his jacket behind, especially not in this weather, and when she lifted it up off the chair, she could see that he had left his wallet in the inside pocket.

'Terrance, ya still 'ere somewhere?' she called out. She waited, but there was no reply. 'Terrance?' she called again, but there was still no answer, so she carried on singing and spraying polish onto his desk.

'I dunno, this man is so mucky,' she muttered to herself. She tugged on a pair of blue nitrile gloves before she picked up Terrance's half-eaten coleslaw sandwich and dropped it into her bin.

Now she picked up her glass cleaning spray, wiping underneath his computer keyboard and over its keys, with a soft rattling sound. She polished the monitor screen and after she had swiped her yellow duster over it, she peered into it to see her own reflection. Almost at once, though, her face began to change, as if it were made of melting wax. She stared at the screen with ever-increasing bewilderment and horror as her hair shrank shorter and her cheeks turned pale and she realised that she wasn't looking at herself any more but Terrance. His eyes were closed but his mouth was slightly open, as if he were finding it difficult to breathe.

Mavis turned around, sharply, expecting to see Terrance standing behind her, but there was no one there.

'This man,' she said shaking her head. 'He give me the creeps. The right royal heebie-jeebies. Something not right with him, ya know.'

She turned back to the screen, expecting his face to have vanished, but it was still there, almost as if it were pressed up against the glass from the inside. Now, though, he opened his eyes and stared directly at her, and his lips moved as if he were trying to say something, and she was sure that she could hear a faint, tiny voice calling out to her. She felt a shivery tingle all the way down to her feet, and she rubbed hard at the screen with her duster, trying to wipe his image away. As furiously as she wiped, though, she couldn't erase him, and she could still hear that tiny, muted voice.

In all the time he had worked at the library, Terrance had never once said hello to her, even though he expected his desk to be clean every morning. Yet here he was, calling out to her, as if he desperately needed her to help him.

It was then that the temperature in the library suddenly dropped like a stone, and Mavis felt as if all the blood in her body had become so cold that it had was as thick as treacle. The bookshelves started to creak, and a freezing draught made her arms go prickly with goose bumps.

'What ya doin', ya horrible, horrible man!' she screamed at Terrance's face. 'Stop starin' at me, will ya? Stop starin'!'

She wiped the monitor screen around and around, harder and harder. It was then that the duster began to squeak and slime, and before long she realised it was becoming soaked in red and that she was swirling wide red streaks all over it. The harder she pressed, the more red liquid seemed to swell from the seams of the monitor frame, and she realised from its metallic smell that it was blood. She had been a trainee nurse once, and she knew what blood smelled like.

Blood was not only oozing from the frame of the monitor but now it started to dribble from the ventilation holes underneath the screen and drip all over the keyboard. Within seconds it was pouring out, sliding across the desk and pattering in blobs and sticky glops onto the carpet. Mavis flung her blood-soaked duster to one side and tried to take a step back, but the interior of the library was now so cold that the blood had coagulated and it stuck to the sole of her shoe. Her shoe came loose and her stockinged foot slipped sideways on the blood-soaked laminate floor. She fell to her knees, grabbing for support from her trolley, but that toppled over with a crash.

With her pinafore drenched in blood, she managed to climb to her feet and hobble out of the non-fiction section and make for the library doors. She unlocked them and then she stumbled out onto the forecourt. The street was deserted so she reached into her wet pinafore pocket and took out her phone. Even though it was tacky with blood she managed to prod out 999.

'What's your emergency?' the operator asked her.

'Police. I'm at Broadbent Library. There's nobody here but it's like somebody got murdered.'

'I'm sorry. I don't understand you. There's nobody there but you think that someone's been murdered?'

'I seen Mr Colman's face, but he wasn't there! He wasn't

there but there's *blood*! There's so much blood! It keep on comin'! Blood, blood and more blood!'

Two police cars arrived, their blue lights flashing, in less than ten minutes. When they climbed out, four uniformed officers found Mavis sitting on the library steps, shivering. She had been too frightened to go back inside to fetch her coat.

'What's your name, love?' asked a female officer, squatting down beside her.

'Mavis. I do the cleaning here.'

'And you reported that you saw blood?'

'It's in there. In the library. So much blood! It's everywhere. All over the floor.'

'Whose blood, Mavis?'

'I don't know. There's nobody there.'

'Didn't you tell the emergency operator that you saw somebody's face?'

'I did. Mr Colman. I seen his face but not him. Only his face. I try to wipe it away but it wouldn't be wiped. And then all that blood come pourin' out his computer! Blood, blood, blood, but nobody there!'

The female officer looked up at her fellow officer. She said nothing, but raised her eyebrows in that expression that meant 'nutter'.

'Are the library doors still open?' the male officer asked her. 'We'll take a butcher's inside, okay? Just to see what's what.'

At that moment, another car arrived and parked behind the police cars. Its door opened and out stepped Inspector

Riley, wearing a thick sheepskin coat with the collar turned up. He came up the library steps and said, 'What's the SP? I was just on my way to Morden nick and I heard the shout on the radio.'

'This is Mavis, the cleaner,' said the female officer, standing up straight. 'She says that there's blood in the library but nobody there.'

'Mavis?' said Inspector Riley. 'You mentioned somebody called Colman. Did you mean Terrance Colman?'

Mavis nodded. 'Terrance Colman. That's him. I seen his face in his computer but he wasn't there.'

'*In* his computer?'

'Yes. Like he's inside it. Like a goldfish in a bowl. But then all that blood.' She pressed her hand against her mouth and then she said, 'I think I'm going to bring up me lunch.'

Inspector Riley turned to the female officer. 'Take care of Mavis, would you?' he told her, and then he beckoned to the other officers and said, 'Come on. Let's go in and see what the bloody hell this blood is all about.'

He pushed open the library doors, and they gave a high, soft groan, like a child having a nightmare. The library was brightly lit, but it was still so cold that the officers' breath smoked.

'Blimey,' said one of them. 'It's like a bleeding fridge in here.'

Inspector Riley walked straight across to the non-fiction section. He saw the blood as soon as he entered the alcove. It had spread halfway across the floor, all around the upturned cleaning trolley, and Mavis' footprints were still clearly visible, as well as her abandoned shoe.

'Hold on,' said one of the officers. 'I'll go and get some overshoes.'

Inspector Riley waited at the edge of the pool of blood while the officer went off to fetch some plastic forensic shoe covers. He noticed that it was still creeping across the floor, until it was almost touching the toes of his suede Hush Puppies.

He could see Terrance's blood-smeared PC on his desk, but apart from the crimson circles where Mavis had wiped it, the screen was black and blank.

Once they had all pulled on their blue plastic overshoes, Inspector Riley told two of the officers to make a thorough search of the library, including the book storeroom, the staffroom, and the toilets.

'Somebody must have been killed to produce all this blood, unless it was brought in here in a bucket, and I don't think that's very likely. There's no footprints apart from the cleaner's, and no tracks to show that a body was dragged out of here, so presumably the deceased is still on the premises.'

He went up to Terrance's desk, his shoe covers making a sticky-tape sound on the floor.

'It looks like the blood came from *inside* the computer. How weird is that?'

The sergeant standing beside him shook his head. 'On a weirdness scale of one to ten, guv, I'd say about seventy-three.'

At that moment – even though Inspector Riley hadn't touched the keyboard – the computer screen switched itself on. At first it lit up bright and blank, but then the scene of a local park appeared, with flower beds and thick bushes.

A pretty young girl of about twelve appeared, with blonde plaits, a pink blouse, and jeans. She was laughing as she ran into the bushes and disappeared, but the camera followed her. It looked as if she were playing hide-and-seek and whoever was holding the camera was trying to find her.

After two or three minutes, the camera found her crouching down behind a bush. The cameraman's hand appeared, seizing her arm. She laughed again, but then the camera was dropped onto the ground and she stopped laughing and said, 'No – no – *no*!' Her voice became muffled and then her pink blouse fell onto the ground, in view of the camera, followed a few moments after by her jeans.

Inspector Riley and the sergeant watched in silence as they heard the crackling of leaves and twigs, and then grunts and cries and finally the thin, pathetic sound of sobbing. The camera was picked up and focused on the girl lying beside the bush, naked.

'*Emily Wilson, July the twelfth, Dulwich Park,*' said a clear, childlike voice.

'Jesus,' said the sergeant. But the videos continued, showing one young girl being molested after another, sometimes in parks, sometimes in alleyways, sometimes indoors. At the end of each video, the same childlike voice would announce the girl's name. There must have been well over forty in all, but at last the screen went blank.

'So *this* is where Terrance Colman hid all his images,' said Inspector Riley. 'Right here in his library computer. We searched his home PC and his laptop but we never found anything to incriminate him.'

'But where is he?' asked the sergeant. 'And what's all this blood?'

The other two officers came back. 'We've searched the whole place, guv. Not a sausage. No dead bodies, either.'

'Well at least we've got enough evidence to take him back to court, if we do find him. That's if this blood isn't his. I'll give forensics a bell so that they can—'

Before he could finish, the computer screen cracked diagonally, from one side to the other, and then it shattered completely, with sparkling glass spraying across Terrance's desk. Out of the broken screen, something greasy and pale and bloody came bulging. To begin with, Inspector Riley thought it was a firehose, but then there was a slopping noise, and yards and yards of this blood-streaked tubing came piling out of the computer and onto the floor at his feet. It smelled rich and foetid, like the inside of an abattoir when dead cows are disembowelled, and it was then that he realised that it was human intestines.

As soon as the last of the intestines had slithered out, a dark brownish liver dropped onto the desk, followed by a sagging stomach and deflated lungs, and then a heart, with all its arteries sprouting out of it. After that, there was a clattering sound, and a shower of bones came tumbling out, almost all of them broken into pieces. A pelvis, a ribcage, shoulder blades, and then a spinal column, which rattled out like a skeletal boa constrictor.

When the spine had collapsed onto the floor, a head appeared inside the screen. It was deathly pale, with gingery-grey hair clotted with blood. Its hazel eyes were open and it was staring blindly but accusingly at Inspector Riley as if it blamed him for its dismemberment.

Inspector Riley was shaken, and he could hardly find the breath to speak. As the head rolled onto the desk, though, and lay on its side, he managed to say, 'Terrance Arthur Colman,' as if he were arresting him.

'Is that really him?' asked the sergeant, in awe.

'That's him all right. We couldn't catch him, could we? But all those children he abused – it looks like they managed to cut the mustard.'

A PORTRAIT OF KASIA

As Leonard was walking back to his car he glanced into the Pond View Café. A woman with tangly blonde hair was sitting in the sunlit window seat with her back to him.

He carried on a few steps, but then he stopped and turned around to look at her again. Although he couldn't see her face, her hair was so much like Kasia's that she could almost *be* Kasia. She herself had jokingly said that she had 'lion's hair'.

Yet Kasia was in Wrocław, in Poland, more than eight hundred miles away. It was impossible that she could be sitting in this café, in Walton-on-the-Hill, in Surrey, in England, especially since she had given him no indication that she might be coming over to see him.

All the same, Leonard was so intrigued by her resemblance that he went back, pushed open the café door and went inside. The young woman behind the counter was steaming milk for a cup of cappuccino, so the noise was deafening, but she gave Leonard a smile and a wave, as if she knew him, even though he had never been in here before.

He went over to the window. For an instant, he was blinded by the sunlight, but then he saw that it *was* Kasia.

It had to be Kasia. He had never met her in person before, but she had sent him twenty or thirty photographs of herself already – either at home, or walking in the woods, or standing on the Piaskowy bridge overlooking the Oder. The sun made her wild hair appear to be on fire, and she was looking up at him over the rim of her coffee mug with mischievous green eyes.

'Kasia?' he said.

'Of course,' she said, putting down her mug. 'I've been waiting for you. You said three o'clock, didn't you?'

Leonard drew out a chair and sat down next to her. 'I don't remember. I didn't expect you to be here.'

'You are going to show me your studio. You haven't changed your mind, have you?'

'No, well, no, of course not. But when did you get here? I can't believe that I invited you and then clean forgot about it. How on earth did I forget about it?'

'It doesn't matter,' she said, and laid her hand on top of his. Her fingernails were painted silvery green to match her eyes and she was wearing a green pearl bracelet. 'I'm here now and nothing else is important. As we say in Poland, "*Miłość pozostaje świeża nawet wtedy, gdy ser pleśnieje.*"'

'Oh, yes? And what does that mean?'

'Love stays fresh even when the cheese goes mouldy.'

Leonard laughed and shook his head. He couldn't believe that this was really Kasia. Yet here she was, with her feline eyes and her high cheekbones and her pouting pink lips that glistened as if she had just finished kissing. He could even smell her perfume, both flowery and fruity. One of Calvin Klein's, unless he was mistaken.

She was wearing a short white jacket that seemed to have fine silvery threads in it, with a dark green T-shirt underneath it.

'Latte for you too, sir?' asked the young woman behind the counter.

'No thanks. I think we'll take a walk.'

In the blink of an eye he found that they were no longer sitting in the café, but standing under the beech trees that surrounded Mere Pond. He couldn't remember paying the bill at the café, or crossing the road, but here they were, by the water's edge, their hands loosely held together, as relaxed with each other as if they had been together for years.

Mere Pond was curved and wide, and the usual crowd of squabbling ducks had been joined by three haughty swans. On most days there were at least half a dozen other people here, tossing torn-off bits of bread to the birds, but this afternoon there was nobody. In fact the entire village seemed to be deserted, with no cars parked at the side of the road, and nobody walking dogs on the heathland opposite. There was only him, and Kasia, and the cloudless sky, which the pond reflected without a single ripple, like a mirror.

'So what are you painting now?' asked Kasia.

'Oh, some fellow's portrait. He's the chairman of the local golf club. His cheeks are so red I ran out of carmine and I had to nip out to the art shop and buy another tube.'

'I love your country scenes. The forests, and the seaside. And your nudes.'

'Yes, well I much prefer painting landscapes and women.

But portraits pay well and I have to pay the mortgage. And of course I have to eat.'

'The women you paint are always so lovely. But not only that – they have so much feeling about them. It seems like you can capture their inside as well as their outside. How can I put it? You understand that behind those beautiful breasts there is a heart beating. That is why I was attracted to your paintings in the first place.'

'I should paint you one day, Kasia. How long are you staying here? And where are you staying?'

Kasia looked away from him, out across the pond. The sky seemed to be growing darker, even though there were still no clouds. A chilly wind began to rise, and suggestively whistle. It stirred up the dry autumn leaves so that they blew across the pathway and rattled against their ankles, and then danced off across the surface of the water.

Suddenly and unexpectedly, Kasia turned back to him and said, 'Leonard, I don't want to lose you.' There were tears sparkling in her eyelashes. 'I need you in my life. Please tell me you're never going to leave me.'

Leonard wrapped his arms around her and held her close. Her tangled mane tickled his face but he kissed it. He lifted her chin so that he could kiss her forehead, but he found that he wasn't lifting her chin at all, only the lapel of his overcoat.

He opened up his arms and took a step backward, but Kasia had gone. He turned around and around, looking for her, but he couldn't see her running away, not in any direction. She had simply vanished.

'Kasia!' he called out, but for some reason his voice didn't carry, and the only person who could hear it was him – not that there was anybody else around.

'*Kasia!*' he called again, and this time he woke himself up.

'You were talking in your sleep again,' grumbled Bartek. 'That's about the tenth time you've woken me up in the middle of the night.'

'I'm sorry,' said Kasia. 'But honestly – I don't know I'm doing it.'

Bartek rolled off the bed and stood up, scratching himself under his hairy armpits.

'You're still doing it, whether you know you're doing it or not. It's all right for you – all you have to do is sit on your arse all day, and you can catch up on your sleep whenever you like. I have to stay awake and crunch numbers. If I dozed off, they'd fire me like the crack of a whip.'

Kasia pulled the duvet right up to her neck and stared at the side of the bedside table. She felt worn out, as if she had hardly slept at all. She could remember dreaming that she had met Leonard beside a pond somewhere, and that Leonard had been wearing a long, oatmeal-coloured overcoat, but that was all. Even now, as she heard Bartek banging up the toilet seat and urinating with a seemingly endless clatter, she could feel the details of the dream sliding away, like an ebb tide sliding away down the beach.

She could recall Leonard saying, in that warm bass voice of his, 'I should paint you one day, Kasia,' and the way he had lifted one mahogany-brown eyebrow when he said it, and smiled.

'I'm taking my shower now!' Bartek called out, from the bathroom. 'Come on, Kaska, get your lazy backside out of that bed and make my breakfast! And my *drugie śniadanie*, too, to take to work! Jesus!'

Kasia threw back the duvet and sat up, furiously shaking her tangled hair. Then she padded through to the kitchen, barefoot and wearing only her nightshirt with its pattern of green oak leaves. The kitchen was cramped, more of a galley than a kitchen, with a counter where they would sit to eat their meals, with two tall stools.

Bartek always wanted the same for his breakfast, every day. Three open-topped sandwiches with kiełbasa and tomatoes and quark cheese with radishes, and three scrambled eggs. He always wanted the same for his *drugie śniadanie*, too, his second breakfast: sandwiches with smoked sheep's cheese and those little dry sausages called *kabanosy*.

Kasia made his sandwiches and then she cracked three eggs into a dish and whipped them up with a fork. She had just poured them into the frying pan when Bartek came into the kitchen. His reddish hair was still damp and sticking up, but he was dressed now. He was wearing tight grey trousers with his belly bulging over the belt and the white shirt that Kasia had ironed for him yesterday evening, and he was tightening the knot of his purple company tie.

'Aren't those eggs ready yet?' he asked her, coming up close behind her and peering over her shoulder, his belly pressing against her back.

'Almost. You can sit down now.'

Instead of sitting down, though, he lifted the hem of her nightshirt and slid his hand up between her legs.

'Bartek! Don't!' she protested, and twisted her hips to shake him off.

Bartek laughed. 'What? You don't like a little stimulation while you're scrambling eggs? I bet they'll be even more scrambled if I turn you on!'

'You're *not* turning me on! You're just being a nuisance! Go and sit down!'

'Hey! You're all prickly! You need to shave again! I hate it when you're all prickly!'

Kasia swung around and pushed him away. As she did so, she knocked the handle of the frying pan and it tipped off the top off the stove. It hit Bartek on the left knee and the scrambled eggs splattered all the way down his trouser leg and onto his shoe.

Bartek took two or three steps backwards, looking down at his trousers in horror. Then, without a word, he stepped forward again and slapped Kasia on the side of her head, so hard that she fell sideways against the stove and hit her forehead on the knobs.

'You stupid, *stupid* bitch! Look what you've done! These are my only trousers for work! What do you think I'm going to do now? Go to the office in my underpants? You're so fucking stupid I can't believe it!'

Kasia was on her knees on the vinyl-tiled floor. Her head was ringing and her right eye was already beginning to swell.

'Look at my fucking trousers!' Bartek screamed at her. 'How can you be so useless? How? But then you've always been useless! Kasia the Fucking Useless, that's what they should have christened you! You can't cook for shit, you can't sew, your hair's like a fucking bird's nest! You can't even give us a baby, because you're barren!'

He smacked Kasia across the face, both ways, and then he seized her tangled hair in both hands and wrenched her violently from side to side before throwing her backwards. She hit the back of her head against the leg of one of the stools, and for a few seconds she blacked out.

When she opened her eyes again, she could see tiny white sparks circling around her. She lay there for a while, listening, not daring to move. She could feel something cold and damp against her bare legs but she didn't want to lift her head to see what it was in case Bartek hit her again.

After about a minute, though, she heard the front door slam. Bartek must have stormed out. He might have been angry, but she knew that he was terrified of losing his job.

She raised her head, and then reached up for the crossbar of the stool to help herself to sit up. The cold and damp feeling on her legs was Bartek's sandwiches, tomatoes and cheese and slices of ham. He must have swept them off the counter in his rage.

Kasia climbed to her feet. Her lips were tightly pursed but she was still making a thin mewling sound, and tears were running freely down her cheeks. She had never felt so lonely and so helpless in her life. She had already told her sister Ola how badly Bartek treated her, and how he was always shouting and hitting her, but Ola had simply shrugged and said it was her fault for having married him.

She had told her mother, too, but her mother had said that she had always obeyed her father when he was alive. '*Kobieta powinna znać swoje miejsce.*' 'A woman should know her place.'

She picked up the sandwiches and dropped them into the bin, then she scraped up the scrambled eggs. When she had cleared up, she limped into the bathroom and stared at herself in the mirror over the washbasin. Her right eye was crimson now, and completely closed up. She thought she looked as if she had been in a road accident. Perhaps that was what she could tell her friends. *I was driving to Nysa and I swerved to avoid a dog and hit a tree.*

Henry Walters knocked at the door and when Leonard opened it, he blurted out, 'So sorry to be late, old boy! It was the annual club dinner last night and I'm afraid I overdid the brandy!'

'Don't worry,' said Leonard, as he followed him along the corridor into the studio. 'I didn't get up until half past eight myself. I slept like a log but I was dreaming all night.'

'Well, you know what that's a sign of, don't you?'

'It's probably a sign that I should have downed a few brandies before I went to bed, like you.'

He helped Henry to struggle out of his velvet-collared Crombie overcoat and hung it up behind the studio door.

'No,' said Henry. 'It's a sign that there's something lacking in your life. Something unfulfilled. That's what dreams are all about. I used to have dreams that I was Henry the Eighth. Honestly – Henry the Eighth! Night after night, eating chicken legs and throwing the bones over my shoulder! Ordering people who annoyed me to have their heads cut off – all that! Then they elected me chairman of the golf club, and I never had that dream again.'

Leonard thought about Kasia, and the way she had looked up at him with tears sparkling in her eyes, begging him not to leave her, but he said nothing. Henry went over to the high-backed armchair where he was sitting for his portrait, while Leonard crossed over to the sideboard where he kept all his paints and his brushes and his bottles of linseed oil.

His studio was a glass conservatory that was built onto the back of his semi-detached Victorian house. The roof panels were painted white to subdue the sunlight, so that it looked already like a painting of a studio, rather than a real studio. It was cluttered with at least half a dozen easels and stacked with canvases and various props that Leonard used in his portraits. Over the years he had acquired a pot-bellied Etruscan vase filled with purple ostrich plumes, an antique cello, a stuffed golden Labrador with only one eye, and even a human skull (ideal for portraits of amateur actors who wanted to look like Hamlet).

'My goodness!' said Henry, as he made himself comfortable in his armchair. 'Is that your new model? She's a cracker!'

Leonard was struggling into his paint-spattered smock, with both arms lifted up in the air. 'Who do you mean?' he asked.

'That young filly there!'

Henry nodded his head towards an easel that was angled towards him, but from where he was standing Leonard couldn't see the canvas on it. He was slightly baffled, because had no recollection of starting another painting, and he hadn't hired a model for over two months.

He tugged his smock straight, and then he picked up his palette and his brushes and walked around so that he could see what Henry was talking about. The picture on the easel was only half-finished, but there was no doubt that it was in his own idiosyncratic style – the underpainting with burnt sienna and the blocking with a dry flat brush.

It was a nude girl, sitting in the same armchair that Henry was sitting in now. Her face was not yet recognisable, although the outline that was painted so far suggested that she had wide, distinctive cheekbones. However, it was her wild blondish mane that gave away her identity. He had underpainted it already and used the scratching technique called sgraffito to give it a fine hairy texture.

'Wouldn't mind taking a sneaky look in here, the next time that she's sitting for you!' Henry chortled.

Leonard stared at the painting, speechless. It was Kasia. It had to be Kasia. But when had he started painting this picture of her, and how? He had plenty of photographs of her, but she had never sent him any nudes, and he had never asked her for any or expected them.

Five months ago, she had sent him a friend request on his Facebook page – Leonard Slater, Illustrator and Fine Artist. She had told him that she was a librarian and had admired his book illustrations for years, especially the pictures he had painted for the Polish-language edition of *Alice Through the Looking-Glass*. He had checked her Facebook page before accepting her as a friend, as he did with every request, but when he had seen her profile picture he had been struck by how attractive she was – that tangly hair, and those impish eyes.

He had written back to her, and she had written back to him, and over the weeks and months that had followed, their correspondence had grown warmer and closer, until they were writing to each other every day. She was married, apparently, to an accountant called Bartek, but she told Leonard that since their marriage three years ago he had become increasingly cold and uncaring. In her own words, she felt 'broken'. She needed someone to make her feel whole again, and valued.

He had dreamed about meeting her, but the travel restrictions imposed by the Covid-19 pandemic had so far made it impossible for him to fly to Poland.

He was still staring at the nude painting when Henry said, 'Come on, then, old boy! Are you going to crack on painting? I'm sorry I'm late but I don't have all day!'

'Yes, of course,' said Leonard. He went over to Henry's portrait and squeezed some phthalo blue onto his palette so that he could finish painting his golf club tie.

He started to paint, but then he paused to stare again at the picture of Kasia, his brush poised an inch from the canvas. Henry noisily cleared his throat, to show that he was becoming impatient.

Leonard put down his palette and his brush. 'You'll have to accept my apologies, Mr Walters. I'm afraid that I'm not feeling very creative this morning. Do you mind if we call it a day? I'm sure I'll be firing on all cylinders by Monday, if you can come back then.'

'"Not feeling very creative?"' Henry blustered. 'What's creative about painting my portrait? You've almost finished it, haven't you? And for God's sake, it's not as though you're painting *The Fighting Temeraire* or *The Rape of the Sabine Women!*'

'I'm sorry, but I'm just not with it today. There must be days when you're off your game of golf.'

'Well, of course. But painting a fellow who's sitting right in front you, not moving a muscle, that's not exactly like knocking a ball into the rough.'

Leonard didn't argue. He went over to the door and came back with Henry's overcoat.

'I can't do Monday,' Henry told him, pushing his arm aggressively into his right sleeve. 'I have to go to Leicester to see my sister. In fact I don't think I'll be back until Thursday at the earliest.'

'Just let me know. The paint will be nicely dry by then, anyway. Good for adding detail.'

'Bloody waste of time, coming here today. And with the Devil's own hangover, too.'

Once Henry had left, still grumbling under his breath, Leonard went back to the picture of Kasia.

I must be losing it. When did I start painting this? Don't tell me I've been painting in my sleep.

He left the studio and went into his living room. His laptop was lying open on the coffee table, so he picked it up and tapped out a Hotmail message to Kasia.

'*Good morning, my darling. Did you have any dreams last night? For instance, did you dream that I painted your picture?*'

After a few minutes she sent him a message in reply.

'Dear Leonard. I had no dreams last night. I took two pills to help me sleep. I will tell you why later.'

Leonard sat back. He felt unreal. Was he asleep or was he awake? Yet there was another message in his inbox. It was from Helen, his ex-wife, so he must be awake. She wanted to know if she could come round and collect the Villeroy & Boch dinner set that she had forgotten to take the last time she had raided their joint belongings.

'*Take whatever you like,*' he wrote back, and signed it '*L*'.

That night, about a quarter to midnight, it started to rain. Leonard was sitting in his studio, wondering if he ought to continue painting the picture of Kasia or whether to abandon it. He had found a picture of her face on his laptop that closely matched the position and the lighting of the model in the painting. He had printed it out and pinned it to the top of the canvas, so that he could copy it.

But to finish this painting seemed like a kind of madness. He had grown to love Kasia, but so far it was only a distant relationship, like penfriends. To paint a nude of her seemed obsessive, almost creepy, the kind of thing that a stalker would do.

Thunder rumbled in the distance, over the Downs, and then the rain began to lash down even more heavily, rattling on the glass roof of his studio and gushing from the gutters. He stood up. He would leave the painting for now and think about it again tomorrow. What he needed was a good night's sleep.

He was just about to climb the stairs to his bedroom

when there was a knock at his front door. Who the hell was knocking at this time of night?

He called out, 'Who is it?' and a faint voice answered, 'It's me, of course.'

He slid off the chain and opened the door. To his astonishment, Kasia was standing in the porch, wearing a wet pink raincoat, her tangled hair dripping over her shoulders.

'Kasia? Come in, come in, you're soaking. How did you get here? You didn't tell me you were coming.'

He looked up and down the street to see if there was a taxi disappearing, but the street was deserted.

'You said midnight,' Kasia told him, shaking her hair. It was then that Leonard was disturbed to see that her right eye was swollen and purple and almost completely closed up.

He closed the door and took off her raincoat. 'Kasia, sweetheart – what happened to your eye? You haven't been in a fight, have you?'

'I left one of the kitchen cupboard doors open. I turned around and hit myself on it.'

'No, you didn't. Was it Bartek?'

'All right, yes. But it was my fault. I spilled eggs on his trousers.'

'And he hit you? For spilling eggs? You should have called the police.'

'The police would not have helped. They would have said, "Look what you have done to your husband's trousers, no wonder he lost his temper." They probably would have arrested *me*, for assaulting him.'

'I can't believe it. I feel like getting on a plane right now and beating him up.'

'Forget it. The bruise will fade away. But you and me, we will always stay together.'

'When did I say midnight? I didn't even know you were coming. Where did you land? Heathrow, or Gatwick?'

She took hold of his hands, stood up on tiptoe and kissed him. 'You said midnight, my dearest Leonard, so here I am. All ready to pose for you. You don't have to paint my bruise, do you? I think I should dry my hair, though, don't you? You don't want me looking like a drowned mongoose.'

'Come through. The gas fire's on – you can warm yourself up. Would you like a hot drink? Coffee, or tea? Or a glass of wine, maybe?'

'A small glass of wine would be welcome. Do you have red?'

'Malbec, yes. Come through.'

He ushered her into the living room and she sat down close to the fire. He poured glasses of wine for both of them, and then he went upstairs to bring down the hairdryer that Helen had left behind. He sat watching her while she fluffed up her hair, but he didn't ask her again when he had invited her here, or how she had flown to England, or when. The hairdryer was too noisy for conversation like that.

When her hair was dry, she stood up, smiling, and said, 'Are you ready to carry on painting?'

'I'm not sure. I mean, are *you* ready to sit for me, what with that black eye and everything?'

'You were so keen last night. You haven't changed your mind?'

She was wearing a bottle-green, rollneck sweater and a sandy-coloured skirt, and dark-brown leather boots. She pulled off her sweater and dropped it onto her chair, and then she unzipped her skirt and stepped out of that. Underneath she was wearing only black tights.

'Would you unfasten my bra for me?' she asked, turning her back to him.

Leonard hesitated. *Is this a dream? No, it can't be a dream. The painting is real, so she must have come last night and I must have started to paint her then. If it's a dream, though, it doesn't matter if she's asking me to undress her, because it's only a dream. And if it's real, she's asking me to undress her, she wants me to, so how can that be wrong?*

He slid open the catch of her bra and she dropped that on the chair, too. Then she sat down and levered off her boots. Finally she rolled down her tights, and kicked them off her feet, so that she was completely naked.

When she stood up again, she faced up to Leonard and opened up her arms. He took hold of her, and held her close, and kissed her – first her forehead, and then her lips, and then they were kissing like hungry wolves, clinging on to each other as if they were trying to tear each other apart.

Leonard gasped, 'I need you, Kasia! You don't know how much!'

He steered her gently backwards towards his large Victorian sofa, which was upholstered in soft purple velvet. He laid her head down on one of the pink toile cushions with her wild blonde hair spread out, and kissed her again. She reached up and started to unbutton his shirt, and tug it out of his waistband. He pulled his shirt off and dropped it onto the floor, while she was already unbuckling his belt.

'What is that?' she said. 'On your shoulder? Is that a tattoo?'

'No. It's a birthmark.'

'It looks like a bird, with its wings spread out. And it has a pointed beak, like a hummingbird.'

Leonard glanced at it. The birthmark was dark brown, a little over four inches wide, which was the wingspan of a real hummingbird.

'It's hereditary, which is quite unusual. It gets passed down from one generation to the next.'

Kasia stroked it with her fingertips, as if it were a real bird.

'Really?'

'My mother has one, and my grandfather has one, too. And, yes, it does look like a hummingbird. We always thought that, too. My grandfather said that God probably gave us that mark because the hummingbird is the only bird that can fly backwards, and we were the most backward family God had ever created.'

Kasia laughed. Even though her right eye was puffed up, her left eye was shining with delight. She tugged down the zip of his trousers and slid her hand inside his briefs. He was already hard and she gripped him tight as if she were holding a baton in a relay race, or had won an Oscar.

He stood up. He peeled his socks off first, because his father had always told him that there are few sights that women find less sexy and more comical than a man wearing nothing but his socks. Then he dropped his trousers and pulled down his navy blue briefs.

When he climbed onto the sofa, Kasia took hold of him again, and rubbed him up and down. 'You're the same as me,' she said, feeling with her other hand between his legs. 'You have no hair. I've never seen that on a man before. It's beautiful. You look like one of those Greek sculptures.'

He kissed her again and again. 'It's a long story.' He smiled. 'The very first girlfriend I ever slept with was Anglo-Indian, and she insisted that I shave off all my pubic hair. I don't know why – it was for some religious reason I think. But after that it became a habit. My ex-wife liked it, although she didn't like it enough to stay faithful.'

'Well, you have enough gorgeous, dark-brown hair on your head, my dearest Leonard. And such luxuriant eyebrows. Is that the right word, "luxuriant"? And dark-brown eyes like my favourite chocolates.'

Leonard kissed her breasts until her nipples crinkled, and ran his hands lightly down her sides so that she shivered. Then he parted her thighs and peeled apart the lips of her vulva, as gently as if he were opening up two damp rose petals on a drizzly day. She was glistening with juice, and he dipped two fingers inside her so that he could use it to make himself even more slippery. Then, very slowly, he slid himself into her, as deep as he could, until their bare skin was pressed together, and they could hardly tell where one of them ended and the other one began.

Kasia shivered again as Leonard touched the neck of her womb.

'Oh my God,' she breathed. 'Oh my dearest darling. Why didn't I meet you years ago?'

'Kasia,' whispered Leonard, close to her ear. 'You're an angel.'

Their lovemaking went on and on. The sofa creaked rhythmically and the clock on the wall behind them ticked in time with every stroke of their bodies. Now it chimed one. Leonard had never felt so close to a woman before, the way he felt now with Kasia. He imagined that he could see right inside the star-sparkling darkness of her mind, like the sea at night, and that he could share with her the rising waves that were bringing her closer and closer to a climax.

It took all of his self-control to hold himself back as she started to shudder, and then pant, and grip his shoulder so hard that her nails dug into his hummingbird. Then she quaked, and he couldn't stop himself any longer, and they held on to each other as if they were falling hundreds of feet from the top of a burning building, and would die together when they hit the ground.

At last they lay together on the sofa, side by side, panting.

'*You*,' said Leonard. 'You are amazing.'

Kasia gave him an impudent smile. 'Do you have enough strength left to paint me?'

He stood up and retrieved his trousers from the floor. 'How about another glass of wine first? And then maybe an action replay?'

'Oh, so you're *not* exhausted?'

Leonard went into the kitchen to fetch the bottle of Malbec.

'Are you hungry at all?' he called out. 'I could knock up a plate of cheese biscuits and olives if you like.'

Kasia didn't answer, so when he went back into the living room, he said, 'Would you like something to eat?'

Kasia was no longer there. Not lying on the sofa, not

sitting by the fire. Her clothes had gone, too. Her sweater and her skirt and her boots.

Leonard felt a chilly crawling sensation down his backbone. Still holding the bottle of Malbec, he opened the door to his studio. The rain continued to rattle on the roof, but there was no sign of Kasia, neither naked nor dressed.

He went through to the hallway, where he had hung up her wet pink raincoat. The hook was empty. The front door was locked, with the chain on.

Please don't say that this was all a dream. Please don't say that Kasia didn't come here at all, and that I only imagined that we made love. But she had that black eye. Why would I have dreamed that she had a black eye?

He returned to the living room and stood there for over a minute, frowning at the sofa.

'Kasia,' he said. 'Where in the name of God are you?'

Then he woke up. He was lying on the sofa, fully dressed. The lamps were still on, and the gas fire was still alight. The bottle of Malbec was standing on the coffee table next to him, three-quarters empty. As he sat up, the clock on the wall struck five.

He stood up and went over to the fireplace, staring at himself in the large gilt-framed mirror over the mantelpiece. Perhaps she had climbed into looking-glass world, like the illustrations he had painted for *Alice*.

Perhaps he had been dreaming of somebody he could never have.

Bartek returned from the office at a quarter past seven.

Kasia was standing in front of the stove, stirring a saucepan of spaghetti Bolognese. Before he took off his black Puffa jacket, Bartek came into the kitchen and dropped a bunch of white roses onto the counter.

'These – well, these are to say that I'm sorry I hit you. But I think you can understand why I did it. I was late for work as it was, and I can't afford to lose this job, Kaska. They've already given me two warnings.'

Kasia looked at the roses. He had obviously bought them on his way home at the Biedronka supermarket, only two minutes away on Kozańowska Street. They all looked sad and limp, and several of their petals were already turning brown at the edges. Bartek hadn't even had the wit to peel off the sticker that said *przecena* – reduced in price.

'Aren't you going to put them in a vase?' he asked her. He was still standing in the kitchen doorway, and his tension was obvious. Until she had accepted them, he wouldn't feel that she had forgiven him.

Kasia opened up one of the kitchen cupboards and took out a cheap cut-glass vase that the previous tenant had left behind. She filled it with water, and then tore the cellophane off the roses and stuck them into it, without bothering to cut the stems or arrange them.

'If you ever hit me again, Bartek, I will walk out of here and I will never come back.'

He took off his jacket and hung it up in the dark, cramped hallway. 'Don't be stupid, Kaska. Every couple has their arguments. And anyway, where would you go? And what other man would have you?

He came into the kitchen again and stood close behind her, playing with the fronds of her hair.

'How long is that supper going to take? I'm dying of hunger.'

Kasia thought, *You can have your supper right now, if you don't mind my throwing it against your crotch.*

'Another ten minutes. Once the spaghetti's cooked.'

'Jesus! How many times a month do we have to have spaghetti? You don't have Italian blood in you from somewhere, do you? Maybe your granny was gang-raped by a battalion of Eyeties, during the war.'

I love my grandma. I love her dearly. Don't you dare to say disgusting things like that about her.

'Spaghetti's cheap. If you brought home a bit more money, we could have steak.'

Another moment of tension. Bartek wound his finger around her hair and gave it a sharp tug – not hard enough to pull it out, but hard enough to hurt.

'Okay. Bring it through when it's ready. I'm going to watch the football. I've missed half of it already.'

That night, in bed, Bartek punched her in the back and shouted, 'Who the fuck is Leonard?'

Kasia opened her one good eye. Her bruised eye had oozed rheum and so her eyelid was stuck. She struggled with the sheets to sit up, and then she switched on her bedside lamp. It was raining outside, hard, and that added to her feeling of fear. Occasionally in Kozanów, the Oder would burst its banks and the 1970s blocks of flats would be flooded.

'Come on!' Bartek demanded, and he was almost screaming. 'You were bouncing up and down like somebody was fucking you, and calling out "Leonard! Leonard! Oh God, Leonard!"'

'I'm sorry. I must have been having a nightmare. Please, Bartek, I'm sorry. I'll take some Zolpidem.'

'That was no nightmare! You were loving it! For Christ's sake, you were practically coming off! Come on – who the fuck is Leonard? Have you been seeing somebody while I've been at the office? You have, haven't you? You've been seeing some *dupek* behind my back and fucking him, right here in this bed!'

Bartek hurled back the duvet cover, pulled up Kasia's nightshirt and thrust his hand between her legs. Then he took his hand out again, sniffed his fingers, and held his hand up, right in front of her face, so close that he was almost touching the tip of her nose.

'There!' he roared at her. 'I know another man's *sperma* when I smell it! That's proof! You and this Leonard, whoever he is! I should knock your fucking head off!'

Kasia was trembling now, her arms crossed protectively across her breasts. 'Bartek, it's just your imagination! I had a shower before I came to bed, anyway! I don't know any Leonard, and I would never cheat on you, I swear to the Holy Mother!'

'You don't know any Leonard? So why do you keep calling out his name? "Oh, Leonard! Oh, Leonard! Stick it in me, Leonard!"'

'I'm sure I never said anything like that.'

'You didn't have to, the way you were bouncing up and down! You weren't dreaming about bouncing on a trampoline, and that's for sure!'

'I don't *know* any Leonard!'

Bartek swung his legs out of bed. 'Oh, no? Well, why don't you prove it to me? Why don't you show me what you've been typing on your laptop, day after day, and night after night? You never stop typing, and you always have a stupid smile on your face when you're doing it.'

'I'm writing a story for children, I told you that. *Luke the Rabbit*.'

'In English?'

'I told you that, too. Books sell much better all around the world if you write them in English.'

'It's a pity I don't know any English. But why don't you prove it to me, and show me what you've been writing? Then I can Google translate it, and see if you're telling the truth.'

'It's the middle of the night! I'm tired out! I'll take two Zolpidem and go back to sleep! I must be stressed, Bartek, that's all. I'll show you in the morning.'

'I want to see your laptop, bitch. I want to see your laptop now. Not tomorrow. *Now!*'

Bartek came around the end of the bed and seized the sleeve of her nightshirt, so that she heard the seam tear, under her arm. He lifted his fist and said, 'How would you like it if your left eye matched your right eye? Hah?'

She sat on the bed for a moment, staring up at him. She was trying to read his expression, trying to understand what made him so violent and aggressive. Sitting all day in front of his computer screen, she imagined, totting up columns of figures that his bosses had told him to calculate, like the downtrodden clerk Akakiy Akakievitch in Gogol's story about the overcoat. She could almost see the endlessly rising columns of figures reflected in his stone-grey eyes. She couldn't see herself reflected in them, even though she was sitting right in front of him.

It was then that she thought: *He really doesn't love me, not in the way that I understand love. He thinks only of himself, and his own uncertainty. He married me only to show off to his family and friends that he could capture a pretty woman, and to bolster his own lack of self-esteem. He has never once asked me what I want out of my life, and what makes me feel happy.*

Well, now I am going to stop being afraid of him, no matter what he says and no matter what he does. If he hits me again, just let him hit me and get it over with. I haven't cuckolded him, not physically, but at last I have found a man who appreciates me and respects me and loves me for who I am.

'All right,' she said, at last. 'If that's what you want. I'll show you. Let go of me and I'll fetch my laptop.'

She went into the living room and returned with her computer. She sat on the bed and Bartek sat beside her, his hip pressing uncomfortably against hers. His breath still smelled of stale beer, because he had forgotten to brush his teeth before he rolled into bed. His underarms smelled, too, like onions.

'If you want to know the truth,' she told him, trying to keep her voice steady, 'I *have* been in touch with a man named Leonard.'

'What? You just swore to me that you didn't know anybody called Leonard. You just fucking swore to me!'

'I have been writing to him but I have never met him. He

lives in England and he is quite a famous artist. Well, not exactly famous, but well-known. I don't suppose I will ever meet him, but we have become friends, that's all. I haven't been unfaithful to you, Bartek. Leonard and I write to each other about ordinary things – what we've been doing during our day, what we've had for breakfast, nothing more than that. He sends me pictures of his paintings and I send him pictures of me.'

'Not sex pictures? Not pictures of your *cipa*?'

'Of course not. I love his paintings and that is why I wanted to become friends with him on Facebook. After that somehow we started sending each other messages. That's all.'

She showed Bartek the screen, with her latest emails from Leonard. He pulled her laptop away from her and started to scroll downwards, faster and faster.

'You've sent him hundreds of messages! Hundreds! They go on and on! And he's sent hundreds back to you! And you say you haven't been unfaithful? This is out-and-out evidence that you've been unfaithful! You bitch!'

'I only wanted somebody to talk to, during the day! Somebody who understood me and enjoyed the same things that I enjoy! The same books, the same music. You never let me go out and you never take me anywhere! All you ever want is your supper and sex.'

'What else is a wife for? Go on, tell me! What else is a wife for?'

'It wouldn't be so bad if you didn't gobble your supper like a pig and you were any good in bed.'

'Oh, I'm no good in bed, am I? Is that why you're having

dreams about fucking this Leonard? I suppose you're giving him ice-cream cones, are you? More than you ever do for me! You're such a bitch!'

Kasia tried to take back her laptop, but Bartek hurled it across the room so that it clattered against the dressing table and knocked off one of her favourite ornaments, a porcelain angel by Karolina Szelag. The angel dropped onto the floor and broke into three pieces.

Kasia stood up, quivering with anger. 'Go on, then. Aren't you going to hit me? Lost your nerve, have you? Or are you afraid that I'll tell Leonard about the way that you treat me?'

Bartek shook his head and spat. 'Leonard. Pah! Don't you worry about Leonard. I'll sort out your Leonard, don't you worry about that. No *dupek* fucks my wife. Not my wife. Not even in her dreams!'

Leonard was walking back across the Downs when he saw Kasia waiting for him under the trees by Langley Vale. It was a fine, warm day, without a cloud in the sky, although it was windy. He had been to the Rubbing House pub next to Epsom Racecourse for a pint of beer and a ham salad sandwich and now he was on his way home to finish an illustration for *Fairy Wars*.

He could tell it was Kasia, even from a distance, because of the way her blonde hair was waving in the wind. Not only that, but she was wearing the same silvery-white jacket that she had been wearing when he met her at Walton-on-the-Hill, and the same red trousers. And, strangely, he could see nobody else on the Downs, not even jockeys taking their racehorses out for exercise around Tattenham Corner.

Even the pub had been practically empty, apart from the bar staff, and four or five other customers sitting in the dining room. On a sunny day like this, it was usually crowded.

'Have you been waiting long?' he asked Kasia, as he walked up to her.

'Not long. And anyway, I didn't mind waiting for you. It's such a beautiful day.'

'Your eye's looking better,' he told her, as he took her hand and they started walking up the path together. The purple bruise was fading, and turning yellow, and the swelling had subsided.

'I pressed a raw potato on it.' She smiled. 'That was my grandma's cure.'

'My mother was always into herbal remedies. Arnica, and calendula tea, that kind of thing.'

'I wish there was a herbal remedy for me,' said Kasia. They had reached the top of the hill now, where the grass was knee-deep and dotted with wild ox-eye daisies and the frothy yellow petals of lady's bedstraw. The wind was blowing strongly up here, so that the grass rippled and whispered as if gleeful ghosts were running across it. Yet there was nobody in sight, all the way across the Downs, and even further into the distance, all the way across Surrey and Berkshire.

'Don't lose hope,' said Leonard. 'I'll be your remedy.' He held her in his arms, and then brushed back her flying hair and kissed her forehead, and her lips.

'I think my only remedy would be a cup of poison, for Bartek.'

'You could leave him, couldn't you?'

'But he's right. I don't have anywhere to go. My sister Ola doesn't have room, with all her kids, and my mother's not well. And I have hardly any money of my own. I feel like a mouse that was tempted by a piece of cheese and now I find that I'm trapped.'

'You said yourself that love stays fresh while cheese goes mouldy.'

'I feel so helpless that I can't even cry. I swear to you, Leonard, I have run out of tears.'

Leonard kissed her again. 'I'm here for you, Kasia. I will always be here for you, no matter how things turn out.'

She looked around. 'It's so warm. It's lovely up here.'

Without saying anything else, she took off her jacket and dropped it into the grass. Then she crossed her arms and lifted off the pink T-shirt that she was wearing underneath, reaching behind her back to take off her bra.

She bent down to ease off her slip-on shoes. Then she stood up on tiptoe to kiss Leonard with a flurry of tiny kisses, like a bee sucking pollen from a flower. While she was kissing him, she unfastened her belt and tugged her trousers down over her hips.

Leonard could only shake his head at her in wonder and amusement as she sat down amongst the grass and the yellow flowers to kick off her trousers, and then pull down her lacy white thong. She tossed that into the grass, where it was caught on an ox-eye daisy.

'Now, you celebrated artist, it is your turn,' she said. She stood up again to unbutton his shirt, unbuckle his belt, and take down his trousers. Soon they were both standing in the warm wind, naked. Kasia kissed the hummingbird on Leonard's shoulder.

'Time for another beautiful flight, little bird.'

She knelt down in front of him and took hold of his penis. He was already so hard that it was curving upwards, but she rubbed it again, slowly, three or four times.

'It looks like a plum from my grandma's garden,' she said, looking up at him. Then she licked it, and took it into her mouth, and sucked it, bobbing her head backward and forward. 'It even *tastes* like a plum from my grandma's garden.'

Leonard laid his hands on her shoulders. 'No, stop,' he said. 'If you do that to me, I won't last more than ten seconds! Here… lie down. Let me give *you* some pleasure. It's about time somebody pampered you!'

She looked up at him again, her eyes mischievous, wiping her lips with the back of her hand. Then she said, 'Okay… yes. I'd like that.'

She lay back in the grass and the flowers, and opened up her legs for him. He knelt down and parted those rose-petal lips again. Her anus was like a tightly knurled rosebud, and he licked it with the stiffened tip of his tongue. Then he parted her thighs a little wider, and tasted the clear juice that was flooding her vagina. Kasia had told him that he had tasted like a plum, and she tasted like no woman he had ever tasted before, like a cocktail of peaches and sweet pomelos.

He started to strum her clitoris with his tongue and she let out a long sigh of contentment, one hand resting on his hummingbird birthmark. He stimulated her as lightly as he could, barely touching her, so that her arousal would last as long as possible. He wanted to bring her to a climax before he entered her, so that she might then have another climax, and then another. Just like the first time they had made love, he could almost feel that he was sharing the dark, warm sensations that were rising inside her, like a flood tide.

The wind whistled softly across the Downs, so that the grass was blown against their bare skin, and the wildflowers all around them nodded, as if in approval. Here are two lovers who really adore each other, as close as two people can ever be.

Kasia moaned, and began to lift her hips. Her eyes were closed, and Leonard's were closed, too, as he licked her ever more quickly. Neither of them saw the man climbing the hill towards them, or the determined way in which he was stamping towards them, like a man on a mission.

Kasia reached her climax, and gasped, and gasped, and shuddered from head to foot as if she had been electrocuted. When she lay still, Leonard laughed and dropped his head down against her stomach, kissing her navel.

'You are my superman,' said Kasia, running her fingers into his thick brown hair. 'You really are.' But it was then that she opened her eyes and was shocked to see that the man who had been climbing the hill was now standing right over them. He was wearing a black Puffa jacket and jeans. And it was Bartek.

'*Leonard!*' she screamed, but it was too late.

Leonard said, 'What?' and lifted his head. As he did so,

Bartek raised a long-handled axe and struck him at an angle, just above his left ear. Leonard pitched backwards and sideways, and Bartek stepped over Kasia and hit him again, in the centre of his forehead, so that his skull was split apart and his brains were spattered into the grass.

Kasia scrambled to her feet and tried to pull Bartek away, but Bartek was too angry and too determined, and violently pushed her aside. He swung his axe like a bell-ringer, chopping Leonard in the face, again and again. He cracked Leonard's jaw and scattered his teeth, and then he stove in his nose and bashed in his eye sockets, until each of his eyes was dangling on either side of his face, staring downwards.

He didn't stop there. He hacked open Leonard's breastbone and broke all his ribs. He chopped up his lungs and his heart and then he split open his stomach and chopped up his liver and his stomach and his intestines. Then he turned around to Kasia, who was kneeling in the grass not far away, hysterical with terror.

'Is this what you wanted him for?' he shouted. 'Is this why you wanted him more than me?'

With that, he brought his axe down between Leonard's legs, over and over and over, until his genitals were reduced to a bloody arrangement of string.

The next morning, after Bartek had eaten his breakfast and gone off to work, Kasia went next door to her friend Kinga and asked if she could borrow her laptop.

'Mine's not working. I don't know why.'

Kinga looked at her narrowly. 'Nothing to do with all that shouting we heard last night, and all that crashing and banging?'

'I just need to send an email, Kinga. But it's urgent.'

She went into Kinga's kitchen and sat on a stool at the counter. Kinga's golden Labrador came trotting up to her, and snuffled at her leg. Then he cocked his head to one side and made a mewling sound in the back of his throat, as if he realised that she was worried about something.

'You and Bartek have been having a lot of rows lately,' said Kinga, watching Kasia as he quickly typed a message to Leonard. 'I don't know why you don't kick him out. I know it's not my place to say so, but I don't think he's the right kind of man for you at all. My Piotr calls him a *zbir*, if you must know. A right thug.'

'Our apartment's in Bartek's name, so I can't kick him out. And if I left him he would probably hunt me down and drag me back. He wouldn't want his friends to think that he wasn't man enough to keep his wife.'

Dearest Leonard, I had a terrible nightmare about you. Please write back at once and let me know that you are all right. XX Kasia.

She waited for more than five minutes, but there was no response. Kinga went into the living room to vacuum-clean the carpet and then she came back into the kitchen, followed by her Labrador. Both of them looked at Kasia sympathetically.

'Perhaps he's out somewhere. Perhaps he's driving.'

Kasia didn't ask Kinga how she knew that she had been sending a message to a man, and that she was anxiously expecting a reply. Kinga had been through an abusive marriage herself before leaving her husband and finding Piotr.

'Can I come back and try again later?' Kasia asked her.

'Stay for coffee. Stay for coffee and tell me everything that's been happening to you. Don't worry. If this man has any feelings for you, he will call back as soon as he gets your message.'

Kinga brewed two cups of strong coffee, and set out a plateful of dark cherry biscuits, and then they sat together in the living room, while the Labrador lay down between them as if she too wanted to listen to Kasia's problems.

Half an hour went past, yet Leonard didn't answer. She tried again, in case there had been some technical glitch and her first message hadn't reached him. She also sent him a message on his Facebook page. Another twenty minutes went past, but there was still no reply.

'Do you have his phone number? Or do you know any of his friends?' asked Kinga.

'There's a phone number for his gallery on his Facebook page, and their email. I'll try them, if you don't mind me using your phone.' She paused for a moment, and then said, 'My phone's broken. Bartek stamped on it.'

She tried ringing the Surrey Arts Gallery, but it rang and rang and nobody picked up. She sent them an email asking if they could call her, but since there was nobody there to answer the phone, she doubted if they would.

Kinga's Labrador stood up and rested her head in

Kasia's lap. Kasia stroked her ears and wished that she could cry.

On Thursday morning, Henry Walters arrived at Leonard's house to have his portrait completed. He had emailed Leonard to tell him that he was coming, and yet when he knocked at the door, Leonard didn't answer.

He knocked again, and when there was still no response, he bent down and shouted through the letterbox, 'Leonard! Are you in there? It's Henry Walters! And for a change I haven't got a hangover!'

He was still waiting outside when a neighbour appeared from next door to take out her rubbish.

'You haven't seen Leonard this morning, have you?' asked Henry. 'Mr Slater, I mean. He's supposed to be painting my portrait. I've been knocking for the past five minutes.'

The neighbour shook her dreadlocks. 'I haven't seen him since – I don't know – Sunday, I think. Maybe he gone away somewhere. Usually he always say hello.'

Henry bent down again and opened the letterbox flap. He could see inside the hallway, and although it was a sunny day, it looked as if the ceiling light was still on. He breathed in, and as he breathed in, he could faintly smell a ripe, rotten odour. Ten years ago, he had been a senior medical officer during the British Army's operations in Afghanistan, and he knew at once what it was.

It was another two days before Kasia received an email

message from the Surrey Arts Gallery, informing her that, sadly, Leonard Slater was deceased. When she googled his name, she read that he had been found murdered in his house in Epsom – brutally dismembered in his bed. Surrey police still had no idea who might have killed him, or why, and there had been almost no forensic evidence. No murder weapon had been left behind, although it appeared likely that he had been hacked to pieces with an axe.

The detectives investigating his homicide admitted that they were 'baffled' by the fact that the front door was locked, with the security chain still fastened, and that there had been no sign of forced entry into the studio at the rear of the house.

Kasia sat staring at the screen of Kinga's laptop. She not only felt chilled, she felt as if she had become invisible, as if she existed only as a dream about herself.

Kinga came up behind her and laid a gentle hand on her shoulder.

'Bad news?' she asked her.

Kasia nodded. 'Yes. The worst. But how can you miss something you never had?'

Nine days after that, Kasia missed her next period. She had been feeling tired and hypersensitive, and suffering from headaches and stomach cramps.

Kinga bought her a pregnancy test kit, and the result was positive. She could hardly believe it.

'We tried so hard for a baby when we first got married.

I wanted to go to the doctor to see why I couldn't get pregnant, but Bartek said not to bother. It was my fault, I was barren, and that was all there was to it.'

'Well, it's obvious that you're not. I'll bet you a thousand zlotys that Bartek has a very low sperm count. But hooray! At last one little fellow has managed to wriggle his way through!'

'Kinga – I'm not sure that I even want his baby.'

Kinga gave her a motherly hug. 'Don't you worry. Whatever happens, you always have me.'

Agata was born on May 7 the following year, at the Hospital Medfemina – a private maternity hospital, which Kasia's mother paid for. Bartek had been unable to afford it, and went to work that day instead of attending the birth, telling Kasia that a private hospital was a waste of money.

But Kasia's mother came to support her, and stayed beside her all through the two-hour birth, holding her hand. Her mother was sitting next to her in the sunny room with its sloping ceiling when the nurse brought in Agata, washed and wrapped in a white blanket, for Kasia to hold.

'Three kilos and twenty-eight grams,' the nurse said with a smile, handing her over. 'A very healthy weight. And I think she will be quite tall, too, when she grows up. Perhaps she'll be a model.'

Kasia was exhausted but happy in a way that she had never experienced before. She had actually created a little girl, and brought her to life, and here she was in the sunshine, her eyes closed, as pink and sweet as if she were formed out of rosy-coloured marzipan.

'Oh, she's adorable,' said Kasia's mother. 'Who do you think she looks like?'

Kasia folded down the blanket that covered Agata's head. Her fine hair was sticking up, but it was quite thick for a new-born baby, and it was dark mahogany brown.

'I'm not sure. At least she's not a redhead, like Bartek.'

She folded down the blanket a little further, and it was then that she saw Agata's left shoulder. It bore a birthmark like a tiny bird, with its wings spread out, and a pointed beak.

Kasia's mother leaned forward, peering at Agata over her rimless spectacles.

'What's that mark on her?' she asked. And then she turned to Kasia and said, 'What's the matter, darling? For goodness' sake, sweetheart – why are you crying?'

THE GREATEST GIFT

'O would some power the giftie gie us
To see ourselves as others see us.'
Robert Burns

'You're mad, do you know that?' Cathy laughed, as the speedometer needle touched eighty. 'You're totally, utterly, irre*deem*ably crazy!'

'What do you mean, crazy? I'm not crazy, I'm just *practical*!' Robin shouted back, over the buffeting of the slipstream. 'Life is too damn short to go slow!'

They were driving north on Bedford Road towards Katonah. It was a bright day in early October, unseasonably warm, and so Robin had put down the roof of his silver Mustang so that the slipstream would ruffle their hair. As they sped along, overtaking every other car on the highway, they left behind them a whirling cyclone of crimson and yellow leaves.

Robin was always frightening Cathy, which was one of the reasons she loved him so much. He was tall and sculpted and handsome, with brushed-up, black hair, a strong jawline and sapphire-blue eyes that always looked as if he was finding life amusing. If they were eating outside on a restaurant balcony, he would jump up when the check was put in front of him, and throw himself over the railings, regardless of how far down he might fall. If they were swimming in the Housatonic, he would climb up to the bridge and dive off it headfirst into the water, even though the river was dangerously shallow. He would challenge anybody who annoyed him – parking attendants, shop assistants, cops, other drivers. Cathy had never met anybody so fearless. He always seemed to be daring the world to stand up to him.

'We can stop at Willy Nick's before we go to your sister's,' Robin shouted. 'I'm jonesing for some of their crab cakes!'

'Okay, but *careful*!' Cathy shouted back, as Robin had to swerve to avoid an oncoming bus.

'Careful? What does that mean?' Robin retorted.

Those were the last words he spoke before they neared the intersection with Parkway, and a huge maroon truck pulled out across the road in front of them. He stood on the brakes but they were driving twenty miles an hour too fast and the Mustang was nose-heavy and slid sideways with its tyres screaming in a shrill operatic chorus.

Cathy clung on to the doorhandle, and all she could see was trees and road signs rotating around her, and then the huge white letters: *Moving Man Inc*. They slammed broadside into the truck with a deafening bang, although Cathy didn't hear anything at all. Her door was flung open and she was thrown out onto the road, almost as if somebody had taken hold of her arm and forcibly yanked her out of the passenger seat. She tumbled over and over, grazing her shoulder and knocking her head hard against the concrete.

She lay on her back for a moment, shocked and concussed, staring up at the sky. She could hear a high singing noise in her ears. Then she heard a stentorian roaring sound, and a wave of heat rolled over her. She managed to turn over onto her side, and prop herself up on one elbow, and it was then that she saw that the Mustang was burning fiercely, and that orange flames were leaping up the side of the removal truck.

The driver and his mate were climbing down from their cab, two black men wearing maroon overalls. They tried to approach the Mustang but the heat was too intense and they had to raise their arms to shield their faces, and back away.

At first Cathy couldn't see Robin, and she thought that he must have managed to jump out. Surely he had managed to jump out, in the same way that he jumped off balconies and bridges, but she couldn't see him anywhere. At that moment, though, the wind fanned the flames to one side, and she saw him still sitting in the driving seat, a scorched black figure with his brushed-up hair alight, frantically wrestling to free himself from his seat belt. His eyes were still white, but circled with red, so that he looked more like a Hallowe'en demon than a man who was being burned alive.

'*Robin!*' she screamed, or thought she screamed. She climbed to her feet and made her way unsteadily towards the blazing car, but as soon as she came within twenty feet of it she found that the heat was unbearable, hotter than an open oven, and like the two removal men she couldn't venture any closer.

Meanwhile, though, the removal truck's driver had run to his cab and now he was hurrying back swinging a large yellow fire extinguisher. While his mate was calling 911 on his cell phone, he unfastened the nozzle and started to spray the burning Mustang with foam. He sprayed Robin first, turning him instantly from a black demon into a struggling parody of a snowman. Flecks of white foam were whirled upwards by the heat, and blown up into the trees by the wind, where they clung like blossom.

A station wagon stopped not far away, and a stockily built man in a tan suede jacket ran up, carrying a smaller fire extinguisher. Between him and the removal van driver they gradually managed to subdue the flames, and at last they guttered out, although the tyres were still smouldering, and so much acrid grey smoke was billowing from the upholstery that the Mustang was intermittently lost from sight.

Cathy cupped her hand over her nose and mouth and made her way into the smoke, as close to the car as she could, even though it was still far too hot for her to try and open the driver's door.

Through streaming eyes, she saw Robin sitting behind the steering wheel with his head bent forward, still clutching his seat-belt buckle. His hair looked like a yard broom that had been burned right down to the last few spiky bristles, and the skin on his hands and forearms had blackened and split, so that the scarlet flesh showed through.

The removal truck driver came up through the smoke behind her and laid one hand on her shoulder. 'Ain't nothing you can do for him, lady. I'm sorry. We've called for the paramedics and the po-lice. You'd best take care of yourself, make sure you ain't got no bones broken nor done yourself any other kind of mischief. I saw you come flying out of that car and it was almost like the Angel of the Lord reached down and hauled you out of there hisself.'

Cathy nodded, although she was too shocked to be able to say anything. She found it almost impossible to believe that this grotesque figure sitting in the car was actually Robin – the same Robin who had made love to her this morning, just as it was growing light. The same Robin with whom she had been laughing and joking only minutes ago. They were supposed to be going to Willy Nick's, and then to visit her sister Jeanette. How could this have happened? How could this incinerated effigy be him?

'Come on, lady, come away,' said the removal truck driver. 'Like I say, there ain't nothing you can do to help him now. Nothing that nobody can do for him, nohow.'

Cathy was about to turn away when Robin lifted his head. His face was a ghastly mask, with rags of burned skin hanging from it, but he opened his red-rimmed eyes and stared at her.

'*Cathy?*' he croaked, between cracked and bleeding lips. '*Cathy, save me.*'

It was early on a Friday morning in the second week in January when Cathy's iPhone warbled. She was standing in the kitchen, filling the kettle to make tea. It was still dark outside, and a light but steady snow was falling.

'Cathy? This is Megan.'

Megan was Nurse Megan Wing from the burns centre at Bridgeport Hospital, where Robin had been taken after the crash, and where he had been undergoing specialist treatment ever since. She sounded emotional, and Cathy's heart sank.

'What is it?' she asked. She could see her own face reflected in the kitchen window and she thought she looked like a ghost, standing in the snowy yard outside, staring in at her herself. 'What's happened?'

'It's good news, Cathy. Robin has come out of his coma. He opened his eyes for the first time about an hour ago, and he's actually managed to say a few words. He asked where he was and he also asked where *you* were.'

'Oh my God, really?' said Cathy, and her eyes were instantly crowded with tears. 'Is he still conscious now?'

'He's under heavy sedation, of course, but he's been drifting in and out. I'm sure that when you come over today he'll be able to speak to you.'

'I'll come right now. It's snowing some but it doesn't look too bad.'

'Just take it easy on the turnpike. I saw on the news that there was a multiple pile-up at the route 1 intersection.'

'Oh, you can bet I will. I've had enough car wrecks for one lifetime. Thank you, Megan. I'll see you later.'

Cathy hurriedly dressed in her pink rollneck sweater and jeans and then shrugged on her dark-brown duffel coat. She was sitting on the stairs pulling on her Ugg boots when her cousin Holly came out of her bedroom door, yawning.

'You're not going out already? It's only ten after six! And look out there – it's snowing!'

'The nurse at the burns centre just called me. Robin's woken up. He opened his eyes and he actually spoke.'

'He's awake?' said Holly. 'That's amazing.' She made no effort to sound enthusiastic. They had argued about this over and over again. Even if Robin survived, Holly had insisted, he would never again be the handsome athletic daredevil that Cathy had fallen in love with. He had suffered over seventy per cent burns, especially to his head and arms and upper body, which should have been more than enough to kill him. It would take years of intensive therapy for him to be able to perform the most rudimentary functions, such as feeding himself and keeping himself clean, and apart from that he would be hideously scarred. Even Nurse Wing had warned Cathy that underneath the pressure mask that was protecting his face, he no longer had a nose or lips, and his ears had been burned off. Even the most skilful of reconstructive surgeons would never be able to give him his good looks back.

But Cathy had said, 'I don't care how much he's changed. He's still Robin underneath. Can't you understand that? His *soul* is still Robin. Nurse Wing said the first thing he asked was: where was he, and the second thing was: where was *I*?'

As she went to the front door and opened it, Holly followed her and said, 'You know how much I care about you, Cathy. You really need to think about what you could be letting yourself in for. You're only twenty-two, for Christ's sake. You're clever, you're pretty. You have so much to look forward to. Don't saddle yourself with a cripple for the rest of your life.'

'Holly! How can you use a word like that? I love him!'

'You love the *memory* of him, sweetheart. The way he used to be. But he'll never be like that again. And being all burned up like that, it will have changed his personality, too. There's no way he's ever going to be the same. How could he be? Would *you* be, if you hadn't gotten out of that car and you'd burned up with him?'

Cathy sat in the driveway in her scarlet Sonic, with the engine running and the windshield heaters switched on to full blast to melt the thin layer of pearly frost that had formed overnight. She knew how much of a challenge it would be, to take care of Robin. But he was still alive, and now he was awake, and he had asked about her, and that was all she could possibly ask for.

Nurse Wing was waiting for her in the smart open-plan reception area at the Bridgeport burns centre. She was tall and Swedish-looking, with blonde hair scraped back into a short ponytail and pale-blue eyes. As soon as Cathy came through the doors, she walked across and took hold of both of her hands.

'Oh! You're so cold! But I hope this news will warm you up a little! Doctor Fremont says that he cannot believe that Robin is making such a strong recovery. He is still very sick, of course, but we have taken him off the danger list.'

'Is he awake now?' asked Cathy.

Nurse Wing smiled and nodded, and led her by the arm along the corridor. 'I told him that you were coming and he said that he couldn't wait to see you. When I told him how long he had been unconscious, and yet you had come every single day to sit by his bedside, he couldn't believe it. I think if he still had any tear ducts, he would have cried.'

They reached the end of the corridor and Nurse Wing opened the door labelled *Staff Only*. Inside there was a small changing room, and just as she had done every day when she visited the burns centre, Cathy took off her coat and tied on a green surgical gown, as well as a surgeon's cap and a mask. She took off her boots, too, and replaced them with pale green theatre clogs.

When they were ready, they crossed the corridor to a room labelled *Mr Robin Starling. Sterile Area. Strictly No Unauthorised Admittance.*

The room was dimly lit, and the venetian blinds were drawn down, although Cathy could still see snow clustering on the windowsill outside. Robin's bed was in the centre of the far wall, with a softly bleeping monitor beside it, and two drip stands. Robin was propped up by two large pillows. His face was covered with a transparent TFO mask, which allowed his doctors to see how the healing of his face was progressing. Cathy had already been told that even after reconstructive surgery he would have to wear this for twenty hours a day for at least the next two years.

Both of his arms and his chest were still wrapped in white mummy-like dressings.

Cathy approached the side of his bed and he turned his head towards her. All she could see underneath the plastic was a knotted mass of reddened weals, but his eyes were open and glistening and she could see that through the holes in the mask he was staring at her.

'You shouldn't have come,' he whispered, although his voice hadn't changed.

She pulled up a blue plastic chair and sat down close to him. 'How can you say that? I love you. I've been coming every single day.'

'Megan told me. I don't know why you bothered. Look at me. And the same could have happened to you.'

'Robin, it's going to take time. I know that. Years, even. But I've talked to your doctors and they'll be able to give you a whole new face.'

Robin's eyes rolled uncontrollably. 'They've told me that, too. But what kind of a face? I don't have a nose any more. My ears were burned off. I've seen people whose faces have been burned as bad as mine. It doesn't matter how good the surgeons are. They all look the same. Like monsters.'

Cathy laid her hand on his bandaged arm, and he grunted in bitter amusement. 'You won't even be able to hold my hand, do you know that? I've lost all of my fingers. Oh, I think my left thumb managed to survive. I won't be much use to you in bed, either. Not unless you like your wieners extra-well-done.'

Cathy shook her head and she couldn't stop her eyes from filling up again with tears. 'I don't care, Robin. I love you. I'm not going to walk away from you, ever.'

Robin started to cough, harsh and phlegmy, and Nurse Wing came forward with a plastic bottle of water so that he could sip some through a straw. 'Thanks, Megan,' he said, when he could speak again. He turned his gleaming masked face back towards Cathy and added, 'Megan... she's been sent directly from heaven. She treats me like I look normal.'

'You *do* look normal, Robin, for a severe burns victim,' said Megan. 'And from now on, you can only begin to look better.'

'Hunh,' said Robin, and then lapsed into silence.

Cathy didn't really know what to say to him. Should she tell him about everything that she had been doing since the accident? How she had moved from her parents' house in New Milford to stay with Holly in Fairfield, so that she could be closer to Bridgeport? Somehow it seemed rather petty and self-congratulatory to tell him about that. *I'm such a martyr. You look hideous but I haven't abandoned you.*

After a long silence, Robin lifted up both of his bandaged arms like a frustrated teddy bear and then let them drop back onto the bedcover. 'The first thing I thought about when I woke up, Cathy, was you. To tell you the truth, sweetheart, I haven't been able to think about anything else.'

Cathy smiled and said, 'I don't care how long it takes, Robin. I'll always be here for you.'

'That's what I've been thinking about,' said Robin, and coughed again, but when Nurse Wing came forward with the water bottle he waved her away. 'You're such a pretty girl, Cathy. I can't expect you to devote the rest of your life to a man who looks like me. I'm going to be a freak, no matter how good they try to patch me up. What do you think people are going to say when you walk into a room with me? They're going to pity you, that's what. They're going to whisper about you behind your back and they're really going to feel sorry for you. You don't deserve that.'

'Robin, my feelings for you, they haven't changed at all. If anything, they've grown even stronger.'

'Well I'm afraid that's just too bad, Cathy, because I'm not going to let you waste yourself on me, not the way I am now. God made you beautiful, and you need a handsome prince in your life, not a burned-up mess like me.'

'Robin—' Cathy began, but he started coughing again, and his coughing was so hard and so harsh that it sounded as if he were ripping his oesophagus into shreds.

Nurse Wing touched Cathy's shoulder and said, 'I'm afraid I think you should leave him for now, Cathy. He's very distressed.'

Robin went on coughing and coughing, gasping for breath at the end of each spasm, and so Cathy pushed back her chair and stood up.

'Please,' said Nurse Wing, and so she left the room, feeling both guilty and abandoned. *Does Robin really not want me any more, or is he just saying that to spare my feelings? How can he possibly understand how I feel? I don't understand it myself. I should walk out of this hospital now and drive home to New Milford and forget I ever knew this man. But for some reason I can't. He touched the very core of me, not just because he was so good-looking, but because he was always prepared to challenge everything that was ordinary and boring and conventional. He set me free, and I can't just turn my back on the man who set me free, no matter what he looks like now.*

She sat down in the reception area and after a few minutes Nurse Wing came out to join her.

'Robin's reaction is only to be expected,' she said, taking hold of both of Cathy's hands. 'Most of our patients with severe facial disfigurement feel the same way. We call it Disturbed Body Image. They have a preoccupation with the change in their appearance and the loss of their normal looks. They also develop a strong fear of other people's reaction and of being socially rejected.'

'Is there anything I can do to help him to cope with it?' asked Cathy.

Nurse Wing shrugged. 'You can continue to tell him that you still love him. But that's only if he allows you to go on visiting him. He just told me that he doesn't want to see you again. I'm sorry, I really am. But he feels so strongly that you're a beautiful young woman and that you would find somebody else.'

Cathy said, 'I'll come back tomorrow anyhow. Maybe he will have changed his mind.'

'Why don't you give it three or four days? Even a week. Doctor Fremont and Doctor Mazdani will be talking to him tomorrow about facial reconstruction, which may give him much more hope of returning to a normal life. Besides, if you leave him for a while he may start to realise that he misses you.'

When she turned into the driveway of Holly's single-storey house on Rowland Road, Cathy saw that Holly's car was missing, leaving criss-cross tyre tracks in the snow. When she went inside, she found that Holly had left her a note on the kitchen table.

Mom not well. Gone to Darien for the weekend. Probably back Tues or Weds. XX

She went to the kitchen window and looked out. Although the backyard was still blanketed in snow, and the sky was still slate-grey, the snow had actually stopped falling and the wind had dropped. The world was silent and very cold, as colourless and motionless as a black-and-white photograph.

So what do I do now? thought Cathy. *Do I forget Robin? Or is there a way in which I can make him think differently about me? His one reason for telling me that our relationship is over is my looks. I know I'm pretty, but supposing I wasn't? Then he wouldn't have any reason to end our relationship. Supposing I was just as monstrous as him?*

She opened the cutlery drawer. Inside there was a clutter of corkscrews, slotted spoons, potato peelers and spatulas. There were also several kitchen knives, including a very sharp knife with a six-inch blade which Holly used for cutting up chickens and trimming steaks.

If I can still recognise Robin underneath his disfigurement, then he'll be able to recognise me, no matter what I look like. He said he loved me, that morning before the accident. He told me that he had never felt the same way with any other girl.

She took out the six-inch knife and cautiously ran her fingertip along the edge. It cut into her skin, although not deeply enough to draw blood. It was so sharp that she didn't even feel it.

She took the knife into the bathroom and stood in front of the washbasin, staring at herself in the mirror. There would be blood. There would probably be a lot of blood, so she pulled one of the bath towels off the heated rail and folded it over the rim of the bath, well within reach. Then she took off her pink sweater and unfastened her bra, so that she was bare-breasted.

Her face in the mirror was pretty but it was totally expressionless. There was no appeal in her eyes for her to change her mind, to forget Robin and find somebody else. She took hold of her left ear and pulled it outwards, and then she positioned the edge of the knife in between the top of her ear and the side of her head.

The knife hadn't hurt her when she had cut her finger and it didn't hurt her now. She drew it downwards and forwards at a slight angle and in one stroke it sliced her ear off completely. Blood immediately flooded down the side of her neck, and she dropped the ear into the washbasin so that she could reach for the bath towel and press it against the side of her head. She felt hardly any pain at all, more of a chill, although the blood was warm as it ran over her collarbone and dripped off her breast.

The flow of blood, though, stopped surprisingly quickly. Cautiously, she lifted away the sodden bath towel and turned her head to one side so that she could examine what she had done. Her ear was nothing more now than a bloody hole, although it still looked neater than the shrivelled-up bacon rind of Robin's ears. She looked down at her own severed ear lying in the washbasin. It could have been some kind of mollusc, and she found it hard to believe that a few moments ago it had actually been part of her.

She changed hands with the sticky-handled knife and now she pulled out her right ear. She was quicker and more decisive this time, because she knew that it wasn't going to hurt very much, and she sliced it off without any hesitation. Again, she let it drop into the washbasin, and again she pressed the blood-soaked towel against the side of her head. She looked at herself defiantly in the mirror, with runnels of blood all down her chest, and she thought, *Yes, I can do this. I can change myself so much that Robin will love me for what I am.*

Her hands were trembling, and she realised that her system was beginning to show signs of shock, but she was determined to continue. Now she leaned forward closer to the mirror and lifted up the tip of her nose between finger and thumb. *Look at you, little piglet*, she thought. Then she placed the knife underneath her nostrils like a shining steel moustache.

She cut upward into the septum, but this was much harder and much more painful than cutting off her ears. She couldn't stop herself from letting out a strangled moaning sound as she was forced to cut upward again and again, until at last she reached the bone. Blood poured over her upper lip into her mouth and dripped off her chin.

Gagging and shaking, she sliced the knife across the bridge of her nose so that she could twist the nub of flesh away from her face. She staggered backwards, dropping the knife with a clatter onto the tiled bathroom floor, and when she reached out to stop herself from falling over, her hand left a crescent-shaped smear of blood across the wall.

She stood in the middle of the bathroom, giddy with shock. It took her almost a minute before she was able to approach the washbasin again and look into the mirror. Where her nose had been there was a gory cavern, and she could see right into the dark recesses of her sinuses. As she breathed, she made a thick bubbling sound, and she could feel the blood pouring down the back of her throat, which made her retch.

She had begun her self-mutilation, but she knew that what she had done was not enough. Robin was disfigured much worse than she was – well beyond any chance of ever having his original good looks restored. He was suffering third-degree burns over most of the upper half of his body, and as he had told her, he wouldn't be much use to her in bed, so his genitals must have been shrivelled up, too.

Cathy bent down with blood still spraying out of her sinuses with every breath and picked up the knife. She felt numb and detached now, as if she were having an out-of-body experience, or watching another young woman in a horror movie. Her hair was sticking up in a tangled fright wig and her entire chest was varnished red with gradually drying blood.

She took hold of her left nipple and stretched it outwards in the same way that she had stretched her ear. She hesitated for a moment while she swallowed a mixture of blood and vomit, and then she sliced upwards and cut her nipple clean off. She dropped it into the basin along with her ears and the lumpy remains of her nose.

Next, she cut off her right nipple, and she stood there with both breasts bleeding as if she were ready to wet-nurse an infant vampire.

She let the knife fall into the bath and then she shuffled back into the kitchen, leaving a trail of bloody footprints behind her. Robin had suffered burns to turn him into a monster, so she had to suffer burns too. She went to the cupboard where Holly kept her blender and her weighing scales, and also the chef's blowtorch that she used for melting the sugar on top of crème brûlée.

She took the blowtorch down from the shelf and slowly made her way out of the kitchen and along the corridor to her bedroom. She sat down on the bed, and as she did so she could see that it was snowing again. She was finding it very difficult to breathe now, and she kept making a terrible snorting sound.

It seemed to take her hours to wrench down her jeans and push them off her feet. Her head was throbbing and her breasts hurt so much that she couldn't stop the tears from running down her cheeks. Robin would have to love her, after she had suffered so much. When he saw what she had done to keep him, he would have no choice.

She dragged down her thong although she left it dangling around one ankle. Then she picked up the blowtorch, thumbed off the safety catch, and pressed the button to light it. She sat there for a long time, staring at the pointed blue flame, while the snow continued to fall outside. She wondered if she secretly wanted the blowtorch's butane gas to run out, so that she wouldn't have to do what she intended to do next.

This will ruin me forever, she thought. *But then I'm ruined already. I'm a monster and so there's no going back.*

She leaned forward and played the flame of the blowtorch up the inside of her left calf. The skin reddened and blistered instantly, and she gave a honking scream of agony through her noseless face. But somehow the sheer intensity of the pain made her even more determined to do it again, and now she directed the flame at her knee, and then her inner thigh. As she burned away the outer layers of skin, and then her nerve endings, she felt as if she understood completely what Robin must have experienced when he was burning in the driver's seat of his Mustang – unbearable pain, but then a strange absence of any sensation at all. She continued to direct the flame at her inner thigh, and felt nothing.

She lay back on her pillows, where her Raggedy Ann doll was lying with her ginger hair and her fixed, silly smile. She opened her legs wide and turned the blowtorch onto her vulva, so that it looked for a moment as if she were being penetrated by a penis made of blue fire. She smelled burning hair and burning flesh and her lips curled up like living worms thrown onto a hotplate.

There was no name for a pain like this, but Cathy lay back and continued to hold the blowtorch between her legs until her brain shut itself down. The blowtorch dropped to the floor. The snow fell. Cathy twitched and shuddered, her eyes half-open, but only the whites showing. She dreamed that she was dead, and in a way she was, because her brain refused to let her wake up.

It was the second day of June when Nurse Wing came into Robin's room at the Bridgeport Hospital. He had undergone his third operation to remove the keloids on his face and to rebuild his nose, but he was still wearing his transparent facial orthosis. The sun was shining and white cumulus clouds were hurrying north-eastwards, as if they were panicking.

'Robin, I have a visitor for you,' said Nurse Wing.

Robin was sitting in a chair by the window, wearing a

thick maroon dressing gown. His bandaged wrists peeked out of his sleeves. The time to fit him with prosthetic hands would come later, when his burns had completely healed.

'Really? I'm not expecting anybody, am I?' Robin had caught something in the tone of Nurse Wing's voice. Usually, when his sister or one of his friends came to visit him, she sounded cheerful and upbeat. Not now, though. She sounded almost as if she were trying to give him a warning.

Before Nurse Wing could say any more, the door behind her opened wider and a young woman walked in. He couldn't recognise her at first, because her face was completely covered by a flesh-covered mask, made out of the same material as pressure bandages. She could have been a giant doll. She was wearing a flowery summer frock in red and blue and yellow, but her legs were also covered by flesh-coloured pressure bandages, and she was pushing a walking frame.

Nurse Wing attempted a smile, and said, 'I'll leave you two together then. Call me, Robin, if you need me.'

She left the room and closed the door behind her. The doll-like young woman stood unmoving for a few seconds, and then she pushed her walking frame up to Robin and before she could say anything he knew who she was. It was the perfume she was wearing, the same perfume that he had given Cathy the week before the accident. Miracle, by Lancôme.

'Cathy? You *are* Cathy, aren't you?'

The doll-like woman nodded.

'Holy Christ, Cathy, what's happened to you? Did you get involved in another auto wreck?'

Cathy sat down in the chair next to him. 'No,' she said, in a strangely hollow voice, as if she were speaking through a megaphone. 'Nothing like that.'

'Then what? What's happened to your face?'

'I did it myself, Robin. I did it for you. Well, that's not really true. I did it for *us*.'

'I don't understand, Cathy, You did *what* for us?'

'You said you didn't want to see me again because you were going to turn out to be a monster and I was pretty.'

'I know,' said Robin. 'I know I did. But I only wanted to be fair to you. You shouldn't have to spend the rest of your life a gargoyle like me when you could pop your fingers and have any man who takes your fancy.'

'That's why I did it,' said Cathy. 'I love you, Robin. You and me, we're soulmates. Now we're more than that. Now we look like each other, too.'

With that, she reached behind her pressure mask and unfastened it. She bent her head forward and carefully eased it away from her face, and then looked up at Robin, her brown eyes bright, her lips smiling.

Robin couldn't speak. He simply stared at her in revulsion. Her brown eyes may have been bright and her lips might have been smiling, but there was nothing but two triangular caverns where her nose had been, and she had no ears. She looked like a ghastly parody of Lon Chaney playing *The Phantom of the Opera*.

'That's not all,' she said, and she eased herself up so that she could lift her dress and show him the purple braided scars between her legs. 'No other man is going to want me now, Robin, so you don't have to worry about me. We can be together forever.'

Robin said, 'Cathy, pull your dress back down. And, please, put your mask back on.'

'Aren't you happy?' said Cathy. 'Aren't you pleased I did this? I still have a whole lot surgery to go through. But they're treating me here at the Bridgeport too. I come here two or three times a week, so we can see each other all the time.'

'What in God's name have you done to yourself?' said Robin.

'I did it for you, Robin. I thought you'd be pleased. You *are* pleased, aren't you?'

'Cathy – just because I look like this doesn't mean that I want a partner who looks like this. I might be a freak myself but that doesn't mean that I'm going to be attracted to another freak.'

Cathy's eyes filled with tears. 'What are you saying? You're not saying that I shouldn't have done this? Robin – I did it for you!'

Robin closed his eyes for a moment. While he did so, Cathy replaced her pressure mask and fastened it. When he opened his eyes, he said, 'I'm going to have to be truthful with you, Cathy. What you've done to yourself, I think you must be psychotic. You look inhuman, and that's the kindest thing I can say. And don't blame me for it.'

He reached across and pressed the bell beside his bed. After a few moments, Nurse Wing came in.

'I think visiting time's over,' said Robin. 'I don't know what to say to you, Cathy. I'm totally shocked.'

Nurse Wing came across and helped Cathy to stand up. Cathy's shoulders were quaking with grief, although she wasn't audibly sobbing.

'I don't know what's going to happen to you now, Cathy,' said Robin. 'All I can do is wish you the best of luck, and say that I'm very, very sorry for you.'

'So there's no chance at all?' said Cathy, in a choked voice.

Robin shook his head and lifted one of his bandaged stumps towards Nurse Wing. 'Me and Megan, we've got really close. She's been taking care of burns patients all of her life, and they don't put her off. And I have to say that she's beautiful, like you used to be.'

Holly was waiting for Cathy in the reception area. She didn't say a word as they walked out into the windy afternoon, and across the parking lot to Holly's car. She could guess what had happened, and she didn't want to say 'I told you so'.

They were speeding back to Fairfield on the turnpike when Cathy said, 'Well. It seems like I have only two choices now. I could join a circus. You know roll up, roll up! Come and see the Noseless, Earless, Unfuckable woman.'

'Oh, Cathy. What's the other choice?'

Cathy sat quite still for a while with her hands in her lap. Then she unbuckled her seat belt, opened the car door and threw herself sideways out of the car and onto the road. She bounced, and bounced again, her arms and legs flying, and then she was hit by a huge Mack truck and disappeared from sight.

Later, when the police and the ambulance had arrived, Holly went over to the truck driver, who was sitting on the steel divider in the middle of the road, still badly shaken.

'It wasn't your fault,' Holly told him.

The truck driver shook his head. 'Never seen nothing like it. Your car door come flying open, and do you know? It was like the Angel of the Lord plucked her out of there, in person.'

EPIPHANY

The instant she stepped out onto the sidewalk, the sky cracked open and thunder echoed all around the office buildings like a car bomb. A few large spots of rain started to patter onto the concrete, and so she ran to the corner of 49th Street and waved frantically for a taxi. She was wearing her new cream linen suit and her new Manolo Blahnik shoes and she had just had her hair cut at Vidal Sassoon.

Like a happy miracle, a taxi with a lighted FOR HIRE sign came jouncing down Lexington Avenue towards her, and she stepped out into the road with her arm still lifted. As she did so, however, a sandy-haired man in a loud green summer suit pushed right out in front of her and let out a piercing two-fingered whistle. The taxi pulled over and the man opened the door, just as the rain began to lash down in earnest.

'*Excuse me!*' Jessica screamed. '*Excuse me! That's my cab!*'

The man was half-in and half-out of the taxi door. He blinked at her as if he couldn't understand what she was talking about.

'This is *my* cab,' Jessica repeated, possessively gripping

the top of the door. The rain was clattering onto the taxi's yellow roof and soaking her shoulders.

'*Your* cab?' The man looked around in mock-bewilderment. 'I'm sorry. I don't see your name on it anyplace.'

'It's mine because I hailed it first – the driver was slowing down for me.'

'Listen, I think I was nearer to the cab than you were. What do you want me to say?'

Still she clung onto the door. 'You asshole. You unmitigated *asshole*! You know this is my cab.'

'Hey, lady, you getting in or what?' the taxi driver wanted to know.

'You saw me first, didn't you?' Jessica demanded. 'You were stopping for me.'

'I just want to get the hell out of here, all right?'

Jessica tried to seize the sandy-haired man's shoulder but he twisted his arm away and slammed the door, breaking her middle fingernail. The taxi pulled out into the traffic and sped off down Lexington, leaving her standing in the middle of the road.

She tried to hail another taxi, and there were dozens of them, splashing across the intersection like shoals of bright-yellow dolphins, but the rain was really hammering down now and every one of them was occupied. She had never hated anybody in her life, not really, but when she saw those smug, dry people sailing past in their taxis, she wished they would all have cardiac arrests over their lunch tables, or choke on a fishbone. Her linen jacket was almost transparent, her strappy little shoes were filled with water, and her hair was sticking to her forehead. There was another flicker of lightning, followed by a deafening thunderclap.

Miserable, furious, she retreated to the nearest doorway. Even here the rain bounced against her shins and the temperature was beginning to drop so that she started shivering. She turned around to see if she could find any shelter inside the building. It was a small private art gallery with heavy glass and stainless-steel doors. She pushed her way inside and immediately found herself in a world that was hushed and warm, thickly carpeted, with bronze mirrors all around, and elegant arrangements of arum lilies in glass Japanese vases. The walls and the furnishings were pale and beige and restful.

She took off her shoes and wiped the insides with a Kleenex. Three hundred and eight dollars, and they were ruined.

Two young men were sitting talking at a creamy marble desk, both of them dressed in expensive suits, their shirts gleaming white and their hair glossed back. The taller one turned and stared in surprise at her bare feet. '*Ye-e-es?* May I help you?'

'I, er... I just came in to take a look around, if that's okay.'

'Please do... you're more than welcome. My God, you poor thing, you're *soaked*! Listen – why don't you go to the restroom and dry yourself off. We have some lovely Turkish towels in there.'

'Well, thank you, I appreciate it.'

She went into the silent, expensively fitted restroom. The mirror was tinted a flattering pink, but she still looked as if the coastguard had just fished her out of the East River with a billhook. She opened her purse and tried to comb her hair, but her feathery brunette bob had been ruined, and all she could do was slick it straight back in a style that was strangely reflective of the two young men.

When she came back out the two young men were waiting for her, smiling. 'Better?'

'Much, thanks.'

The taller one opened a drawer in the desk and took out a thick shiny catalogue. 'Here... you'll probably want one of these. Seventy-nine fifty, I'm afraid.'

'*How* much?'

'Oh, don't worry. It'll be worth *twice* that in six months' time.'

She took the catalogue and somehow she felt like a Dayak tribeswoman being handed a Manhattan telephone directory.

The young man smiled and said, 'The prints are all for sale, too, starting at twenty-five.' He gave a little cough and added, 'Thousand.' Then: 'Each.'

Jessica looked down at the catalogue. On the front cover there was a black-and-white photograph of a young Mexican man. He had gappy teeth, and he was smiling wide-eyed and mocking at the camera. About twenty feet behind him, on a wide verandah, a silver-haired white man in a light-grey suit was looking over a garden of impossible lushness, crowded with orchids and ferns and amaryllis. The brochure was entitled: *Queer Nation: the photography of Jamie Starck*.

Oh my God, she thought. She had read about this exhibition only yesterday. Jamie Starck had been a protégé of the notorious homosexual photographer Robert Mapplethorpe, and this exhibition had been furiously and publicly condemned by Mayor Rudolph Giuliani. The mayor had tried to close it down, but there had been demonstrations in Gracie Square by hundreds of gay rights activists, and in the end the mayor had been forced to give way. Or at least to come up with the grudging acceptance that 'graphic depictions of alternative lifestyles, in context, may not be wholly deleterious to the city's moral fabric'.

'I ah – I seem to have made a mistake,' she said, trying to hand the catalogue back.

'Of course you haven't,' the young man replied. 'Or, even if you *have*, how will you know unless you see for yourself?' He was handsome in an other-worldly way and perfectly groomed. His skin was exfoliated and honey-tanned, and his fingernails were lightly polished. His necktie was silk, an Impressionistic splash of carmine and gold. His spectacles were fashionably lozenge-shaped, and immaculately clean. He wore a loose gold wristwatch by Jaeger-LeCoultre and a spicy and expensive cologne. Jessica could imagine that his underwear was Calvin Klein, blindingly white, without a single stain.

'I've come to the wrong gallery, that's all.'

But the young man said, 'Does it matter?' and took hold of her arm, and guided her towards the exhibits.

'Honestly,' Jessica protested, 'I only came in here to shelter from the rain. I really didn't…'

It was then that she saw the first photograph. It was black and white, as all of them were, taken on a high-intensity film that gave startling clarity to every single hair, every single goose bump, every single blemish. It was a picture of two young men – one black, one white, facing each other with their arms loosely linked over one another's shoulders. They were both slim, muscular, and almost laughably good-looking. Both of them had fully erect penises, and their glans were touching each other, almost kissing each other. The photograph was labelled *Racial Accord*.

Jessica stood and stared at it for nearly ten seconds. Then she turned to the young man in the lozenge-shaped spectacles and looked in his face for an explanation.

'You're looking for a meaning,' he said, as if he could read her mind.

She shook her head in confusion. 'I never thought that—'

'I know. This exhibition strikes everybody the same way, men and women both. They come here with all kinds of preconceptions, "I hate queers" or "I'm straight but curious", but they all walk out enlightened. Like Saul, you know, on the road to Damascus.'

Jessica moved to the next photograph, and the young man followed her, although he kept his distance. The photograph depicted a naked Arab, kneeling in the desert, his cheek pressed against the hot sand as if he were listening for the sound of distant hoofbeats. On the far horizon there were sand dunes, ribbed by the wind, and a cluster of palm trees. Close to the palm trees stood a white-bearded man wrapped in Bedouin black, holding the halter of a highly uninterested camel.

The Arab was pulling apart the cheeks of his bottom to expose his anus, in a gesture of extreme submission. His penis was erect and the glans was seasoned with grains of glittering sand. The title of the photograph was *Abid*.

'In Arabic, *abid* means "slave",' said the young man, although he still kept his distance.

'I, ah – I think I should go now,' said Jessica.

'Well, that's up to you. But you'll never see anything like this again, ever. Jamie's dying of AIDS, and he's already lost eighty per cent of his sight.'

As if she were dreaming, Jessica moved to the next picture. It showed a very thin middle-aged man lying naked on a chaise longue. His eyes were half-closed as if he were dozing, and his hair was long and blond and wavy, like a woman's. On the elaborately tiled floor beneath him lay a Borzoi dog, sulking, as Borzois do. A young Moroccan man in a huge, top-heavy, silk turban was kneeling next to the chaise longue. His turban was draped with strings of pearls and he wore large dangly earrings. The young man's lips were closed around the Englishman's penis, while one long-fingered hand was cupping his testicles. The young man wore an embroidered waistcoat, but he was naked from the waist down, and semen was dripping like strings of pearls down his thighs.

'What does it mean?' said Jessica. 'Is it just perversion, or what?'

The man in the glasses gave her a strangely confidential smile. 'Perhaps it means that people should be free to express themselves in whatever ways they wish, no matter how bizarre.'

'Oh, yes? And perhaps it's nothing but hard-core porn, masquerading as art.'

The man approached the photograph, and said, 'You see it though, don't you? Each picture is a mystery but each picture is also an answer.'

'So what's this picture an answer to? Some bony old faggot's prayer?'

The man laughed. 'I like you... you're very direct. That's unusual.'

'I think I should leave now,' said Jessica. 'I recognise the quality of this photography, and I guess it's arguably art. But if you really want to know, I find it embarrassing.'

'All right. At least you're honest.'

She gave him the catalogue back. 'Good luck, anyway.'

On her way out, she caught sight of a photograph that she hadn't seen before, because the light had been shining on the glass, and obscured it. She stopped, even though she didn't really want to. The man in the glasses waited so close behind her that she could hear his measured breathing. *I'll bet that even the hairs in his nostrils are immaculately trimmed*, she thought.

The photograph had been taken on the landing of a grand marble staircase, with high leaded windows that let in a thin, restrained light. A young man of nineteen or twenty, naked except for thong sandals, was leaning languidly against a marble pillar. He looked Thai, or Cambodian, and his hair was fastened with chopsticks in a geisha-like bun.

His skin shone with a silky, almost unearthly radiance. His nipples were like ripe sultanas. His penis was half-erect, with a foreskin that looked as if it were just beginning to slide back, and his scrotum was the texture of crumpled silk. A single sparkling drop of liquid quivered on the end of his penis, like a diamond.

More than anything else, though, it was the expression on his face that caught Jessica's breath. He had high cheekbones and large, dark, unfocused eyes, as if he were drugged, or hypnotised. He was utterly exquisite.

'Ah,' said the man in glasses. 'All our women fall in love with Lo Duc Tho.'

'That's his name? Lo Duc Tho? Who is he?'

'He was actually Viet Namese. Jamie found him in a grand house in Paris, next door to the apartment building where Marlene Dietrich used to live.'

Jessica approached the picture and touched one finger lightly against the glass. Lo Duc Tho stared back at her enigmatically. *Each picture is an answer, but each picture is also a mystery.*

'What was he doing in Paris?' she asked.

'He was a toy. I think that's the best description. The house was owned by a very wealthy lady whose father had made a fortune in Viet Nam when it was still owned by the French. After the battle of Dien Bien Phu in 1954, when the French were forced to give up all of their possessions in Indo-China, her father came back to Paris – bringing not only his daughter but also the orphaned son of one of his servants, a child of ten years old, and that was Lo Duc Tho.

'Lo Duc Tho was fed well and educated by private tutors and pampered in every way that you could think of. But in 1962, when he was eighteen, the father died suddenly of a stroke, and his daughter took over Lo Duc Tho's upbringing completely.'

'You called him a toy.'

'Exactly so. Lo Duc Tho was mademoiselle's plaything. After her father's death, she expected him to amuse her all day, playing the violin for her, singing for her, dancing for her. She also expected him to be nude at all times, except when they went out.'

'Nude? Like, all day?'

The man leaned against the wall beside her and nodded. 'She made him pose for her in all kinds of exotic positions and sit close to her so that she could fondle him whenever she felt like it.'

'That's extraordinary. What did Lo Duc Tho think about it?'

'I don't have any idea. But he didn't appear to mind, because he never attempted to run away. He hardly ever spoke, and when he did he used to refer to himself in the third person, as if he were talking about somebody else.'

'What a strange life.'

'You don't have any idea. Mademoiselle used to invite her friends for afternoon tea, and Lo Duc Tho would be sprawled on a chaise longue next to them, so that these thirtyish ladies could kiss him and caress him and even fellate him, if they wanted to. Jamie told me that madame's friends use to smear the boy's private parts with raspberry preserves so that they could lick it off.'

'My God. Talk about decadent.'

'I don't know. I've heard about worse in New York. Guinea pigs, being used in all kinds of inventive ways, things like that. And at least the French make very decent preserves.'

'You're teasing me.'

The man gave her the faintest of smiles. 'Tell me now that you won't leave here feeling enlightened. Or *different*, at least.'

'Well, I guess you're right. I will. Do you know what

happened to Lo Duc Tho? He must be middle-aged himself now.'

'Mademoiselle became very ill and the house had to be sold. Jamie made some inquiries, but nobody found out where Lo Duc Tho disappeared to.'

The man accompanied Jessica to the front door. It had stopped raining now and the sidewalks were blinding with reflected light.

'Thank you,' she said. 'It's been very interesting. Possibly obscene, but very interesting.'

'The pleasure,' he assured her, 'is totally mine.'

'So how was *your* day?' asked Michael, pouring himself another large glass of chardonnay.

'Unusual,' she said.

'Oh, yes? Unusual in what way?'

'I did something I never imagined that I would ever do in a million years. I went to see that Queer Nation exhibition. Well, I didn't actually go out with the intention of seeing it, but I got caught in the rain and that's where I ended up.'

Michael blinked at her. He was thirty-one, two years younger than she was, but his short-cropped, iron-grey hair made him look much older. He had very pale blue eyes, the colour of bleached denim, and a broad, Scandinavian-looking face. He was wearing a blue-and-white striped, English-tailored shirt and a pair of expensive fawn slacks, and no socks. His ankles were still tanned after two weeks' filming in Bermuda.

'And?' he said, at last. 'What did you think of it? The exhibition?'

'I was… corrupted, I think.'

'Seriously? You're serious?'

'It was strange. I don't know exactly what I felt. Some of the pictures were very beautiful and they were all technically brilliant. But there was something *poisoned* about them.'

'Maybe you'll make a point of taking an umbrella next time.' He checked his heavy steel wristwatch. 'Jesus, look at the time. I have to call Bertrand in Vancouver.'

'Can't you just finish your dinner?'

'Listen, I'm going to miss him if I do. He's flying to Montreal this evening and I have to talk to him about the Harrington account.' He took his glass of wine and left his half-finished tagliatelle on the plate. He went across to the living area and sat on the large black leather chair next to the window, where the phone was. Jessica stayed at the table with its shiny black glass top and continued to eat and watched him while he talked. Outside the window she could see the sparkling lights of the Jersey shoreline, and two helicopters circling like fireflies.

Both Michael and she worked in advertising. He was a freelance director for TV commercials while she was a senior copywriter at Nedick Kuhl Friedman. They had lived together for eleven months now, renting between them this huge condominium overlooking the Hudson. They had furnished and decorated it in minimalist style, but very expensively. On the opposite wall, discreetly lit, hung a dot painting by Damien Hirst for which they had paid $78,000.

Michael said, 'We could meet up in Cancun on the twenty-fifth. Yes, that's right. I need that very special light they have on the beach there. No, the Gulf Coast is no good at all. Far too harsh. What are you talking about, filters? If you want perfection you have to *start* with perfection.'

Jessica wound her tagliatelle around her fork. She couldn't help thinking about Lo Duc Tho, and how he had wandered around naked all day. She could almost imagine him sitting in the large leather chair opposite her, his hair pinned up like a geisha's, one leg insouciantly slung over the armrest, his eyes as dark and blurry as a court portrait by Velázquez. He would be idly playing with his half-erect penis, rolling his foreskin backward and forward in a slow, dreamy rhythm.

'I need at least two lighting cameramen. Well, I'd prefer David Weill, but if you can't get him... yes, I know all about budget, Jim. But you're talking false economy here.'

Perhaps she would beckon Lo Duc Tho and he would rise from his chair and walk across to the table. He would lay one long-fingered arm on her shoulder, respectfully, as lightly as a hummingbird. She would beckon him again to stand even closer, so that she could see every vein beneath his ivory skin. His pubic hair was like shiny black silk, and pomaded, and combed, so that it stuck to his stomach in waves.

'I'm telling you, if we shoot it and it doesn't work, which it *won't*, the way you're describing it, then we'll have to shoot it over, and that's going to cost us more than double.'

She took hold of Lo Duc Tho's penis and gently massaged it. It grew harder and harder, until the foreskin peeled right back and the glans swelled as dark as a damson plum. She gripped it even tighter, as tight as she possibly could, but when she looked up at Lo Duc Tho he did nothing but give her the most abstract of smiles, as if he were thinking about something else altogether.

Between finger and thumb, she lifted a strand of tagliatelle from her plate. She encircled the shaft of his penis, and tied the tagliatelle in a slippery little bow. Then she took another strand, and another, until his erection was decorated with eight or nine ribbons of pasta.

'Now for some sauce,' she told him. She took a handful of garlic and tomato sauce out of the bowl and smeared it all over his scrotum and between the cheeks of his taut, rounded bottom. 'You like that?' she asked him, gently rolling his testicles between her fingers. 'Now you're a meal in yourself.'

She leaned forward and licked his wrinkled, tomato-tasting skin. She nuzzled him and sucked him, sucking each testicle one after the other. 'You're beautiful, aren't you?' she said. 'You're absolutely gorgeous.'

She took the swollen head of his penis into her mouth and slowly slid her hand up the shaft, so that one by the one the ribbons of tagliatelle slipped over his glans and into her mouth. When she had swallowed them she stuck out her tongue and probed the hole in his penis with it. As she did so, she rubbed him harder and harder. 'Come on, you can give me my dessert now. Don't be shy.'

It was then that she became aware that Michael had finished his phone call to Bertrand and was standing staring at her. Immediately, embarrassed, she sat up straight, and it was then that she realised that there was nobody there, no Lo Duc Tho, and that she had been smearing tomato and garlic sauce all over her chin and her cheeks and beating with her fist at nothing but thin air.

Michael slowly pulled his chair out and sat down, still staring at her. 'What the hell are you doing?' he asked her, at last.

'I'm, ah – I seem to have made a bit of a mess.'

'What is this? Some kind of attention-seeking stunt? Listen, I'm sorry I had to call Bertrand right in the middle of dinner, but for Christ's sake, look at you.'

Jessica wiped her face with her napkin, and then stood up. 'I was – I don't know. I was trying to eat it the Italian way.'

'I've been to Italy six times and I never saw *anybody* eat like that. I never saw anybody eat like that *ever*. Maybe my sister's two-year-old kid.'

'Well, I just wanted to relish it, that's all. Like really, really relish it.'

With that, she threw down her napkin and walked stiffly to the bathroom. She stood in front of the mirror staring at herself. She still had tomato and garlic sauce in her hair, and the front of her cream cotton blouse was spattered all over, so that she looked as if somebody had hit her in the nose.

How could I have done that? she thought. *I was sure that I could see Lo Duc Tho. I was sure that I could actually* taste *him. God... maybe I'm working under too much pressure. Maybe I'm cracking up.*

She looked down at her hand, and slowly reproduced the rubbing motion she had used to stimulate Lo Duc Tho's penis. She could still feel his hardness. She could still feel his foreskin, as slippery and pliable as a wonton. She took a deep breath and then she unbuttoned her blouse, filled up the washbasin with cold water, and pushed it in to soak.

***

When they went to bed, they both read for half an hour. Then Michael abruptly slapped his book shut, put on his American Airlines sleep mask, and heaved himself sideways, with his sun-freckled back to her.

'Goodnight, then,' said Jessica, but Michael didn't answer. He didn't like weirdness, or anything unpredictable (like his partner smearing her face with tomato and garlic sauce) and he was obviously making a point. One of the things that had first attracted her was his solidity, the feeling of security he had given her, but as time went by she was beginning to find it increasingly repressive, like living with a disapproving parent.

She had been reading Coleridge, an old dog-eared copy she had found in a cardboard box in the cellar. It wasn't easy to understand. Yet she felt that it was just like Lo Duc Tho's photograph, a mystery and an answer, both at the same time.

'*In his loneliness and his fixedness he yearns towards the journeying Moon, and the stars that still sojourn, yet still move onward; and everywhere the blue sky belongs to them, and is their appointed rest, and their native country, and their own natural homes, which they enter unannounced, as lords that are certainly expected and yet there is silent joy at their arrival.*'

She felt as if Lo Duc Tho had been waiting in the wings of her life ever since she had first felt sexual stirrings. Thinking back on her reaction this afternoon when she had first seen his picture, she realised now that what had stopped her in her tracks was *recognition*. Here was the man who would sit beside her under the journeying moon and the lordly stars, and offer his nakedness and his docile beauty so that she could discover the true meaning of pleasure.

She laid her book on the nightstand and switched off the light. In the darkness she could hear the plaintive mating call of a ferry crossing to the Jersey shore. Michael had started that persistent *pish, pish, pish*, which meant that he was already asleep.

She was very tired. Before she had been caught in the rain she had been working for more than five hours with her creative team, trying to develop a series of magazine advertisements for Moist-Your-Eyes anti-wrinkle cream. Then – after she briefly come home to change – she had gone down to Ray MacConnick's studio in the Village to supervise a three-and-a-half-hour photo shoot.

All the same, she found it difficult to sleep. She couldn't stop thinking about Lo Duc Tho, and the way in which he had seemed to materialise in front of her. She couldn't stop thinking about his strange, detached smile, and the feeling of his skin.

She turned over, and as she did so she felt fingers trailing gently down her back. 'Not now, Michael,' she murmured. But the fingers kept on tracing patterns around her shoulder blades and down her spine, and back again. The touch was so light that it made her skin tingle.

'Michael—' she said, but then she heard him grunt and stir and start that monotonous *pish – pish – pish*.

'Michael?' She propped herself up on one elbow, and looked around. Michael still had his back turned towards her, and he was deeply asleep.

She looked around the darkened bedroom, frowning. She

even slapped the comforter, as if there could be somebody hiding underneath it. Nobody. She must have imagined those fingers, or maybe they were nothing more than the draught from the air-con unit.

Uneasily, she lay back down again. It was true that she had been working far too hard for the past three months, but she knew that if she could pull off a really successful campaign for Moist-Your-Eyes there was a vice-presidency waiting for her, and $25,000 more salary. She didn't want to come to pieces, not now. Not when everything for which she had sacrificed so much time and so much effort was right within her grasp.

She tried to empty her mind, the way that she had been taught at her yoga class. Imagine your thoughts pouring out of your ear, and soaking into your pillow. Imagine blackness, infinite blackness. No sound, no sensation, just seamless darkness and total detachment. But then she felt the fingers again, delicately teasing her shoulders, and following the curve of her body so that she shivered as they reached her hips.

She turned onto her back. Immediately – without a sound – Lo Duc Tho materialised out of the darkness and lightly climbed astride her. She let out an '*ah!*' of shock, but he pressed his fingertips against her lips. He sat gazing down at her, his face barely visible in the gloom.

'You're not real,' Jessica breathed. 'There's nobody here but me and Michael.'

Lo Duc Tho leaned forward and kissed her lips, and she was sure that she could taste lemongrass on his breath. As he kissed her, he took hold of her right hand and guided it towards his penis, so that she could feel it rising between her fingers. He showed her how to roll it against her nipples, round and round, and it gradually grew so hard that it felt as if it were carved out of polished ivory. Her nipples stiffened in response.

Her breathing began to grow shallow. With her left hand she reached between Lo Duc Tho's thighs and fondled his testicles, tugging at the skin of his scrotum with her sharpened fingernails. She tugged harder and harder, but Lo Duc Tho didn't utter a sound, although the head of his penis was slippery now, and so were her nipples.

This was a kind of heaven… to have a beautiful and exotic young man who didn't speak or argue or complain. A young man with whom she could have any variety of sex she wanted, whenever she wanted. She closed her eyes and already she could feel a dark, compressed sensation between her legs. It was the first stirring of an orgasm that she knew would be almost unbearable. She pressed his penis harder and harder against her breasts, and kept up her rhythmical pulling at his scrotum.

He suddenly arched his back and ejaculated. Warm sperm flipped against her cheek, and then anointed her neck, and then her breasts. Lo Duc Tho sat utterly still for a moment, and then he began to stroke her face and massage her breasts until the sperm began to dry. She closed her eyes and she could smell him and she felt as if she had never been so pampered in her life.

Then he disappeared. She didn't know how he did it, but he simply unravelled in the darkness like a knotted silk sheet, and he was gone. She sat up again, trying to see if he was hiding behind the armchair, or buried in the shadow of the armoire, but there was nobody there.

She couldn't have imagined him. She touched her breasts and she could still feel his sperm drying on her. She waited for a long time, almost five minutes, to see if he would reappear. She didn't call out.

At last, exhausted, she lay back and closed her eyes. Michael grunted and turned over again, and his arm dropped heavily across her.

'Got to call Henry,' he mumbled.

During her lunch break the next day, Jessica went back to the gallery. The smart young man with the glasses was still there, but this time he was alone. Jessica went directly to the picture of Lo Duc Tho and stood staring at it, as if she expected it to talk to her.

'You're back, then?' said the man, circling around behind her. He was wearing a smart navy blazer and a very white shirt and his aftershave had strong notes of vetiver grass.

'I wanted to take another look, that's all. You were right. This exhibition is a revelation. The trouble is, I can't work out what it's a revelation *of*.'

'I think you will, if you give yourself time.'

'Tell me more about Lo Duc Tho.'

'There's nothing more to tell. He was content to be used, that's all. Whatever mademoiselle asked of him, he obliged. I suppose you and I find it difficult to imagine anybody being so docile. But there can be great spirituality in such docility. I think that Lo Duc Tho was closer to heaven than we can possibly imagine.'

'You knew him yourself,' said Jessica.

'Yes, I did.'

'In fact… you're Jamie Starck, aren't you, and you're not dying of AIDs at all.'

The man gave her a smile that was almost coy. 'Well guessed. I tend not to advertise my identity. When they find out, some people react in a very negative way. Negative – I suppose that's a joke, for a photographer.'

'I need to find out who Lo Duc Tho actually was.'

Jamie Starck took off his glasses and looked at her seriously. 'You *need* to?'

'Yes, whatever you know. Anything.'

'You've seen him.'

'No. But I imagined that I saw him.'

'It counts for the same thing.'

'Who is he? *What* is he?'

'I can't really explain.'

'Is he a ghost? Is that it?' She didn't even know how she could bring herself to think such a thing, let alone suggest it out loud, on a bright summer day.

Jamie Starck shook his head. 'I don't think that I believe in ghosts. But perhaps I believe in the overwhelming power of human desires – particularly sexual desires. Think about it – sometimes we can almost bring ourselves to orgasm, can't we, just by thinking sexual thoughts. Lo Duc Tho is one of our desires, and that's what gives him such a grip on our imagination.'

Jessica said, 'You've seen him too, haven't you? I mean, after you took his picture? Did he come to your bed?'

Jamie Starck said nothing. Jessica hesitated for a moment, and then she said, 'He's very alluring. I'm not sure what to do.'

'No, it isn't easy, I'll admit. It's that mixture of absolute innocence and absolute corruption. Let me tell you... I walked into mademoiselle's salon one afternoon when she and her friends were gathered for tea. Lo Duc Tho was sitting on the chaise longue, wearing a girl's velvet hat, his cheeks rouged, his eyes made up with eyeshadow, his lips painted with lipstick. His legs were wide apart and he was erect. An elegant woman in a Balenciaga suit was sitting beside him, a truly classic French beauty of a certain age, and she was slowly pushing her long pearl necklace into his anus, pearl by pearl, right up to the clasp, and then slowly pulling it out again, over and over, until he climaxed all over her skirt. She laughed with delight.'

'Is he dead, do you think?' asked Jessica.

'I don't know. Probably. Even if he isn't, I wouldn't even know where to start looking for him.'

That night Michael had to take three of his clients to Le Cirque, so Jessica spent the evening alone, washing her hair and giving herself a pedicure. At 11:00 pm, Michael called to say that he was going to be very late, so not to wait up for her. She went to bed with the television switched on but the sound turned right down and tried to read, but she was too tired to make much sense of Coleridge.

'*And all should cry, Beware! Beware! His flashing eyes, his floating hair! Weave a circle round him thrice, And close your eyes with holy dread, For he on honey-dew hath fed, And drunk the milk of Paradise!*'

Without realising it, she fell asleep, and the book dropped out of her hand and onto the comforter. And it was only a few minutes afterward that a young long-fingered hand gently lifted the book away, and stroked her forehead and her hair, and kissed her cheek.

She opened her eyes. Lo Duc Tho had climbed onto the bed next to her, on all fours. His glossy black hair was hanging loose, so that he looked like a wild young animal. He was staring at her intently, his lips slightly parted, but he didn't speak. She could see between his thighs that his penis was already stiff, and that his testicles were as tight as two walnuts.

'What do you want?' she asked him, and her voice seemed unnecessarily loud. The light from the television gleamed on his naked back. 'Are you alive? Or dead? Or am I going mad?'

He kissed her again, and then he drew down the comforter. She was wearing a pink sleep-T, and he reached down with both hands and softly squeezed her breasts through the warm brushed cotton. She no longer felt frightened. She could see now that Lo Duc Tho was everything that Jamie Starck had described. He was everything that she had secretly desired, and never dared to tell anybody, come to life.

She sat up in bed, crossed her arms and took off her T-shirt. She stroked Lo Duc Tho's cheeks and upper lip, and pushed the tips of her fingers into his mouth, so that he could kiss them and lick them and nip them with his perfect white teeth. Strongly but gently she pushed him onto his back, and then she sat astride him, as he had sat astride her. With both hands, she moved his penis up and down, quite forcefully, so that on her downward stroke his foreskin was stretched right back.

'Are you never going to talk to me?' she said. Lo Duc Tho gave her his abstract smile, but still didn't speak.

'I suppose that's the nature of fantasies,' she told him. 'They don't argue with you and they don't involve you in idle conversation.'

She leaned forward so that her nipples touched his chest, and she swung her breasts from side to side. 'I think we're going to have to decorate you a little,' she said. 'How about some silver rings through your nipples, and some tattoos? You'd look gorgeous with a few flowery tattoos.'

She kissed him and ran her fingers deep into his clean shining hair. His skin was absolutely flawless, except for a tiny, star-shaped scar on his right shoulder. 'Touch me,' she said, sitting up again; and he slid one hand beneath her thigh and stroked her clitoris with the tip of his middle finger, so lightly that it was almost like being licked. She was so aroused that his stroking made a wet clicking noise like somebody softly smacking their lips.

She raised her hips, and took hold of his penis in her hand, and positioned it between her thighs. Then she sank down on it, all the way down, until she could feel his scrotum squashed against the cheeks of her bottom, and she let out a long quavering moan of absolute pleasure. If this was nothing but a fantasy – if this was nothing but her own desire – it was a fantasy of unbelievable intensity, and she didn't care if she was going mad or not.

'Lo – Duc – Tho—' she breathed, again and again. 'Lo – Duc – Tho—'

He felt so long and hard and slippery that he seemed to penetrate deeper into her body than any man who had ever made love to her before. She could almost believe that the head of his penis would nudge her heart.

'You're driving me out of my mind,' she gasped. 'You're killing me.' They were both glistening with sweat and yet Lo Duc Tho still didn't appear to be exerting himself, or involved in what he was doing to her in any way. She rode up and down on his penis even more forcefully, *smack*, *smack*, *smack* against his thighs, and she caught him closing his eyes for a moment, as if at last he was beginning to feel something like the same pleasure that she was.

Exhausted, she lifted herself off him and rolled onto her back. Lo Duc Tho rose up next to her, as if he was going to climb on top of her, but she threaded her fingers into his hair and said, 'You're *my* fantasy, remember? I want you to lick me.' This time, *she* wanted an orgasm, too. This time she urgently needed one.

In silent obedience, Lo Duc Tho crawled down the bed and lay between her thighs. She watched him enthralled as his narrow tongue flickered on her clitoris, and he watched her back, never taking his eyes off her once. The feeling he gave her was so strong that she felt as if they were on a raft, on the ocean, at night, being washed out on an overwhelming swell.

Jessica had an orgasm that made her deaf and blind. It went on and on, until she couldn't tolerate any more back-breaking spasms, and she reached down to push Lo Duc Tho away from her.

Except that Lo Duc Tho wasn't there any more. She was lying alone on the twisted sheets, with the silent television still flickering, and her book of Coleridge lying on the floor where she must have dropped it.

She couldn't move. She knew that she should have got up, but she couldn't. She lay staring at the ceiling and breathing like a marathon runner. She thought: *What's happening to me? I've never had sex like that before, ever. But maybe I haven't had it even now.*

She was still lying there when the bedroom door and Michael came in, tugging off his stripy silk necktie. 'Hey, there! You still awake? Jesus – I thought those guys were going to go on drinking all night.'

He came over to the bed and sat down beside her. 'You look hot. Are you okay?'

'I'm fine, I'm okay.'

He reached out and touched her forehead. 'Jesus, you're burning up. I'm not kidding you – you look like you're going down with the flu. You should keep yourself warm, not lie here undressed like this.'

She couldn't think what to say. She couldn't stop trembling and she was still short of breath.

'I'll call Dr Biedermeyer first thing. And there's no way you're going into work tomorrow.'

He came back with two glasses of milk. 'How are you feeling now? I should have known something was wrong when you had that accident with the pasta sauce.'

She was sitting up straight in bed in a black silk kimono, with her hair in a towel turban. 'That was no accident, Michael.'

'I don't get you. You didn't make all that mess on purpose?'

'Michael, there's something I have to tell you.'

He took off his robe and climbed into bed next to her. 'You're very stressed out, honey. I know that. That's why I'm going to call Dr Biedermeyer. He can give you something to keep you together until this Moist-Your-Eyes account's all wrapped up. You know, maybe Prozac.'

'I don't need Dr Biedermeyer, Michael, and I don't need Prozac. I've been seeing somebody.'

Michael had just taken a mouthful of milk but now he slowly put his hand to his throat as if she had told him that she had poisoned it. 'You've been *seeing* somebody? Who?'

'It's not what it sounds like. I haven't been having an affair. I've been seeing somebody, like a hallucination. Here in the house.'

'*What?*' he said, with a disbelieving laugh that was almost a bark. 'I don't understand you. A hallucination? Like, a mirage?'

'More like a ghost. Except that he doesn't walk through walls or anything like that. I can feel him. I can actually smell him.'

'A *ghost*? For Christ's sake, Jessica. I thought you were the most pragmatic woman I ever met.'

She was tempted for a second to tell him the truth, but then she decided that he wouldn't be able to take it. Apart from being very straitlaced about sex, he was also fiercely possessive. Even the thought of a *ghost* making love to her would upset him.

He took hold of her hands. 'Listen, sweetheart… I still think this is definitely a stress thing. You know and I know that ghosts don't exist. What you're seeing, what you're feeling, it's all in your head. You remember Chet Lewis, who used to work with Langton & Clarke? He got so overworked that he started believing that black dogs were chasing him down the street.'

'Please, Michael. I don't want to see Dr Biedermeyer and I don't want Prozac. This is nothing to do with stress. I guess the best way to describe it is that it's some kind of epiphany.'

Michael looked completely baffled. 'An epiphany? Like a *revelation*? The burning bush, something like that? Jesus, you *do* need a doctor.'

'There's only one way I can explain it to you, and that's to show you. Meet me tomorrow lunchtime on 49th and Lex.'

'This is crazy, Jessica. This doesn't make any sense at all.'

She leaned forward and kissed him on the lips. 'Michael, I love you. When you see this for yourself, I promise you, you'll understand.'

'I don't know... I'm supposed to be meeting Ron Shulman at twelve.'

'Meet me at eleven-thirty then. Please.'

He puffed out his cheeks. 'Okay, if you insist. But I still think you need some help with this. Really.'

It was raining again when she met him outside the gallery. He stepped out of a cab, paid the driver, and came over with his coat collar turned up. Then he saw the poster outside announcing *Queer Nation* and even before he said 'hello,' he said '*Here?* This is where you had your epiphany? I can't go in here.'

'Please, Michael, you must.'

He looked around uneasily. 'For Christ's sake. Supposing somebody sees me.'

'It's a legitimate photography exhibition, Michael, and you're a professional photographer.'

'I don't think so, sweetheart. This kind of thing really isn't my scene.'

'I need you to understand, Michael. Please.' She grasped his hand and led him through the door into the softly carpeted interior. Jamie Starck wasn't there today, but his young assistant was. He came over with a wonderfully hip-swaying, hands-flapping walk and said, 'Hel-*lo*!'

'Hi,' said Michael, in the gruffest of voices, and held on to Jessica's hand as tightly as he could.

'Come for another peek?' the young assistant said. 'You're in luck; we close tomorrow. Next week it's the Reuben French, the Grey Period. Very *dour*, Reuben French.'

Jessica said, 'My partner and I just want to take a quick – you know—'

'Professional interest,' put in Michael. 'I'm photographic director for J.D. Philips.'

'Oh, I *am* impressed,' the young assistant told him. 'Do feel free, won't you? And if you need anything...' and here he gave Michael a long, lingering look '...you won't shy away from asking me, will you?'

'Yes,' Michael told him. 'I mean, no, we don't need anything.'

As they walked into the gallery, Jessica said, 'You're not coming down with a cold, are you?'

'No, why?'

'You were talking like *thurss*,' she said, mimicking his gruffness.

'I always talk like that.'

'You mean you always talk like that when you think another man's taken a fancy to you.'

They reached the photograph of the Arab boy bending over in the desert. Michael stopped and said, 'Oh my God.'

'*Abid*,' Jessica explained. 'That means slave.'

Michael didn't say anything but slowly shook his head.

'Anyhow,' said Jessica, 'that wasn't what I brought you here to see.'

She led him around the corner and there was the photograph of Lo Duc Tho. Michael looked at it for a moment and then turned his back on it.

'This?' he said, pointing his finger over his shoulder. 'This faggot is your epiphany?'

'You don't see it?'

'I see a dirty picture, that's all.'

Jessica approached the photograph and stared into Lo Duc Tho's unfocused eyes. 'He was a plaything,' she said. 'He would allow women to do anything they wanted.'

Michael turned back. 'I can't see what you're trying to show me.'

'He was naked all day, so that women could touch him and kiss him and pet him. Don't you understand? He was completely open, completely unthreatening, completely compliant. Men expect that in women, but sometimes women need that in men.'

'I'm sorry, Jessica, I really don't get it.'

'Look at him, Michael. Look at his face. Look at his eyes.'

Michael looked at him, and then he shook his head. 'You've lost me, sweetheart. You've completely and utterly lost me.'

***

Michael took her to the Park Bistro on Park Avenue that evening, where she toyed with sautéed skate wing in vinegar sauce while he had a messy saddle of rabbit, and kept tearing off large lumps of bread and stuffing them into his mouth.

'They have the best bread here. They fly the flour in from France.'

'I'm sorry about today,' she said. 'I guess you're right. I've been trying to take on too much.'

'Don't even think about it,' he told her, with his cheeks full like Chip 'n' Dale. 'You ought to try some of this rabbit – it's out of this world.'

That night she thought about Lo Duc Tho, but she was too tired to want him to visit her. All the same, she wondered what it would be like if she tattooed him all over – his back, his buttocks, his thighs, his face. She would cover him in large blue chrysanthemums, like the chrysanthemums on her silk scarf from Galeries Lafayette. She would decorate his nipples with gold rings, and his belly button with a gold stud. Then she would have a large, gold ring pierced through his foreskin, so that she could lead him all the way around the apartment by a long silk cord.

In his sleep, Michael grunted, '*Won't.*'

The following evening she had to stay late at the office to finish off the last of the Moist-Your-Eyes layouts. She didn't finish until way past one o'clock in the morning, and she was hyped up with too much coffee. She caught a cab home, and the seats were sticky and smelled of sick.

The apartment was in darkness when she let herself in, apart from the silent-movie flickering of the television under the bedroom door. She went into the kitchen and poured herself a large glass of Evian water. She could see herself reflected in the window, and she thought that she looked almost like a skull. White face, high cheekbones, dark rings under her eyes. She finished the water and rinsed the glass under the faucet.

She opened the bedroom door and at first she couldn't understand what she was looking at. Michael was crouched on the bed on all fours, and he didn't see her at first because his face was turned away from her. It was only when he slowly turned around and lifted up his head that she realised that he wasn't alone. There was a slight, mottled figure crouched beneath him.

In the stroboscopic light from the television, she saw that it was Lo Duc Tho, his long black hair hanging loose on the pillow, his thin elbows propping him up. He was decorated all over in chrysanthemum tattoos, and she saw the sparkle of nipple rings. Michael was hunched over him in the way that a stallion covers a mare.

'*Michael?*' Jessica whispered.

Michael sat up, withdrawing himself, his penis gleaming, one hand laid protectively flat on Lo Duc Tho's slender back. He said nothing at all, but simply stared at her, caught in the act, waiting for her to say something.

Jessica approached the bed. 'Michael?'

Lo Duc Tho turned his head towards her and smiled at her slyly, his face half-covered by his hair, like a girl.

'I fell asleep,' said Michael, in a parched voice. 'I felt somebody touching me and I thought it was you.'

'I never knew you – well, I never imagined you ever wanted *men*.'

'I didn't. I mean I don't.' Michael's penis was sinking. Lo Duc Tho reached around and took hold of it, and started lasciviously to rub it. All the time he kept on smiling at Jessica in that secretive, superior way, as if he knew that she wouldn't do anything to stop him.

Michael said, 'He's not a man, is he? He's just an illusion.'

'If he's such an illusion, why is your cock going hard?'

'You were right. It's just like you said. It's an epiphany. It's like understanding what you want for the very first time.'

Jessica stood beside the bed for the time it took her to breathe in and out, in and out, ten deep breaths. Then she unfastened the buttons of her thin ribbed cardigan, and pulled it off. Neither Michael nor Lo Duc Tho said a word, but both of them watched her unblinkingly.

She unfastened her bra and dropped it on the floor. Last she stepped out of her pale silk La Perla panties. Michael held out his hand to her and she climbed onto the bed next to him. Sweat was sparkling in his sandy-coloured chest hair.

'What are we doing?' Jessica whispered, kissing Michael's lips, kissing his nose, kissing his eyes. All the time Lo Duc Tho kept massaging Michael's penis, deliberately rubbing it against Jessica's thigh, so that she could feel its snail slime on her.

Michael said, 'Maybe this is what we always wanted, both of us. Maybe this is what we always needed.'

He pushed her back gently onto the pillow, and parted her thighs. Then he helped Lo Duc Tho to climb on top of her. With two fingertips he opened her lips and guided Lo Duc Tho inside her. She felt Lo Duc Tho's long smooth penis slide so deep that she couldn't help herself from quivering. Lo Duc Tho's hair trailed all over her face, and when she looked up she could see him staring at her, with that same distant but strangely self-satisfied smile.

It was then that Michael mounted Lo Duc Tho, and forced himself into him in one powerful thrust. Lo Duc Tho arched his back and uttered a single, high-pitched '*oh*,' as if he were practising his pitch for an aria.

After that the three of them were silent, Lo Duc Tho pushing himself as far into Jessica's body as her imagination would allow, and then further; and Michael gripping Lo Duc Tho's hips and rhythmically forcing him backward and downward. Jessica reached down between her legs and felt four slippery testicles jostling with each other, and it was then that she started quite unexpectedly to climax and couldn't stop.

She lay in the flickering light from the television for a long time afterward, staring at the ceiling. When she sat up, Lo Duc Tho had dematerialised, and there was only Michael lying there, already asleep. She started to reach out to touch him, but then she changed her mind. She began to wonder if she still loved him any more.

★★★

The next day she finished work early. She had lunch with her old schoolfriend Minnie at Dosanko noodle restaurant on Madison Avenue and then she went home. When she opened the front door she was surprised to hear music playing from the living room, one of Michael's favourites, 'Samba Pa Ti'.

'I didn't know you were taking the day off,' she called, kicking off her shoes. 'I met Minnie for lunch. You could have joined us.'

She walked into the living room. Michael was lying on the couch, naked except for his Argyle socks. Lo Duc Tho was kneeling on the carpet next to him, his skin still tattooed all over with chrysanthemum patterns. His shining black hair was draped all over Michael's lap and his head was bobbing up and down.

'Christ, Michael, what's going on?'

'What? You're going to start getting all censorious? You were the first one to conjure him up.'

'I know. But I don't know what to say. I never knew you were queer.'

Lo Duc Tho's head kept on bobbing and in the end Michael had to grab hold of his hair to stop him. Lo Duc Tho looked up, and turned around, and when he smiled at Jessica his lips were glistening.

Michael said, 'It's not a question of being gay, is it? It's a question of finding yourself.'

'Don't you understand?' Jessica retorted. 'He isn't even real!'

'Then it doesn't matter, does it? Maybe you'd like to have sex with another woman, but if she wasn't real, that wouldn't make you a lesbian, would it?'

'I don't know. I can't handle this, Michael. I don't *want* to handle it.'

'Lo Duc Tho gave you your revelation, didn't he? He gave you yours! Well, he gave me mine, too! He made me realise what I was and what I really wanted!'

'You want other men? Is that it?'

'For the first time in my life somebody allowed me do what I've always wanted to do. Without any shame. Without any guilt. Without making me feel disgusted with myself.'

'So where does that leave us?'

'Why should it affect us at all, except to make our relationship more exciting, and more honest?'

'You call it honest when I come home in the middle of the afternoon and find you with another man?'

'You said it yourself: he isn't real. We're imagining him, that's all.'

Jessica knew this had to stop. Lo Duc Tho was still kneeling beside the couch, still fondling Michael's softening penis, and the expression on his face told her what she was already starting to suspect. His appearance wasn't a sexual epiphany at all. It was a revelation of something much darker than that. It was the beginning of a downward journey into sexual self-indulgence that could only end in acts so obscene that they could scarcely be imagined. It was the ground opening up, right beneath their feet.

'Jessica! Listen to me!' Michael demanded. But Jessica went through to the kitchen, opened the cutlery drawer and took out the largest knife she could find. She returned to the living room, where Lo Duc Tho had risen to his feet and Michael was standing with his arms wrapped protectively around his narrow shoulders.

'Don't touch him, Jessica. You're not thinking straight. Put down the knife and we can talk this over like sensible adults.'

Jessica approached them with the knife held out stiffly in front of her. 'This isn't something you can talk about, Michael. This is corruption, mine as well as yours.'

'Jessica, put down the knife before somebody gets hurt.'

She came closer. Lo Duc Tho was staring up at her with his dark, inexplicable eyes, his lips slightly parted.

Michael held out his hand. 'Come on, sweetheart, give me the knife, will you?'

Jessica put the knife behind her back. With her left hand she took hold of Lo Duc Tho's erection, slowly massaging it up and down. He grew harder and harder, until he was fully erect. Jessica looked at Michael and Michael looked at Jessica and there was caution in Michael's face but also expectation, as if he were waiting for her to say that everything was going to be all right, and that they could share Lo Duc Tho between them. After all, if he were nothing more than a fantasy, what difference did it make?

Jessica rolled the ball of her thumb around the head of Lo Duc Tho's penis and at the same time she stared into his eyes. She didn't say anything, but she wanted him to know that she understood what he really was.

'Can we—?' Michael began, and it was then that Jessica swung her arm around from behind her back and cut with a gristly crunch clean through Lo Duc Tho's penis.

Michael shouted, '*No!*' Like a curtain caught by the wind, Lo Duc Tho melted away in front of Jessica's eyes but suddenly the world was smothered in blood – the carpet, the couch, the cushions. There was blood all over Jessica's hands and blood all over her blouse and blood was spraying in her face.

'*Oh God! Oh God!*' Michael was screaming and clutching his hand between his thighs. Blood was spurting out from between his fingers and halfway up the wall.

Jessica stepped back. One step and then another. She looked at the knife in her hand and then she dropped it.

'*Call the paramedics! For Christ's sake! Call the paramedics!*'

Michael fell onto his knees, his forehead pressed against the floor. Blood was streaming down his thighs in dark red rivers. He started to sob, but all Jessica could do was stand and watch him.

'*Call me the fucking paramedics for Christ's sake, you witch!*'

She didn't say anything, couldn't understand what was happening. Lo Duc Tho had vanished, but after all he wasn't real and now she had proved it.

Michael collapsed onto his back. He stared up at her glassy-eyed, gasping. 'Help me,' he croaked. 'Jessica, for Christ's sake help me.'

He slowly lifted his hands away from his thighs, and Jessica could see that all he had left was two crimson testicles and a two-inch stump, which was still pumping out blood. '*Jessica, help me!*'

But Jessica couldn't, or wouldn't. She turned away, and there on the arm of the couch she saw her chrysanthemum scarf from Galeries Lafayette, and the gold scarf-ring that went with it. She picked up the scarf and pressed it to her lips, and it was cool and silky and smelled just like Lo Duc Tho.

***

Two months later, a thirtyish woman wandered into the Wabash Gallery in Chicago. She stopped, looking bewildered. An immaculately dressed man rose from his desk and approached her. 'Yes, can I help you?'

'I don't know. I think I must have come to the wrong gallery. I was looking for the Edward Hoppers.'

'Last week, I'm afraid. But you're more than welcome to take a look around here.'

She frowned at the poster. 'Oh, no. I don't think this is quite me.'

The man took hold of her sleeve and guided along the soft-carpeted corridor. 'How will you know, if you never even have a look?'

With a smile, he steered her towards her epiphany.

THE RED BUTCHER
OF WROCŁAW

This year, it was colder in Wrocław than the last winter of World War Two, when the Germans were desperately holding out against the advancing Russian army.

In January 1945, the temperature dropped to minus twenty-seven degrees and blinding blizzards swept across Lower Silesia from the east. Back then, over eighteen thousand people in the city froze to death.

I had expected snow. I had *wanted* snow. But what was tumbling out of the sky every morning was overwhelming, like God and the archangel Gabriel were having some never-ending pillow fight. From the weather forecast, I could see that our filming schedule would have to be put back by a week at the very least, with all of the extra cost and complicated rescheduling that would involve.

I was here in southern Poland to film some critical outdoor scenes for a chilling supernatural movie for Universal, provisionally titled *Chill of the Dead*, but we had already gone two and a half million dollars over budget. Not only that, our lead talent Ada St James was booked to appear in another movie in only three weeks – a beach comedy set in Hawaii.

So here I was, sitting in the bar of the Art Hotel with the movie's male lead, Olly McBane, as well as our director of photography Russ Mulroney and our first cameraman Jimmy Huong and the movie's scriptwriter Cindy Flinders, who also happened to be my current girlfriend. We had chosen to sit in the raised area in the bar, which overlooks the narrow street outside, and we were all trying to pretend that we weren't keeping an eye on the thick fluffy lumps of snow that were endlessly falling past the window, in case they showed the slightest sign of easing off.

'Jesus,' grumbled Russ. 'We could have built Wrocław in the 007 Stage at Pinewood, and called in Snow Business to do the effects, and I bet it would have cost us half of what this is costing. *And* we wouldn't have had to freeze our arses off or eat *pierogi* morning, noon and night.'

'You don't have to eat *pierogi* morning, noon and night,' Olly told him. 'There's plenty of other stuff on the menu.'

'Yeah, but I fecking love *pierogi*. It's that *sledz* I can't stand, that pickled fish. That's enough to make a maggot gag.'

Russ was short and bald with bulging blue eyes and a bristling ginger beard, and he had the thickest Sligo accent you ever heard. Every 's' sounded like 'csh', like: 'Tings will get wush before dey get bettoh.' All the same, he was one of the best DOPs in the business, and two years ago he had been nominated for an Oscar for his cinematography on that horror movie *Blood Season*.

Jimmy Huong was tall and lanky for a Chinese man, but

then his Mandarin father had married a tall and lanky girl from San Clemente while he was working for MGM in the late 1970s as a sound technician. His father was probably a foot shorter than his mother but apparently he used to tell Jimmy that height is irrelevant when you're lying down.

Jimmy had a handsome, Tony Curtis kind of a face, but Asian eyes and short black hair that stuck up on top of his head like a scrubbing brush. If he had inherited one Chinese characteristic from his father, it was his total serenity, and his deep-sounding mottoes. Like: 'You can make as much cheese as you like from spiders' milk, but do not expect to spin webs.'

Ada hadn't joined us. She had wrapped herself up in her faux-fur coat and gone down to Rynek, the city square, to do some shopping. She had rolled her eyes and admitted that, for her, 'Shopping is the nearest thing I have to religion.'

Cindy noisily sipped the last of her negroni and looked across the table at me with those hazel eyes of hers and said, 'We might as well go back to bed.'

Cindy was petite and pretty with a little snub nose and short but messy blonde hair. She was nearly forty but she looked as if she had just celebrated her twenty-first birthday. She was wearing a tight, teal T-shirt with *Despair* printed on it in white letters. Despair was some heavy metal band from Fresno that she knew, and I suspected that she might have had a fling with the lead singer, some messy guy with a nose-ring called Frogg.

'I have to call Bob and tell him we're still snowbound,' I told her. Bob Kaminsky was president of production at Universal and I wasn't looking forward to telling him that we had filmed only three and a half minutes so far, and those were of Ada staring out of the hotel window, and then turning to the camera and saying, 'I'm frightened, Jerry. I'm more than frightened – I'm petrified!'

Bob hadn't been too keen on *Chill of the Dead* from the start. He preferred comedies and musicals and he thought my horror movies were way too extreme. Behind my back he called me 'Gruesome Newsome' and a couple of times he had even said it to my front. My movies made a profit, though. *It's Raining Brains* had brought in $64.3 million, even though the critics hated it.

I was just about to get up and call Bob when my daughter Kathy came into the bar, wearing her pink duffel coat with the pointed hood. Her hood and her shoulders were still speckled with snow, although she brushed it off onto the floor and it melted almost at once. Close behind her came Marcin Sokolowski, who worked for the city promoting culture and sport, and who was supposed to be helping us to find locations and organise our shoots.

'This is the *best* winter ever.' Kathy smiled, perching herself up on one of the chairs. She was eight, skinny and tall for her age, and she had inherited the cheekbones of her Polish grandmother – my mother Saskia. It was because of her Polish heritage that I had offered to bring her along on this shoot to see the land of her forebears for the very first time. It had given my ex-wife Melissa a break, too.

'It's a gas, Kathy, I agree with you,' said Olly, lifting his glass up high so that the waiter could see that he needed a refill. 'In fact I could happily sit here drinking *piwo* for the rest of my life, so long as I was getting paid for it.'

Marcin pulled out a chair and sat down next to me. He was a lean young man with short-cropped hair and a long pointed nose. He was wearing a dark-green nylon jacket and a smart activity tracker on his wrist.

'I have just been to the office,' he told me. 'I am sorry to say that the weather forecast is not at all happy. The temperature is expected to go down even more in the next two days, and the snow will continue.'

'Oh, shit,' I said, and Kathy frowned at me and pressed her fingertip to her lips.

'Oh, *shoot*,' I corrected myself. 'What the two-toned tonkert am I going to tell Bob? If we can't start tomorrow he's going to pull the plug.'

What worried me was that Bob might not only cancel this location shoot, but that he might scrub the whole movie, since we had less than twenty-five minutes in the can so far, and he had never been too hot about it, right from the start. *Chill of the Dead* was a zombie movie set around Christmas, with dead people rising from their graves and bursting into the homes of their still-living relatives while they were opening their presents and singing carols and enjoying their turkey dinners. The tagline was *Merry Christmas, Every Body!*

'Kathy – would you like a Coke?' I asked her. 'And how about something to eat? You only had that *paczki* for breakfast.'

'No, thanks, Dad, I'm not hungry,' said Kathy. She was standing up again now because she could see four or five children out in the street having a snowball fight, and on the sidewalk outside St Elizabeth's Church another two of them were building a huge snowman. 'Can I go outside and play with them?'

'You don't speak Polish.'

'I know, but you don't need to speak Polish to throw a snowball.'

'Okay, but stay where I can see you.'

'I will.'

She pulled on her mittens again, jumped off her chair and went down the hotel steps into the street. I could see her scooping up a handful of snow, packing it together, and throwing it at the nearest boy, hitting him smack on the side of the head. Before I knew it she was right in the middle of a fierce barrage of snowballs, and obviously having the time of her life.

'How about that,' said Russ, shaking his head. 'I haven't had a snowball fight since I was at school in Cleveragh and I had to walk all the way home with my pants and my socks all wringing wet. But I'd give anything to be seven years old again and go out there and chuck a few snocks around.'

'If you were seven years old again you would have to be very careful here, in this street, with the temperature so low,' said Marcin. 'So the legend says, anyway.'

'Oh, I was a *fianán diana* in them days. A tough little cookie, and no mistake, even though my ma said I the brains of a bag of Lego.'

'No matter how tough you were, that would not have saved you from *Czerwony Rzeźnik*.' Marcin smiled.

'And what's that when it's at home?'

'*Czerwony Rzeźnik* means the Red Butcher. His name is famous in Wrocław... especially among the older generation. Near the end of the war, when Wrocław was under siege by the Russians, and it was colder than it had ever been in Lower Silesia in all of recorded history, everybody of course was starving as well as dying of hypothermia.

'But here... right here on this corner outside St Elizabeth's Church, a kind of a temporary stall was set up, with a coal fire, and this is where the Red Butcher was selling sausages. They called him the Red Butcher because he was dressed all in long scarlet robes, with a hood. And that is why this street is still called Kiełbaśnicza, which means "Sausage Makers' Street".

'It was a few days before parents began to come looking around here, saying that their children were missing. Of course it was different then... the city was under constant bombing and shelling and sometimes children wouldn't come home because they were sheltering somewhere, with their friends maybe.

'But more and more children were going out and then never returning home. Their parents searched all around the old town for them, and at last they discovered heaps and heaps of their bones and all their discarded clothes – and guess where?'

Marcin pointed out of the window across the street. '*There* – there is where they found them, hidden in the crypt of Elźbiety Węgierskiej. After that, they knocked over the sausage stall and chased after the Red Butcher, but he escaped into the church and they could not find him. He was never seen again.'

'Oh my God, is that true?' asked Cindy. 'He was really making sausages out of children?'

'You wouldn't believe what people will eat when they're starving,' put in Olly, as the waiter handed him another beer. 'I was in that movie *Forlorn Hope* about the Donner Party, you know those pioneers who got stuck in the Nevada mountains in the middle of winter and ended up eating each other.'

'It sounds like the kind of food they serve up in Chinese markets,' said Jimmy. 'Bat soup, pangolin pie, children sausage.'

'You're one sick dude, Jimmy.' Olly grinned.

I stood up. 'I must go call Bob. If I stretch the truth a little, and tell him we've shot some great snow scenes, maybe he'll go easy on us. Order me another Żywiec, would you, Cindy, and maybe some Kalisz wafers. And a plate of those pickled mushrooms.'

I went upstairs to our room on the first floor and sat on the bed and phoned Bob. He was in a surprisingly amenable mood, which made me suspect that his new discovery Jillie Burnside had been nice to him last night, in spite of being half his age. I made up some story about all the fantastic snow scenes we'd been able to shoot, and how they were going to give *Chill of the Dead* some real class that would lift it way above your run-of-the-mill horror movie. In fact we might even have a chance of winning a Golden Globe.

Actually, I don't think Bob was even listening to me, and I could hear girlish giggling in the background. After a while he interrupted me and said, 'Fine, Dave, whatever – you carry on. I know I can trust you to come up with something truly ghoulish. When do you think you'll be coming back?'

'Let's say a week to be on the safe side, Bob. I don't want to rush a production this good. You know what they say about ships and ha'porths of tar.'

'Ships and what? No. No idea what you're talking about. Jillie – behave yourself, Poppa's on the phone!'

'It's okay, Bob. I'll call you again tomorrow.'

I stood up and went to the window, which overlooked the street. Three boys were still throwing snowballs but the kids who had been building the snowman appeared to have abandoned it, and it didn't even have a head yet. What disturbed me, though, was that there was no sign of Kathy.

I opened the window as far as I could and called out, 'Kathy! Kath! Are you down there?'

The boys looked up at me, but clearly they didn't understand what I was shouting about, so they went back to throwing their snowballs.

I pressed the elevator button but when it didn't open immediately I ran down the stairs. As I passed the bar, I could see Russ, Olly, Jimmy, Cindy and Marcin all still sitting at the table, laughing. I yanked open the heavy hotel door and went down the steps into the street. It was bitterly cold out there, a dry cold that dropped into my lungs as if an icebox had fallen onto my chest, and the snowflakes were tumbling around me so thickly that I could see no further than the end of the high church wall.

I went up to the boys and said, 'A girl. *Dziewczyna*. Have you seen her? She was out here tossing snowballs with the rest of you. A young girl. *Młoda dziewczyna*. She was wearing a pink coat. *Różowy*.'

The boys looked at me blankly. Jesus, I wish I'd listened when my mother was trying to teach me to speak Polish, and even the few words I did know I was probably mispronouncing so badly that they couldn't understand me. *Jiff-chin-ah*, was that right?

I hurried through the snow up to the next corner. There was no sign of Kathy there, or of the boys who had been building the snowman. One of them had been wearing a fluorescent yellow anorak so he wouldn't have been hard to miss. I went all the way around the church and then down to the next street, shouting out 'Kathy! Kathy!' so that passers-by turned and stared at me, all huddled up in their snow-covered coats, while I was wearing nothing but a blue rib-knit sweater.

I stood by the headless snowman, listening. The snow had built up into such a thick carpet in the streets of the old town that I couldn't hear any traffic, only the flat clanging of trams along Nowy Świat at the end of the street.

'*Kathy*,' I said, and then I realised that I had said that almost soundlessly, too.

I walked back quickly to the hotel. As I came into the bar, Marcin looked up at me and said, 'David? What is wrong? Have you been outside?'

'My *God*, Dave,' said Cindy. 'You look like Frosty.'

'Kathy's disappeared. Didn't you see her go? I thought I asked you to keep an eye on her.'

Cindy turned around and stared out of the window. 'Oh, no! She was there only a minute ago. I saw her!'

'Children can vanish in a minute, Cind, and Kathy's vanished. I've looked all around the church and up and down the street and I can't find her anywhere.'

'We will help to you look for her,' said Marcin. 'She cannot have gone very far.'

'I tell you, boy, it was literally only a minute ago that I saw her,' said Russ. 'She was right over there with them lads packing snow onto that snowman.'

Olly swallowed the last of his beer and stood up. 'Come on, guys, we'll all go and look. Grab your coats.'

We all put on our coats and jackets and went outside. Olly, Russ and Jimmy split up, with Olly going down to the market square and Russ heading up to Nowy Świat and the Oder river, while Jimmy went to look along the narrow streets behind St Elizabeth's Church. Cindy stayed with me, and Marcin acted as our guide and our interpreter. I knew 'young girl' and 'pink' and I even knew *zaginiony*, meaning missing, but that was hardly enough.

First of all, Marcin went over to the boys who had been throwing snowballs. They had given that up and now they were demolishing what was left of the snowman by drop-kicking it.

He spoke to them for a few minutes and then came up to Cindy and me and said, 'They said that your Kathy was helping the other boys to make the snowman when a priest came out and said something to them, and they followed him back into the church.'

'But Kathy doesn't speak Polish, and she knows she's not supposed to go off with strange men.'

'Well, he was a priest, so perhaps she trusted him. It seems as if the boys did.'

'They must still be in the church, then. But what have they been doing in there? They've been there for – what fifteen minutes at least.'

I ran up the steps to the church door, nearly slipping over, and Cindy and Marcin followed me. The door creaked when I pushed it open, like the door in a haunted castle. Inside, behind the inner doors, it was gloomy and musty and smelled of stale incense.

St Elizabeth's had been built in the fourteenth century in the Gothic style. It had soaringly high vaulted ceilings and narrow stained-glass windows decorated with angels and a benign-looking Virgin Mary. This afternoon it was almost empty except for a priest lighting candles behind the altar and one elderly woman praying in front of one of the side chapels. Every footstep and every word echoed.

'It does not appear as if they are in here,' said Marcin. 'They could have come in through these doors and then out by the doors on other side.'

My heart was beating hard and I was beginning to panic. What would some priest want with Kathy and a couple of boys playing in the snow? Unless he wasn't a priest at all, but only dressed up to look like one, so that he could gain the children's confidence. Even then, though, surely the boys would protest if he tried anything sexual.

I circled around the church, looking in all of the side chapels and even opening up the confessional. Cindy and Marcin came after me, and our footsteps clattered like horses cantering. When I approached the altar the priest who had been lighting the candles blew out his taper and came up to me. He was short and bald with a cast in his left eye, so that he looked as if he were watching somebody behind my right shoulder, too. He said something but even though it sounded kindly I didn't know what he meant. Marcin came up and translated for me.

'He asks if you have are looking for something, and perhaps he can help.'

I nodded to the priest, trying to work out which of his eyes to look at. 'You bet I'm looking for something. My eight-year-old daughter. She was brought in here by another priest – her and two young boys. She was wearing a pink duffel coat, with a hood. And red rubber boots.'

Marcin spoke quickly to the priest, who listened, but then shook his head.

'He says he has only just come out of the sacristy to prepare for the next service, so unfortunately he did not see anyone of that description come into the church. But he wishes you the best of luck in finding your daughter and prays that you will find her safe and well.'

Cindy said, 'What are we going to do now? I mean, where do you think he could have taken her? And for why?'

'We'll have to call the police, Marcin,' I told him. 'The sooner they start looking for her, the better.'

'Okay, yes of course,' said Marcin. He took out his phone and prodded it, but when he lifted it to his ear he said, 'There's no signal in here. We'll have to go outside.'

We headed quickly back towards the main entrance, but before we reached it Cindy suddenly stopped and tugged at my sleeve and said, 'Dave – *there* – what's that?'

'What's what?'

She pointed through the brick arch next to us, towards a dark oak door.

'There,' she said. 'There's something stuck underneath it.'

I took a closer look. She was right. There was something pink trapped under the bottom sill of the door, and almost at once I realised what it was. With my heart palpitating even harder I dropped to my knees in front of the door and tugged it out. It was one of Kathy's *Frozen* gloves.

'*Marcin!*' I almost screamed at him. '*Marcin!*'

As Marcin came running up I tugged hard at the door handle, but the door was firmly locked.

'This is Kathy's glove. He must have taken them in here! Quick – get that priest to open this door!'

Marcin stared at the glove in horror. 'You are right – I saw her wearing these same gloves.'

With that, he went back across the church, dodging his way around the altar, and just managed to catch the priest before he went back into the sacristy. The priest came hurrying up with a large bunch of jangling keys.

'He prays that they have not left the key in the lock on the other side,' Marcin interpreted, as the priest fumbled through the keys to find the right one. At last, though, he picked out a large key with a bit that was shaped like a demon's sigil, pushed it into the keyhole and turned it. With a complicated clicking, the door opened up, and he pushed it inward. It shuddered on its hinges as if it were warning us not to come in.

On the other side of the door there was a short landing with an iron railing, and then a curving stone staircase. I was tempted to shout out, to find out for sure if Kathy was down there, but I thought it would be safer if I kept as quiet as I could. If that priest was unhinged enough to bring children down here, I didn't want to startle him into doing something crazy that might hurt them.

The brick walls of the staircase were illuminated by a dim, wavering light from below, so presumably there was somebody down there. Cautiously, I started to make my way down the steps. It was chilly down there. Not the bone-dry cold of the street outside, but a damp, breathy kind of a chill. The chill of the dead.

I heard a young boy's voice, and then somebody harshly saying '*sshhh*!' I turned and looked around. Marcin was coming down the staircase right behind me and Cindy was close behind him.

I crept down the last few steps of the staircase and found myself in a low-ceilinged crypt. Two paraffin lamps had been set up on either side of the crypt, and they threw dancing silhouettes on the walls. It looked as if the shadows in the dark recesses all around had mischievous lives of their own, and kept leaping out to frighten anybody who dared to come down here.

Sitting back to back on two upright chairs on the left hand side of the crypt were Kathy and the boy in the fluorescent yellow anorak. They were lashed tightly together with blue-and-white washing-line cord. Kathy turned around and shook her head, her eyes wide, as if she were imploring me not to shout out loud.

She didn't need to tell me. What I saw in the middle of the crypt stunned me into silence, and I heard Cindy let out a squeal of disgust. On a long wooden table lay a partially dissected body, its head removed, its ribcage and its pelvis stripped of flesh, and strips of raw meat heaped up beside it. Where its head had been there was a beige woollen beanie, soaked in blood, and where its feet had been, there was still a single lace-up boot. The other had dropped onto the floor.

I said, 'Right, Kath, let's get you out of here, right now. You and your friend. Marcin – call the cops.'

I made my way around the table to untie Kathy and the boy in the yellow anorak, but as I did so I was stopped in my tracks by a hoarse, high, hair-raising screech. Out of the darkness at the far end of the crypt, a figure appeared – a figure robed in red, with a high pointed hood. Its face was masked in black gauze, so it was impossible to see if it was a man or a woman. It was thin and round-shouldered, but so tall that its hood touched the ceiling of the crypt, and it came towards us with an odd, uneven gait, as if it were walking on stilts or very high heels.

In one hand it was carrying a huge triangular butcher's knife, stained with blood.

The figure stopped at the far end of the wooden table, and brandished the knife at me.

'Marcin – call the cops *now*!' I told him.

Marcin took out his phone but then the figure hissed and whispered something, so that the black gauze was sucked in and out. Marcin held up his hand and said, 'Wait, David—' and spoke to the figure in Polish.

The figure hissed and whispered again. Marcin listened, and then he turned back to me.

'He says he is the Red Butcher, and that he has come back because the winter is so cold and there is an epidemic and the people of Wrocław will soon be hungry.'

'He's killing *children*? He's insane! Call the police!'

'He says he is a man of God, a cardinal. He is only obeying the word of the Lord. When Jesus fed the five thousand, it was with loaves, yes, but "fishes" was a mistranslation of "school". When the people were starving, Jesus fed them children. The young were rightly sacrificed to keep their elders alive.'

'He's crazy! This is like something out of one of my movies!'

'He says you cannot stop him because he has God on his side.'

The red-robed figure started to walk in that odd, stilted way towards Kathy and the boy in the yellow anorak, holding up his knife. Kathy screamed, and the boy let out a terrified moan.

I ran forward and grabbed the Red Butcher's wrist. He twisted and struggled and hit me again and again with his free left fist, although he seemed to have very little strength. I wrenched the knife out his hand and when he tried to claw it back from me I stabbed him as hard as I could, right into the middle of his robes. I dragged the blade upward until I felt it stick against his ribs, and then I pulled it out.

'*No!*' Marcin shouted. 'David – *no!*' and Kathy screamed again.

The Red Butcher staggered, and I stepped back, still holding the knife. Marcin rushed up to the Red Butcher and tore open his robes with both hands. Underneath he was wearing a tight white sweater and jeans, but the white sweater was slit wide open and already soaked in blood, and out of the slit his intestines were cascading like a nest of slippery snakes.

'*Karetka pogotowia!*' Marcin shouted. 'Call for an ambulance! It's 112!'

He was holding the Red Butcher in his arms as the scarlet-robed figure sank to the floor, his legs quivering with shock.

'Who *is* that?' I shouted at him. 'Marcin – what the fuck is going on? Who *is* that?'

I heard Cindy saying, 'Oh my God, oh my *God*!' and then I heard the urgent scuffling of footsteps coming down the staircase. Olly, Russ and Jimmy were suddenly in the crypt alongside me. Jimmy started to untie Kathy and the boy in the yellow anorak. Russ knelt down beside the Red Butcher, unfastening the silk cord around his neck.

'I told you this was a fecking stupid idea, didn't I?' said

Russ, looking up at Olly. '"Oh no," you said, "it'll be the laugh of the century. Let's scare the shite out of the feller who scares the shite out of everybody else!"'

The boss-eyed priest had come down to the crypt to find out what all the commotion was about, and as far as I could understand him, Marcin told him to go outside and wait for the ambulance to arrive.

I set down the knife on the table and knelt down on the cold stone floor next to Russ. He eased off the Red Butcher's hood and carefully peeled the black gauze mask away from his face. To my horror, the Red Butcher wasn't a 'he' at all, but Ada St James. Her eyelids were fluttering and blood was sliding out of the side of her mouth. Marcin was holding his hand pressed against her stomach to stop her intestines from sliding out over the waistband of her jeans.

'Oh Jesus, Ada,' I said, under my breath. 'Whatever you do, please don't die.'

I turned around and saw that Jimmy was ushering Kathy and the boy in the yellow anorak upstairs. Kathy looked back at me and I had never seen such pain and sadness on a young child's face before.

Ada survived, although it was touch-and-go for a while, and she spent months convalescing. She never acted again, and I never directed another horror movie. I was arrested, but I had a very persuasive attorney, and she was able to convince the judge that I had acted in self-defence and in defence of my daughter.

I don't think I'll ever get that scene in the crypt out of my mind, not for the rest of my life. I haven't been able to eat pork ribs again, but that's been the least serious effect that it's had on me. What it showed me was that death and horror are not entertainments, and that the story of human existence has been nothing but an endless succession of appalling tragedies, one cruelty heaped on top of another, from the freezing ruins of Wrocław during World War Two to the misery of refugees in Syria.

I write comedy now, although most of it is bitter-sweet. If I thank God for one blessing, though, it's that I live in Sherman Oaks. I never have to see it snow.

CHEESEBOY

'Ah, look, here he comes now! Stick your clothes pegs on your noses, everybody! Hold your breath until he's gone past! What's the story, Cheeseboy? How many years is it now since you last saw a bar of soap? As if you'd even know what a bar of soap looks like!'

Aidan walked past his tormentors with his head down and the collar of his shabby grey jacket pulled up to stop the rain from running down his neck. As usual Michael O'Reilly and his gang were clustered in the alcove on the right-hand side of the main doors into St Jerome Bunscoil, sheltered from the drizzle by the overhanging roof.

While the pupils were all waiting for the doors to be opened, Aidan had to stand on his own close to the wall on the left-hand side, although that gave him very little protection from the rain, and the occasional splatter of water that dropped down from the overflowing gutter.

'What kind of cheese are you today, Cheeseboy?' called out Sinead Buckley. 'Carlow or Gubbeen?'

'Something extra-ripe, I'll bet you,' said Michael O'Reilly. 'Just don't expect me to stand close enough to smell it. I've just had me breakfast and it'll give me the gawks!'

Aidan looked the other way, across the glossy wet asphalt

of the high-walled playground. He had learned from his first term at St Jerome's not to answer back to Michael O'Reilly or any of his cronies – not even to acknowledge that he had heard them. He was bigger than all of them, because he was a year behind in his schooling, He was ten and they were only nine and individually he could have given them a beating, but when he had tried to claim Michael O'Reilly, six or seven other boys had jumped on him, too. They had pulled him to the ground and kicked him, so that one of his front teeth was knocked loose, and then they had stamped on the packet of Taytos that his mother had given him to take to school.

He endured it. It was the only way. Nothing was ever going to change, as far as he could make out. He had tried hopping off school and he had wandered around the city all day, growing increasingly footsore and hungry, but in the end there had been nowhere else for him to go but home, back to the mobile home at the back of the Spring Lane halting site.

His mother had been drinking as usual, and the air in the mobile home had been almost unbreathable for cigarette smoke. The toilet had flushed and an unshaven man had emerged, buttoning up his jeans. He had smelled of strong body odour and sex.

'Who's this, then, Breda?' he had asked, with a gap-toothed grin. 'Your toy boy, is it?'

'Oh, away to feck with you, Declan,' his mother had said. Then: 'What are you doing back so early, Aid? They didn't throw you out of school again, did they? Or did you shit yourself again? Mother of God, I'll swear there's more skid marks in your cacks than the North Ring Road.'

The man called Declan had picked up his quilted maroon windcheater and headed for the door, but Aidan's mother had sat up and said, 'Hey! Aren't you forgetting something, you stingy scobe?'

Declan had slapped his forehead as if to admonish himself for being so absent-minded, and then he had reached into the back pocket of his jeans, taken out a folded wad of banknotes, and licked his thumb so that he could count out fifty euros.

'Jesus, you're so fecking tight you squeak when you walk,' Aidan's mother had told him.

Declan had stripped off one more ten-euro note and handed it to her with a leer. 'That's for the bonus, do you know what I mean, like? Bonus, bone-arse, like bone up your arse, get it?'

He had left, and they had heard him kick-starting up his motorcycle and go bellowing off towards Blackpool. Aidan's mother had tucked the money into the pocket of her peach satin dressing gown, which was spotted with brown stains and cigarette burns. The last ten-euro note that Declan had given her she had waved at Aidan and said, 'Here, take this, will you, and go along to Elsie's and fetch us both some fish and chips. I'm fecking starving. I could eat the decorations off a hearse, I tell you. But don't you be keeping the cobbage.'

Later that evening, she had finished her half-bottle of Paddy's whiskey and fallen asleep on the couch, snoring softly, with her cigarette still burning between her fingers. Aidan had carefully taken her cigarette away and crushed it out in the tin lid she used as an ashtray. Then he had collected up the half-eaten cod and chips that she had left in their wrapping paper on the floor, and bundled them up, and pushed them into the overflowing waste bin in the kitchenette.

After that, he had tugged her dressing gown across her chest to cover her flat exposed breast, and then he had sat down beside her to watch TV. As usual, he had stayed awake until well past midnight.

There was a photograph of her on the shelf next to the television set, when she was twenty: dark-haired and dark-eyed, with a mischievous smile. Aidan loved that photograph. That was what she had looked like when his father had made love to her, whoever his father was. He had been created because his mother had been beautiful. He never allowed himself to forget that.

He looked at her now and that girl in the photograph had almost vanished, leaving only this skinny, tangle-haired creature, more like a scavenging animal than a woman. It was hard to believe that she was only thirty-one. But she was his mother, and he loved her, because there was nobody else in his life to take care of him. Nobody else wanted to, because he was Cheeseboy.

Once the school doors were opened, the nineteen children in Rang a Tri filed into the classroom, chattering and laughing. The classroom was as gloomy as a fish tank on a wet day like this, and old-fashioned, with battered wooden desks that seated two pupils each, sitting side by side. On the left-hand side of the classroom, nearer the windows, there were two rows of five desks. Then there was an aisle, and on the right-hand side, next to the wall, a single row of five desks.

Aidan sat alone in this single row, in the third desk back, because Miss O'Connell had told him that she didn't want him sitting too close to the front, where she could smell him. All of the rest of the class sat in the two rows nearer the window.

'Sure, this weather's desperate, isn't it?' said Michael O'Reilly. 'You can't open the windies when it's raining like this, and let out the smell of cheese!'

Aidan said nothing, but untied the string that held together the broken buckles of the battered brown leather satchel that he had rescued last term from the school rubbish skip. He took out his geography book and opened it to the last essay that he had finished, *Fishing Off the West Coast*. He had consistently misspelled herring as 'erin' and trawlers as 'trallus'. Miss O'Connell had given him 1/10 for writing neatly, but she had also written *Please wash your hands, Aidan. before writing next essay*, because he had left smudgy black finger marks on the sides of the pages.

They all filed into the school hall for morning prayers. As usual Aidan stood right at the back, by the doors, behind Rang a Sé, who were twelve and thirteen years old and all much taller than him so that he could never see what was going on at the front. None of his own class wanted to stand next to him, and even the older pupils would make a show of fanning their hands under their noses when he appeared.

Mrs Rooney the grey-haired head teacher announced that there was going to be an outing next month for Rang a Dó and Rang a Trí to Secret Valley Wildlife Park in Clonroche, in County Wexford. It would cost €15 each – €7.50 for admission to the park and €7.50 for a packed lunch.

'I pray to holy Saint Joseph that Cheeseboy's not going on the wildlife trip,' said Michael O'Reilly, as they returned to the classroom. 'It would be just my luck to be sitting next to that stinker on the bus. I'd be donkey sick, I tell you.'

'You'd only have to put up with it the one way, though,' said Brendan Hagerty. 'We could leave him behind with the skunks, like. The park-keepers wouldn't be able to smell the difference.'

Aidan didn't rise to that. He knew that he wouldn't be going on the outing anyway. His mother might grudgingly give him the €7.50 admission, but she would insist on making his packed lunch herself to save money, and that would be a Kraft cheese sandwich and a small tin of baked beans with no spoon to eat them with, and a single bruised apple, all folded up in a crumpled Primark bag. He wouldn't be able to sit around a picnic table with his classmates while they were all eating their smart boxed lunches, not with his mother's home-made offering. He had grown immune to their constant comments about how badly he smelled, but he didn't want to hear them insulting his mother. Her life had been hard and she couldn't help how far she had fallen.

As soon as she had become pregnant, her parents had disowned her and packed her off to Saint Winifred's Mother & Baby Home, in Mayfield. There the nuns had constantly impressed on her what a sinner she was, and that she and her child were worth nothing in the eyes of God. Because he was illegitimate, Aidan had never been baptised, and even now he was excluded from catechism classes. He never prayed, because the nuns had told him when he was little that he was a child of Satan and that God would never listen to him. He had come to understand that if he needed salvation, he would have to save himself.

Miss O'Connell came into the classroom and all the children stood up. She was a plain young woman, Miss O'Connell, with rimless glasses and a pale podgy face and ginger hair that was tied back with a ribbon like a chaotic bunch of French carrots. She was wearing a droopy green cardigan and a long fawn skirt and sensible shoes.

'Today, class, we're going to start learning about the weather,' she said. 'We're going to learn about rain, and fog, and thunderstorms, and wind.'

Somebody at the back of the class made a loud farting noise and Brendan Hagerty put up his hand and said, 'Denis has the wind, miss! I just heard it!'

All the children screamed with laughter, but Miss O'Connell rapped her wooden pointer on her desk. 'Who made that *disgusting* noise? Denis Grace, was that you?'

There was immediate silence. Miss O'Connell walked slowly between the desks until she reached a skinny boy with a short scaldy haircut and protruding ears. His eyes were lowered, but he was smirking, and obviously trying not to laugh.

'I said, was that *you*, Denis? And don't you try lying to me, because God knows the truth, and God will find his own way of punishing you, even if I don't.'

'Yes, miss,' said Denis Grace, almost inaudibly.

'"Yes, miss," *what*? "Yes, miss, I made that disgusting noise," or "yes, miss, I'm lying?"'

'Yes, miss, I done the noise.'

'Why?'

'Because you said "wind", miss, and that's what my da always says when somebody lets off. "What was that? The weatherman didn't warn us there was going to be wind, did he?"'

There was more laughter, but Miss O'Connell rapped her pointer on Denis Grace's desk, and again there was silence.

'Well, Denis, if you find it amusing to be disgusting, I'm going to humour you. I'm going to let you sit next to Aidan for the rest of the day.'

Denis Grace looked up at Miss O'Connell in horror. 'Oh, no, miss! Serious?'

He turned around to appeal to Aidan, as if he wanted Aidan to say that he preferred sitting on his own. But Aidan was concentrating on writing the word *Wedder* in his notebook, the tip of his tongue stuck out in concentration.

'Go on, Denis,' said Miss O'Connell. 'Take your books and your satchel with you.'

'Oh, miss, do I have to, miss? I'll do anything else. I'll write out a hundred lines, miss, honest. I'll write out a *thousand*! If I sit next to Aidan I'll get the gawks for sure.'

'Do what you're told,' said Miss O'Connell.

Aidan may not have been looking, but he was listening, and he knew that forcing Denis to sit next to him was as much a punishment for him as it was for Denis. He had tried to have a wash this morning in the toilet block on the halting site, even though the water was a funny colour and freezing cold and there was never any soap. His mother had run out of Dawn dishwashing liquid long ago, even though she rarely bothered to wash up the dishes. He had tried to wash his own vest and underpants the night before last but they had still been damp when it was time for him to get dressed for school and so he had put on yesterday's underwear.

Dragging his feet with reluctance, Denis came across the classroom and sat on the bench seat next to him, right on the very edge, as far away as he possibly could. When Miss O'Connell's back was turned, he stretched his mouth wide open and stuck his finger into it, miming that he was just about to vomit. The class squealed with laughter again, at least until Miss O'Connell swivelled around and glared at them.

'Any more of this now and there'll be less of it!' she snapped.

She started to draw a map of Ireland on the blackboard, with blue arrows to indicate how the Gulf Stream flowed across the Atlantic and kept the Republic's climate very temperate, considering how far north it was, but also very wet.

They were all supposed to copy this weather map in their exercise books, and while they did this there were five minutes of silence, interrupted only by an occasional cough. At this time of the year at least a third of the class would have colds.

Denis was frowning with concentration as he scribbled away with his coloured pencils, but he shielded his exercise book with the crook of his arm so that Aidan couldn't see what he was drawing. After a while, though, he dropped his pencil and slid his picture across the desk.

'There,' he said. 'That's you, boy.'

He had drawn a giant yellow cheese, with arms and legs and bulging red eyes, and a crowd of tiny people running away from it, all holding their noses and bringing up fountains of bright green sick. Underneath, he had written *Cheeseboy!! The Smell from Hell!!*

Aidan was carefully drawing streams of blue arrows across the Atlantic ocean. At first he wouldn't look at the picture that Denis had pushed towards him, because he knew that it was going to be horrible, whatever it was. But then Denis whispered, 'G'wan, Cheeseboy! That's you, that is! You're the stinky manky cheese monster! I'll tell you something – the bang of benjy off of you, it's enough make a maggot gag!'

Aidan glanced at it sideways. Some of his classmates had drawn worse pictures of him, and been far more abusive. But somehow the idea that he was a monster, and not even human, and that he would disgust people so much that they would vomit as they ran away from him, that was more than he could bear. He was cold, too, and shivery, and hungry, and the insides of his thighs were sore because his flannel shorts were damp, partly from the rain and partly from urine. He clenched his blue pencil tightly and he started to cry. He made no sound at all, but tears ran down his cheeks and dripped on to his exercise book.

Denis put up his hand and said, 'Please, miss! Please, miss! I think Aidan has something in his eye!'

The whole class turned around now and saw that Aidan was weeping, and they burst out laughing. Aidan didn't have a handkerchief, of course, so he had to wipe his eyes on the rough damp sleeve of his jacket.

'What in the name of God is the matter with you, Aidan?' asked Miss O'Connell.

'Nothing, miss,' said Aidan, although he had such a *tocht* in his throat that he could barely speak.

'Well, if you're finding that there's something to cry about, I wish you'd share it with the rest of us.'

'It's nothing, miss.'

'And blow your nose, boy, for the love of Jesus.'

Aidan gave a bubbly sniff, and sniffed again. At last Miss O'Connell pulled a Kleenex out of the box on her desk and came over to him, handing it to him at arm's length.

'I don't know, Aidan. The state of you la. I'll say a novena to Saint Joseph when you go up to Rang a Ceathar.'

Aidan didn't answer, but continued to wipe his nose with the tissue until it was nothing but a damp screwed-up ball, and at the same time to draw more blue arrows. Miss O'Connell had drawn only about twenty on the blackboard, but Aidan drew scores of them, until the entire page of his exercise book was a torrent of blue arrows.

Denis looked at what he was drawing and said, 'Jesus. You not only stink, you're a header! That's about a hundred fecking arrows you've done there! If you had two brains you'd be twice as stupid!'

Aidan stopped drawing. He wiped his eyes with his sleeve again, and sat back. What did it matter how many blue arrows he drew? It would make no difference at all. Miss O'Connell would still give him one out of ten, if he was lucky. The highest mark that she had given him all term was three, and that was for singing. He had sung well, in front of the whole school, and he had remembered all the words, but it was a Traveller song – 'The Blue Tar Road' – and that hadn't gone down well with the visiting school inspectors.

'There's a fierce difference between educating children to be Irish and educating them to be Knackers,' Aidan had heard one of them county councillors say to Mrs Rooney.

'The next thing we know, you'll be having bare-knuckle boxing on sports day.'

Mrs Rooney had let out one of her weird, humourless titters, but she had glared at Aidan over the county councillor's shoulder as if she could happily wish that he had never been born.

As he was sitting in the classroom, however, he became aware that Sinead Buckley was staring at him. Sinead was a pretty girl with dark-golden hair braided into plaits, and large china-blue eyes. She always wore six or seven friendship bracelets around her skinny wrists, and she was not only popular but also clever, and consistently top of the class. Her parents owned Buckley's Stores in the Ballyvolane shopping centre, and that was one of the reasons she knew so many varieties of cheese.

He stared back at her for a few moments, thinking that she would turn away, but she didn't. She kept on looking at him with his dirty tear tracks down his cheeks and there was an expression on her face that he couldn't understand at all. It was a sad little pout, the sort of expression that girls give when they see a kitten that's been drenched in the rain. Then her pout turned up at the corners into a sympathetic smile.

Aidan turned his head away and looked at the wall. He could guess what was coming next. She would pretend to be nice to him, and tell him that she wanted to be friends, and meet him after school. When he turned up, though, a whole gang of boys would be waiting for him, jeering and throwing clods of earth, or dog shite. He had been caught like that before and he had sworn that he would never fall for it again.

***

When he came out of school that afternoon, though, Sinead was waiting on the corner, by the green post box. It had stopped raining, although the sky was still grey and the pavements were still wet and shiny.

Aidan stepped into the road to walk past her, but Sinead said, 'Aidan, stall it a moment, would you?'

Aidan stopped and looked at her suspiciously. 'What do you want?' he asked her. 'You're going to ask me what kind of a cheese I am, is that it?'

Sinead glanced back towards the school gates to make sure that none of her friends could see her.

'I saw you in the class today and you were bawling and all.'

'I was not bawling. It was like Denis said, I had a bit of grit in my eyes, that's all.'

'All right, whatever you like. But I saw you weren't happy and I know that I've been one of the worst ones for making you feel like that. And I wanted to say that I'm sorry.'

Aidan said, 'You shouldn't have bothered. I don't give a shite if you're sorry or not.'

'I'm still sorry. And I was thinking that maybe I could help you.'

'What are you going to do? Find me a gun so I can shoot Michael O'Reilly?'

'Don't be an eejit,' said Sinead, still glancing around to make sure that nobody was watching. 'I think it would help you if somebody could talk to your ma. Do you know what I mean, like?'

'How would that help?'

'Well, look,' said Sinead, 'supposing I was to ask my ma

to come home with you tomorrow and have a bit of a chat with your ma.'

'And what good would that do?'

'Aidan, everybody in the school calls you Cheeseboy because you smell. Your clothes are dirty. Your hair is dirty. You have wax in your ears. You look like you never wash, and you look like you never get enough to eat, either.'

'So what if your ma talks to my ma – what difference is that going to make?'

'It could make *all* the difference, Aidan!' said Sinead. 'Your ma never visits the school, does she, so she probably doesn't realise what a hard time you're having. If she did, then maybe she'd change. Maybe she needs some help. You know, somebody to give her a hand with the cleaning and the cooking and all that kind of thing. Maybe she needs money. My Auntie Bridget works for Tusla – you know, the people who help out families when they get into trouble. I'm sure she could do something. You don't want to go on being Cheeseboy for the rest of your life, do you?'

'Don't *call* me that.'

'I won't, not any more. I've said I'm sorry, haven't I? And I won't be calling you any more names, ever again, I promise you. But why don't you let my ma go home with you tomorrow and talk to your ma?'

'My ma has plenty of money. She wouldn't want to talk to your ma, any road.'

'Aidan, please, give it a try. I'll ask my ma today when I go home. I'm sure she'll say yes. Think what it would be like, if you had clean clothes and clean hair and you didn't smell at all. You'd never have to sit on your own in the classroom, not any more. You'd have friends. You might even have *girl*friends.'

Aidan said nothing but stood looking at her and thinking how pretty she was. He couldn't make up his mind if she was being sincere or not, or if this was going to turn out to be another one of Michael O'Reilly's grotesque practical jokes.

A group of girls came out of the school gates, laughing. 'Sinead!' one of them called out. 'What you doing there, girl?'

Sinead immediately said, 'I have to go. But, like I said, I'll ask my ma tonight, and I bet she'll say yes.'

She ran back down the hill with her shiny satchel flapping. Aidan watched her join her friends, and then he started to walk slowly back to the halting site. Sinead had confused him, and depressed him, in a way, because he knew in his heart that his mother would never change. She had lost the will to change a long time ago; and now she no longer had the ability.

Aidan always took a short cut from Spring Lane itself through to his mobile home. There was a hole in the wooden fence that ran along the side of the road, and when he squeezed through that he could climb his way across the dump that was used by the Travellers and also by the factories that bordered the southern side of the halting site.

He clambered over the mountains of rubbish, his shoes squelching into sodden cardboard packing cases and stained and mouldy mattresses. Then he slid down into valleys filled with broken bottles and dirty nappies and armchairs with broken arms. The city council had been promising for over a year to clean up this dump as a health hazard to the Travellers who lived on the halting site, but money was tight and the Pavee people were a very low priority. The toilet block had overflowed twice this autumn already, flooding the site with tawny-coloured sewage.

Almost hidden under the dark overhanging trees on the left side of the dump stood a large old-fashioned household refrigerator, with a domed top. It was slightly tilted to one side and Aidan thought that it looked like a gravestone. He had even written on it once, in black felt-tip pen: *Here Lies Miceal Oreilly*. Over the weeks, however, the persistent rain had washed most of his lettering off, and in any case there was no chance of Michael O'Reilly coming up here to the dump and seeing that Aidan wished him dead and buried.

His mother wasn't home when he climbed back up the steps into their mobile home, although he knew that she wouldn't be far away – probably drinking and smoking and gossiping with her friend Fineena. The inside of the mobile home was chilly and dark and smelled of stale cigarette smoke and cat litter. Their ginger tom Bartley was asleep under the television and when Aidan came in he opened one eye but then immediately closed it again as if Aidan was of no interest to him at all.

Aidan opened the small fridge to see if there was anything for him to eat. On the top shelf there was a lump of hard red cheese with mould on the edge of it, and an open tin of sardines in tomato sauce. If he wanted anything for his tea today he would have to ask his mother for €1.50 so that he could walk to Dunne's Stores and buy himself a hand pie.

He didn't feel distressed. It was very rare for him to come home and find that his mother had been shopping for food, and even when she did she bought the oddest selection of groceries, like chocolate biscuits and a whole melon and a tin of butter beans. If she had ever known how to cook she had forgotten now.

He stood in the kitchenette for a moment, thinking of what Sinead Buckley had said to him. '*You might even have friends. You might even have* girl*friends.*'

Then he went back down the steps of his mobile home and across the muddy stretch of ground to Fineena's caravan, to see if his mother was there. It had started to rain again, a thin fine drizzle, and he turned up his collar.

Sure enough, when he came out of the school gates the following day, Mrs Buckley was waiting for him. She was a small, blonde woman, blue-eyed, like an older version of Sinead, except that her hair was cut short in a geometric bob. She was wearing a smart turquoise raincoat and turquoise rushers to match. She smiled as soon as she saw Aidan and went up to him and took hold of his hand.

Aidan looked around to make sure that none of his usual tormentors could see him with Mrs Buckley, and quickly twisted his hand away from hers. He knew exactly what they would say if they caught sight of him. 'Got yourself a girlfriend, at last, did you, Aid? Bit *old* for you, boy, but that cheesy smell of yours – I bet you'll have her slipping off her chair!'

'I don't need you to come home with me, Mrs Buckley,' he told her.

'Aidan, love, I only want to have a few words with your ma, that's all. Maybe there's some way I can help her.'

'She doesn't need no help. She's grand altogether.'

Aidan started to walk up the hill, as fast as he could, but Mrs Buckley kept pace with him.

'Sinead told me all about you, Aidan, and the difficult time you've been having at school. Don't tell me you wouldn't like all that bullying to stop.'

'I don't pay it no mind at all. Any road, what can I do about it? They'd still say that I was a pew no matter what I smelled like.'

He kept on walking, hoping that Mrs Buckley would soon realise that there was no point in coming home with him, and turn back. But even though she said nothing more to him, she stayed beside him. She even followed him when he squeezed his way through the gap in the fence and climbed across the dump.

At last he arrived at his mobile home. Before he climbed the steps, though, he turned around and said, 'She won't want to talk to you, Mrs Buckley. I know that for sure.'

'Well, Aidan, I can at least try, can't I?'

Aidan didn't know what to say to her. She was giving him such a rueful little smile that he could hardly run up the steps and slam the door in her face.

His mother was sitting on the couch when he went inside. She was wearing only a dark-brown rollneck sweater and a pair of laddered pantyhose and one brocade slipper. She had just lit a fresh cigarette and the mobile home was filled with cirrus clouds of smoke. All the curtains were drawn.

'Ma,' said Aidan. He was praying that none of her men friends would emerge from the toilet. 'Ma, there's somebody come back with me to see you.'

His mother looked up. For a split second, Aidan could see in her face the pretty young woman in the photograph;

but then she frowned, and took a long drag at her cigarette with her cheeks drawn in, and blew out smoke from the side of her mouth, and wiped her nose with the back of her hand; and that vision vanished.

'It's Mrs Buckley, Sinead Buckley's ma.'

'Sinead Buckley? I thought you told me that Sinead Buckley was a right young bitch. What does *she* want?'

Mrs Buckley was standing in the open doorway. 'Is it all right if I come in and talk to you, Mrs Nevin?'

'Talk to me? What about? And it's *Miss* Nevin, if you don't mind.'

Mrs Buckley came into the living area and sat down on the couch. 'My first name's Fionnuala,' she said. 'Would you mind if I called you by yours?'

'Breda,' said Aidan's mother.

'Well, Breda, I hope you don't think I'm being intrusive, or judgemental. I'm the last person in the world to tell another mother how to take care of her own child.'

'So why did you come here? You want to talk about the weather? I wouldn't be able to help you there, because I haven't been outside today.'

'I've come to talk to you about Aidan.'

'What's he done now? Have you been tossing rockers and breaking windies again, Aidan? I know for sure that you haven't been fighting. He never fights, you know that? I keep telling him to stand up for himself but he won't. He's always been funky. Just like his father. One sniff of trouble and he's gone.'

Mrs Buckley said, 'It's about Aidan's hygiene. To be absolutely honest with you, he never seems to be clean, and his clothes are always dirty, and he smells.'

'He's a young lad. What the feck do you expect? All young lads smell.'

'I'm sorry, but they don't. Not as badly as Aidan, anyway. And because of his hygiene problem, he's bullied at school by all of the other children.'

'Including your Sinead, from what Aidan's told me.'

'Yes, you're right. Sinead has been as guilty as all of the others. But now she's realised how unhappy Aidan must be, and she's apologised for being so cruel to him. That's why she's suggested that I come here and talk to you and see if we can't find a way for him to clean himself up, so to speak.'

Aidan's mother took another drag on her cigarette, and when she spoke, smoke came out of her mouth with every word, and out of her nostrils, too.

'I'll say this, Fionnuala. I've been taking good care of Aidan ever since I gave birth to him. His father didn't want to know him, and my family turned me out for getting knocked up without a wedding ring on my finger, and they've never spoken to me since, nor given me a cent of support, not ever. If I hadn't been taken in by a Traveller fellow I wouldn't even have this home to live in.'

'So what's happened to him? This Traveller fellow?'

'He was killed in some fight about a horse – stabbed. Five years ago – six, maybe. I don't know. But at least I have somewhere to live and so does Aidan, and how I bring him up is my business.'

'Breda, you don't understand that Aidan has no friends. His teacher won't even let him sit at the front of the class because he smells so much. Unless we can work out a way of getting him clean, he's going to have no future. Not in school, not in college, not in finding himself a job. Who's going to employ him if he smells so badly that nobody will go near him?'

'All right, for feck's sake,' said Aidan's mother. 'I'll send him along to the shops to buy some soap. I don't suppose you want him to wear perfume as well, do you? I wouldn't want him bullied for smelling like a batty boy.'

'It's going to take much more than soap,' said Mrs Buckley. 'He's in desperate need of new clothes and new shoes and a shower or a bath at least every other day.'

'And how am I supposed to buy him new clothes and new shoes, and how do I pay for all that hot water? I've barely enough to keep body and soul together.'

'You could stop smoking and drinking, Breda, or cut down at least.'

'Well, that's easy for you to say. But if I couldn't have a smoke now and again, and a gat or two, I might as well take myself down to the river and throw myself in.'

'Supposing I give you some money to help Aidan clean himself up?' said Mrs Buckley. She opened her bag and took out her purse. 'They sell packs of three school shirts in Penney's for only twelve euros, as well as really cheap socks and underpants. And he could do with a new sweater too.'

'I don't need charity, thank you,' said Aidan's mother. 'They might be giving Aidan a hard time at school, but I'll not have anybody saying that I'm a beggar.'

'All right, then, let me *lend* you the money. Look, here's fifty euros. Pay me back whenever you can. It's Aidan's well-being I'm worried about, not your reputation.'

'Ah, gone on to fuck,' said Aidan's mother, and spat on the floor. 'I don't know how you have the brass nerve to come around here and tell me how to look after my own son. Go on, get yourself out of here.'

Mrs Buckley snapped her purse shut and stood up. 'I'm serious, Breda. If you don't make sure that Aidan has a regular wash and his clothes are clean, I'm going to report you to Tusla.'

'Do you think I care? You can report me to whoever you like. Now, let me see the back of you, you interfering bitch.'

Mrs Buckley held her ground. 'You don't seem to understand. Tusla have the authority to take Aidan away from here and put him into care.'

'You listen to me,' said Aidan's mother. She reached for her cigarette packet and took out a cigarette. 'Aidan is my son and nobody's going to take him away from me. Now, get out of here, before I slap you in the kite.'

'All right, then,' said Mrs Buckley. 'You don't leave me any choice, do you? I'm going to call Tusla about Aidan and tell them how badly you've been neglecting him. If they don't make an application to the district court to have him taken into care, I'll be amazed.'

She stepped out of the door and down the steps.

Aidan followed her. 'You won't really, will you?' he asked her.

'Report you to Tusla? Of course I will. You can't go on living like this. What's going to happen when you grow up and go to Meánscoil? And after you leave, and try to find yourself a job?'

She started to walk away. Aidan stood still for a moment, watching her, and he then ran after her.

'Please, don't,' he said. 'I don't care what they say about

me in school. I don't want to get my ma into trouble. I don't want to leave her. Please.'

'It's no use, Aidan,' said Mrs Buckley. 'Once Tusla find you a foster parent to take care of you, and feed you properly – once you don't smell so bad any more – your whole life will be so much happier. Your ma needs help, too, the state of her. It's all for the good, believe me.'

Mrs Buckley continued to walk towards the entrance to the halting site, past a broken-down caravan and a tractor with no wheels. The path curved around the side of the dump, where a new load of rubbish had been tipped that afternoon. A flock of seagulls was clustered all over it, flapping and fighting and screaming like frustrated children.

Aidan looked around. There was nobody else in sight, only him and Mrs Buckley. The sky was grey and there was no wind at all. He saw a length of rusty angle iron, about a metre long, which looked as if it had been part of a demolished shed. He clambered up the side of the dump and picked it up, and then clambered back down again.

He ran after Mrs Buckley, his shoes pattering on the path, although the seagulls were screaming so loudly that she probably didn't hear him. As he came closer, he lifted up the length of angle iron, and hit her with it, as hard as he could.

He had tried to hit her on the head, but she was walking fast and he only managed to strike her between the shoulder blades. All the same, she stumbled and fell to her knees, raising both hands to shield herself. Aidan gripped the angle iron in both hands now and hit her again, much harder. This time he gave her a crack on the back of the head, and she pitched forward into the mud.

He looked around again, panting, just to make sure that nobody had seen him. Mrs Buckley was lying face-down, and one side of her curly blonde hair was glistening crimson with blood. Her fingers were twitching and he could see that he was still breathing, so he hadn't killed her. He wondered if he ought to hit her again, but then he heard his mother calling out.

'Aidan! Aid! Where the feck are you, boy? I need you to fetch me some more fags!'

She was just out of sight, and he knew that she wouldn't come out looking for him, not the way that she was dressed, but all the same he realised that he had to hide Mrs Buckley as soon as he could. He gripped the sleeve of her raincoat and heaved her over on to her back. Her eyes were closed, although her eyelids were fluttering, and her face was as white as candle wax. There was gritty black mud sticking to her lips and her eyebrows.

Aidan bent over and took hold of her, underneath her armpits, Gradually, he dragged her across the path to the edge of the dump, and then up the sloping heaps of rubbish. He was gasping with the effort of it, and his nose was running down his upper lip, but he licked at his snot and carried on tugging. Mrs Buckley stayed completely inert as he pulled her over scores of clanking bottles, and then a sodden layer of brown horsehair matting that his shoes sank into, with a squelch.

When he reached the highest point of the dump, he paused for a moment to catch his breath. A mud-spattered Toyota turned into the halting site and drove down the path, but he didn't think that its occupants noticed him. He bent over again and carried on pulling Mrs Buckley across a stinking landscape of baked bean tins and dirty nappies and crumbling plasterboard.

At last he managed to drag her under the shadow of the overhanging trees. He left her lying on the ground and went over to the old domed fridge. He tugged three times at the door handle and managed to open it. Inside it had a pale green plastic lining, and two wire shelves. In one corner there was a small pool of dirty rainwater because the rubber seal around the door had perished.

Aidan slid out the shelves and threw them away, as far as he could. He kept the door propped open with a broken fruit box and then he went back to Mrs Buckley. She was still unconscious, although it looked as if her head had stopped bleeding. He rolled her over and over until she was resting right up against the side of the fridge. Then, inch by inch, mewling in the back of his throat with the strain of it, he humped her up inside it, so that she was sitting upright, although her head was hanging forward.

He wiped his nose on his sleeve and then he wrestled off her turquoise rushers so that he could more easily bend her knees.

'Mrs Buckley?' he said. Then, a little louder: 'Mrs Buckley?'

She didn't respond, and he was glad that she didn't, because he didn't know what he would have said or done if she had. He stood up and knocked away the fruit box with his foot, Then he took one last look at Mrs Buckley before he closed the fridge door. Unlike modern fridge doors, it had a catch, which meant that it couldn't be pushed open from the inside. It went *klikk*, and then he was standing under the trees on his own, beside that battered metal gravestone, with the blurred grey letters RIP still visible on it. It was starting to rain, and the rain made a crackling sound as it fell on the dump, as if it had caught fire.

Aidan buried Mrs Buckley's rushers underneath a heap of rotting compost. Then he climbed back down the dump, and crossed the muddy concrete to his mobile home. Although it was raining harder now, the door was still open, and he could hear bursts of laughter from the television.

'Oh, there you are,' said his mother, her head wreathed in cigarette smoke. 'I was wondering where the feck you'd got to. So long as you didn't go off with that do-gooding Buckley woman.'

'Oh, I would yeah,' said Aidan. 'Do you have anything in for tea or do you want me to go and fetch some pies?'

His mother waved smoke away with her hand and looked at him narrowly. 'Something's bothering you, Aid. What is it?'

'Nothing.'

'Don't lie to me, I'm your mother. I should know when something's bothering you.'

'Nothing. It's just that—' Aidan hesitated, and then he said, 'Just don't let's tell nobody that Mrs Buckley was here, all right?'

'And why would I?'

'I don't want nobody taking me away, that's all.'

'Well, sure, and nor neither do I. What would I do without you? Who would I send to get the messages, like, do you know what I mean? Don't you worry, Aid, so far as I'm concerned I never saw Mrs Buckley in my life, and I hope I never see her again.'

***

That night, at about one in the morning, when his mother was harshly snoring on the couch, Aidan switched off the television. He picked up his mother's cigarette lighter from the floor, pushed it into his pocket, and then went into the kitchenette. There, he opened the cutlery drawer and took out a small sharp knife, the one that his mother usually used for cutting string. Then he reached up and opened the top cupboard where she kept the pie dishes and the saucepans that she never used these days, and took down a screw-top pickle jar. It now contained only fifteen punts, which she said she was saving for the time when the Irish grew sick of the euro and wanted to change back to their own currency. Aidan took the banknotes out and dropped them into the cutlery drawer with the teaspoons.

He put on his worn-down runners although he didn't bother to lace them up. Then, very quietly, he opened the front door and stepped outside, closing the door just as quietly behind him. He needn't have worried: his mother had drunk most of a bottle of Paddy's and a Land Rover could have crashed into the side of their mobile home without waking her up.

It was still raining, but the rain was very fine, more like dandelion puffs than rain – jinny-jos Aidan had always called them – and it sparkled in the few overhead lights that were strung around the halting site.

He climbed up the side of the dump, the soles of his runners slipping on the wet rubbish. The night was quiet except for the distant sound of traffic and the mournful hooting of a tanker on the River Lee far below. When he reached the fridge, he stopped and listened for a while, in case he heard knocking from inside it, or Mrs Buckley calling out for help, but there was silence.

With his heart beating fast, he took hold of the door handle and clicked the latch. He opened the door only a few inches to begin with, taking his mother's cigarette lighter out of his pocket and snapping it into life. The flame showed him that Mrs Buckley was still hunched up inside the fridge with her head hanging down. The blood in her hair had clotted into thick maroon lumps. At first Aidan thought that she might be dead, but when he opened the door wider, he could hear her breath softly rattling in her lungs.

'Mrs Buckley?' he said, not to wake her but to make sure that she was still completely unconscious. 'Mrs Buckley?' he said again, but she didn't stir.

Now he opened the door wide and wedged it with the broken fruit box, and that gave him enough illumination from the halting site lights. He knelt down in the wet leafy soil in front of the fridge and unscrewed the lid of the pickle jar. Then he took hold of Mrs Buckley's left ankle, levering her leg so that it was sticking out straight. He did the same with her right leg, so that she was now sitting, rather than crouching. This enabled him to reach the front of her turquoise raincoat, and twist open the top three buttons. Once he had pulled her raincoat open, he found that she was wearing a bobbly white jumper underneath. Taking out the small kitchen knife, he sawed the jumper open from the neckline right down to the waist.

Mrs Buckley suddenly let a low *urrrhhhhhhhh*. Aidan

froze. His heart was beating so hard now that it hurt, but Mrs Buckley didn't move, and didn't make another sound.

Underneath her jumper she was wearing only a sheer white bra. Aidan wiped his running nose on the back of his hand, and then he began to cut away the elastic between the cups. Once the cups had fallen apart, he pulled her jumper to one side and bared her small right breast.

He hesitated for several seconds, watching her chest rising and falling as she breathed. He could never smell his own bad odour, but he could smell Mrs Buckley's perfume. It was flowery and sweet – jasmine and pink pepper and patchouli, not that Aidan knew what they were. The perfume seemed to fill not only his nostrils but his entire brain, and for some reason that he couldn't understand it made him feel both sad and angry. Sad because she smelled like a happy family life that he could never hope to have; and angry for the same reason. *Why did God choose* me *to be Cheeseboy, and then turn His back on me, as if it was my fault? I was only a baby when I was born – I didn't have any choice. Why me?*

He took hold of her cold right nipple between finger and thumb, stretching it out as far as he could. His eyes began to fill up with tears, and he had to blink so that he could clearly see what he was doing. Very slowly, taking infinite care, he sliced her entire nipple away from her breast, including the pale pink areola. Blood poured copiously out of her breast at first, but after a few moments the flow was reduced to a hesitant but persistent drip.

Aidan dropped the severed nipple into the pickle jar. Then he reached inside Mrs Buckley's jumper and lifted out her left breast. By now he was trying not to sob, but he was determined to do this. He was determined to show everybody that he wasn't some freak of nature, that everybody was just the same as him, except that they had been born under luckier stars. It wasn't *his* fault that he was Cheeseboy, so why did he have to be punished? He wasn't given occasional punishments: for breaking a window, say, or hobbling an apple, or being cheeky to the teacher. He was punished every single day, every single week, every single month – and, as far as he could tell, for the rest of his life, just for being him.

He sliced away Mrs Buckley's left nipple, too, and dropped that into the pickle jar. The folds of her stomach were streaked now with thin parallel runnels of blood.

Once he had screwed the lid back on the jar, he forced both of Mrs Buckley's knees back up. She had slipped down a little since he had opened the door, and he had to wedge his hands under her arms and heave her back upright three or four inches, so that he would be able to close it again. As it was, he had to twist both of her feet sideways before the door would shut completely.

He climbed back down the dump without looking back at the fridge. Halfway down, he slipped on a sheet of rain-slick hardboard and dropped the pickle jar. It fell somewhere in the darkness, and he had to grope around in some stringy wet muck before he found it.

He had almost reached the bottom of the dump when a white Garda patrol car appeared at the entrance to the halting site. It stopped there for a while, and then it turned down the path and started coming slowly in his direction. Aidan jumped down the last few feet to the path, and then ran as fast as he could towards his mobile home. He just managed to reach it and climb the steps before the patrol car came around the curve in the path.

Once he was inside, he pushed the pickle jar into the space under his bed. Then he pulled off his jacket and his shirt, unfastened his belt and kicked off his shorts. By the time he heard footsteps outside, he was wearing only his vest and his pants and his wrinkly grey socks – but then he always wore his school socks to bed in the winter.

He heard thick-soled boots climbing up the wooden steps outside, and then there was a sharp knocking at the door.

'Gardaí!' said a loud voice. 'Would you open up, please! We need to have a word with you!'

Aidan waited, holding his breath. He reckoned that if he answered the door immediately, the guards would wonder why a boy of his age was still awake when it was almost two o'clock in the morning.

There was a long pause, and then another knock, much more insistent this time.

'Hallo in there! Gardaí! Would you open the door please! We have to talk to you urgent-like!'

Aidan went to the door and opened it. A male garda was standing outside in his yellow high-viz jacket, while a female garda was waiting for him at the bottom of the steps.

'Are you Aidan Nevin?' the garda asked him.

Aidan nodded, but didn't speak.

'Is your mother home?' said the garda, trying to see past Aidan into the living area.

'She's sleeping,' said Aidan.

'All right, but would you wake her up for us, please?'

'I can't.'

'What do you mean you can't?'

'Once she's asleep I can't wake her up. Nobody can.'

'Why's that, then? Has she been taking sleeping pills? Or is it something else she's been ingesting?'

Aidan frowned, as if he didn't understand what the garda meant by 'ingesting'.

'Come on, son,' said the garda. 'Has she been sniffing coke, or smoking weed, or drinking?'

'She's beat out, like, that's all,' said Aidan.

'Well, I'm looking for a woman called Mrs Buckley,' the garda told him. 'Her daughter Sinead's a friend of yours from school.'

'No, she's not,' said Aidan.

'She says she is.'

'She's not. Nobody is. I don't have no friends at school.'

The female garda came up the steps behind her colleague and said, 'Sinead says her mother went home with you earlier, Aidan, so that she could meet *your* mother.'

'She didn't,' said Aidan.

'That's what Sinead told us. She said that you'd been having trouble at school. You've been bullied, that's what she said, because you hadn't been able to keep yourself quite as clean as most of the other children – through no fault at all of your own. That's why her mother went home with you, to see if she could help *your* mother.'

'My ma doesn't need no help. My ma's grand altogether.'

'Aidan – you're absolutely sure that Mrs Buckley didn't come back with you?' asked the female garda. 'The thing is, she left home yesterday saying that she was going to meet you, but she hasn't been seen since. Her family's fierce worried, as I expect you can imagine.'

'I haven't seen her,' said Aidan.

The male garda said, 'You know that it's against the law to tell lies to the guards, don't you?'

'Yes,' said Aidan.

'I'm afraid you're going to have to wake your mother,' said the female garda. 'We don't like to disturb her, but this is a very serious matter.'

'I can't,' Aidan told her. 'I could shake her and shake her but she would never wake up.'

The two gardaí glanced at each other. 'I'll tell you what we'll do,' said the male garda. 'We'll send another guard around in the morning, when she's awake, just to make sure. Meanwhile, if you see Mrs Buckley, or you hear from her, you ring us at once, okay?'

'We don't have a phone,' said Aidan.

'In that case, go to the Garda station on Watercourse Road and tell them so.'

'Okay,' said Aidan. 'Can I go back to bed now?'

The gardaí stood looking for a few moments at this white-faced boy with his badly cut hair, standing in the open doorway of this rundown mobile home in his grubby vest and yellow-spotted underpants and sagging grey socks.

Then the female garda smiled at him and said, 'Yes, Aidan. You can go back to bed now.'

At eight o'clock, just before Aidan was due to set off for school, two different gardaí came knocking at the door. They were both male – one tall and one short – and they both looked as if they wished they were anywhere else but here at this halting site. A group of seven or eight Travellers were already beginning to gather around their car, their arms folded and their eyes narrowed as if they weren't going to tolerate the presence of the Garda on their patch for very long, and for their own good health they had better not try to arrest anybody.

Aidan's mother was awake and dressed in a drooping beige cardigan and skin-tight black jeans. She had curlers in her hair and she was standing in the kitchenette spooning her breakfast of meatballs in onion gravy straight out of the tin, and smoking her first cigarette of the day.

Aidan opened the door and said, 'Ma, it's the law.'

'What in the name of feck do they want?'

The tall gingery garda standing on the step outside said, 'We're looking for a missing woman, ma'am. Mrs Fionnuala Buckley.'

Aidan's mother came to the door, holding her tin of meatballs and her cigarette in one hand and a dessert spoon in the other.

'Who did you say?'

'Mrs Fionnuala Buckley. She's the mother of one of the girls in your son's class at St Jerome's. Her family say that she accompanied your son back home last night so that she could have a word with you about some trouble that he's been having at school.'

Aidan's mother sucked at her cigarette and blew out smoke. 'Never heard of the woman, and even if I had she wasn't here.'

'You're sure about that?'

'Of course I'm sure. Why else would I say it if I wasn't? Any road, what trouble?'

The garda looked down at Aidan, who was surreptitiously picking his nose. 'He's been bullied, apparently.'

'First I've heard of it. Aidan can take care of himself, like, can't you, Aidan?'

Aidan said nothing but rolled up the grollier between finger and thumb and flicked it out of the doorway, unaware that the garda had been watching him.

'According to Mrs Buckley's family, your son has a hygiene problem.'

'And what business is that of theirs, whoever they are? Aidan's ten, for the love of God, and what do you expect from a boy of ten? Do they want him to go around smelling all flowery like some fecking steamer? He'd be bullied then all right.'

'So Mrs Buckley didn't come to see you last night?'

'Like I've just said to you, I don't even know the woman. Now, is it all right with you if I finish my breakfast?'

The garda looked around. One of the burliest Travellers was sitting on the bonnet of his patrol car now, and the rest of them were clustered around it as if they were planning to overturn it if the two gardaí didn't soon leave.

'All right,' said the garda. 'But we might be back with a warrant so. For your sake, you'd better be telling me the truth. If Mrs Buckley's been here, we'll be able to tell, no matter what you do to hide it.'

'You wouldn't give Aidan here a lift to school, would you?' asked his mother. 'I don't want him to get into trouble for being late.'

'Sorry, ma'am,' said the garda, who could see that Aidan was digging his finger into his nose again. 'That's against regulations, like. Health and safety.'

'Well if his teacher gives him lines for being late I'll bring them around to the pigsty and you can do them for him.'

***

Five days went by, and there was still no sign of Mrs Buckley. Since both Aidan and his mother emphatically denied that they had seen her, and nobody else at the halting site had seen her, either, the Garda appeared to be convinced now that she had not taken Aidan back home that afternoon, even if she had told Sinead that she intended to.

Detectives interviewed both Sinead and her father, and it turned out that Mr and Mrs Buckley had been having some marital problems – mainly that Mrs Buckley had suspected her husband of having an affair with an attractive young assistant who worked in their store. Mr Buckley strenuously denied it, but the detectives noted that her suspicions might have given Mrs Buckley sufficient motive for leaving him, and not telling him where she had gone.

Her picture appeared in the *Echo*, and on social media, and her disappearance was reported to the National Missing Persons Helpline, as well as the Cork City Missing Persons Search and Recovery Unit, but apart from that there was little that anybody could do. On the day that she had disappeared, there were four thousand two hundred and two people missing in Ireland, and Fionnuala Buckley had simply made it four thousand, two hundred and three.

Aidan went to school every day, and every day he took the short cut over the dump and past the domed refrigerator. He had decided to wait a week until he took a look inside it, by which time he was sure that Mrs Buckley would be dead. The rubber seal around the fridge door was perished, so he knew that she wouldn't have suffocated, but by then he reckoned that she would have died of thirst and starvation.

Every day he sat quietly in his isolated seat on the right-hand side of the classroom, and carried on with his writing and his drawing. As always, he ignored the gibes of his classmates about his smell, although their bullying had become noticeably less vicious since Mrs Buckley had gone missing.

Sinead didn't appear at school until the following Monday, and when she did she looked pale and strained, with purple rings under her eyes. On the first morning of her return, she wouldn't look at Aidan, and whenever she saw him coming along the corridor, or out on the playground, she turned her back on him. She had clearly been warned by her father and probably the Garda, too, not to have any contact with him.

Every night, after his mother had fallen asleep, Aidan would reach under his bed for the pickle jar. He would hold it up to the light, to see how Mrs Buckley's nipples were turning brown, and how an amber liquid was collecting in the bottom of the jar as they gradually putresced.

Having her nipples in his possession like this made him feel strangely calm and powerful. They were a physical trophy to prove that for the first time in his life, he had turned the tables on all of those people who had mocked him and bullied him. Now he was causing them the same fear, depression and anxiety that they had always caused him, and the most satisfying part about it was that they didn't have the slightest inkling *who* was making them feel so distressed. If only they realised that it was him who had made Mrs Buckley vanish off the face of the earth. Him – *Cheeseboy*.

He also relished the fact that he now owned the same

nipples that had suckled Sinead when she was a baby. That would teach her to patronise him, and insult his mother, and try to have him taken away from her. *I have killed the very person who gave you life, and cut off the very nipples that fed you before you even understood who you were – so what do you think about that?*

He knew that what he had done would change his life forever, but whatever happened to him now could hardly be worse than more years of bullying. He could have thrown himself in the River Lee – that was what most people in Cork did if they couldn't bear their lives any longer. But why give Michael O'Reilly and his friends the satisfaction? Sinead might cry if he drowned himself, but then Sinead had always been a drama queen, and the staff of St Jerome Bunscoil would probably breathe a collective sigh of relief.

He could just imagine Miss O'Connell walking into the classroom and sniffing loudly, and then saying, 'That terrible smell seems to have gone now.' And the whole class rocking with laughter.

On Friday morning, when he sat down at his desk, he discovered that he had left his pen in the pocket of his anorak, which he had hung up in the cloakroom.

He left the classroom and walked as fast as he could along the corridor. Running was forbidden. As he turned the corner into the cloakroom, he almost bumped into Sinead.

Aidan didn't know it, but the God who had turned His back on him when he was born decided that now was the moment to click the switch that would set his destiny into motion.

'Sinead!' said Aidan.

Sinead tried to sidestep past him, but he sidestepped, too, to block the doorway.

'Why won't you talk to me?' he asked her. 'Jesus, Sinead. You won't even *look* at me, like.'

'Why do you think?' Sinead retorted.

'Is it because of your ma going missing? I never *saw* your ma. Honest. I told the shades that I never saw her and the shades believe me.'

'It's nothing to do with my ma going missing.'

'Then what is it? Come on, out of everybody in the class, you're the only one who ever talked nice to me. And now you won't talk to me at all.'

Sinead stared at him and even Michael O'Reilly had never fixed him with such a look of total disgust.

'Because you *smell*, that's why. You smell like cheese. In fact you smell worse than cheese. You smell like poo and cheese, all mixed up. Now, let me go, because you're making me craw sick just standing there.'

Stunned, Aidan stepped back to let her pass. He felt as if she had slapped him across the face, twice. She didn't yet know what he had done to her mother, so he thought that she might still feel some sympathy for him. After all, none of this would have happened if she hadn't seen him crying in geography, and taken pity on him.

But he would show her. He would show *all* of them – Michael O'Reilly and Brendan Hagerty and Denis Grace and all the rest of them, including Miss O'Connell. They thought *he* smelled, did they? Well, he had something that smelled even worse – something that would give them the gawks so bad they wouldn't be able to forget it for the rest of their lives.

He took down his anorak and struggled into it. His mother had bought it for him last year in the Irish Cancer Society shop on Princes Street and it was a size too small for him. He opened the door that gave out on to the playground and cautiously looked around. The caretaker was around the back of the school, making a loud clattering noise with the rubbish bins, and all of the teachers were still in the staffroom. He ran across the playground and out through the school gates, and then he pelted up the road, heading home.

'No Aidan today,' said Miss O'Connell, looking around the classroom. 'Well, that's very unusual. Thank Heaven for small mercies.'

She couldn't remember the last time that Aidan had taken a day off school. He always turned up, even if he had a persistent cough or a cold that had him monotonously sniffing snot bubbles all day.

She chalked a sketch map of South America on the blackboard, and then she said, 'Here... this is South America, and today we're going to find out all about El Niño. Now, does anybody know what El Niño is?'

Denis Grace put up his hand. 'It's a South American police car, miss! You know, like *Ni-ño! Ni-ño!*'

The children were still laughing when the classroom door swung open. They all turned around, and there, standing in the doorway, was Aidan. He was still wearing his anorak, and he was breathing hard.

'Aidan, you're very late,' said Miss O'Connell. 'I thought you might not be coming in to school today.'

Aidan didn't answer her, but entered the classroom and walked halfway down the aisle, until he was standing beside Sinead.

'Aren't you going to hang up your coat?' Miss O'Connell asked him.

'Yes, come on, Cheeseboy!' said Brendan Hagerty. 'We're having this cool lesson about South American police cars!'

There was more laughter but it quickly died away. Aidan reached into the right-hand pocket of his anorak and tugged out the pickle jar.

'Aidan—' said Miss O'Connell sharply. 'What are you doing? Take off your coat, boy, and sit in your usual place. Otherwise you'll be writing lines for bad behaviour, I promise you!'

'Yes – sit down, or Miss'll be giving you a cheeser!' called out Denis Grace. A cheeser was what the children called a hard clip across the back of the head with the edge of a ruler. 'A cheeser for the Cheeseboy!'

But Aidan suddenly let out a weird, high-pitched screech, which silenced them all. He held up the pickle jar and showed it around, like a magician demonstrating that he wasn't hiding anything.

'You think that I smell!' he said, and he was very close to tears. 'You think that I have a bang off of me! Well, you *all* will, when you're dead! You'll all go rotten, after you're buried, and nobody will want to come anywhere near you!'

He unscrewed the jar and waved it from side to side.

'Smell the benjy off of this!' he said, and now he was almost screeching. 'This is Mrs Buckley's nips! Yes, I cut off her nips off and here they are! Just smell the benjy off of this!'

The children let out shrieks of horror. Sinead had shifted herself as far away from Aidan as she could, so that she was pressed right up close to her deskmate Kathleen Lynn, but Aidan brandished the pickle jar closed to her face.

'You like the smell of this? This is your ma's own nips, gone rotten! And you say that *I* smell like cheese – cheese all mixed up with poo? Smell this! This is your ma! Smell this!'

With that, he threw the contents of the jar on to Sinead's workbook – two curled-up nipples that had turned blackened and shrunk, and a splatter of amber liquid.

'Aidan!' shouted Miss O'Connell, and came stalking out from behind her desk. She seized Aidan's sleeve and wrenched him around, but he twisted his arm free and then he kicked at her thin, maroon-stockinged shins.

Before Miss O'Connell could grab him again, he ran out of the classroom and along the corridor towards the front door. Mrs Rooney was coming out of her office as he hurtled past her, and she snapped out, 'Nevin! No running!'

But then he was gone, leaving the front door wide open.

Miss O'Connell came panting up to Mrs Rooney. 'We need to call the guards,' she said.

'What's happened?' asked Mrs Rooney. 'Has Aidan been fighting? Is somebody hurt?'

'Worse than that. I think he's murdered Mrs Buckley.'

★★★

Aidan didn't stop running until he reached the gap in the fence. He squeezed his way between the slats and then he climbed over the dump, jumping and bounding like a mountain goat.

He was surging with adrenaline, but he wasn't frightened. He was triumphant. He had shown them at last. He had terrified them, far more than they had ever frightened him. He had no idea what was going to happen to him now, but he didn't care. They would have nightmares about what he had done to them for the rest of their lives.

What kind of cheese are you today, Mrs Buckley? The stinkiest nipple-cheese, that's what! And now I'm going to find out just how much the rest of you stinks!

He slid across a wet sheet of corrugated iron, and then he ducked under the trees until he reached the dome-topped fridge. He took hold of the door handle, gripping it tight, but he hesitated for a moment before he tugged it open. He was excited, and breathless, but he couldn't begin to imagine what Mrs Buckley must look like by now, and he was almost afraid to find out. He was sure that he could smell her, even before he had opened the fridge door.

He opened it, and propped it open with the broken fruit box. Mrs Buckley was crouched inside, as before, and the ripe, cloying smell she was giving off was overwhelming. All the same, she didn't look as decomposed as Aidan had expected. She had been trapped in here for over a week, but because the door didn't fit properly she had been able to breathe, and there was a triangular puddle of rainwater beside her, although now it was stained brown with faeces.

Aidan was strangely disappointed that she hadn't yet turned green, and wasn't enormously bloated like the dead horse that he had once seen lying in the field next to the halting site. He would just have to leave her in here for a few days longer.

He was about to close the fridge door when he noticed the silver necklace she was wearing, with a silver butterfly pendant, decorated with amethysts. If he took that, he was sure that he could sell it, and make enough money to escape somewhere. He was sure that if he could hide out somewhere for long enough, people would forget all about Mrs Buckley, and him, and he would be able to come back and live with his mother, just as before.

He reached out and twisted the necklace around, so that he could open its clasp. The skin of Mrs Buckley's neck was chilly and flaccid and very slightly sticky, but he was thrilled by the feel of it, because she was dead. She was an actual dead body, and he had killed her.

He was still struggling to open the small lobster clasp when her spine suddenly went rigid, as if she had been electrocuted. His first thought was that this was what happened to people when they were dead: they went stiff. Perhaps this was only happening now because he had opened the fridge door and exposed her body to the air.

Before he could react, though, her left arm jerked up like a railway signal and she seized his wrist, digging her fingernails deep into his tendons. He let out a scream of fright and tried to jerk his hand free, but then she gripped his left wrist, too, just as tightly, and pulled him towards her.

He screamed again, but Mrs Buckley screamed back at him, right in his face, a with a blast of fetid breath and a speckling of rancid spit.

The two of them struggled in an awkward see-saw motion – Mrs Buckley trying to pull herself out of the fridge, and Aidan trying to push her back into it.

Aidan had the strength of panic, but Mrs Buckley had the greater strength of sheer desperation. She heaved at him, and he tumbled up against her, and as he did so, he kicked away the fruit box that had been holding the door open. It swung shut behind him, and the catch clicked.

They were tangled close together, the two of them, face to face. Aidan's knees were pushed between Mrs Buckley's legs, and his elbows were digging into her chest. Their foreheads were pressed together, painfully hard. Both of them screamed, and both of them tried to force the door open with their feet, but the catch held firm.

They kept on screaming, for nearly half an hour. Then they stopped, exhausted, and both of them began to sob.

There were sightings of both of them in Limerick, and Kenmare, and somebody reported seeing Mrs Buckley as far away as Dundalk.

The Cork City Missing Persons and Recovery Unit plied their way up and down the River Lee searching for their bodies with their Humminbird sonar scanner. They found the body of a sixty-seven-year-old father from Mayfield who had been missing for five months, but there was no trace of Aidan or Mrs Buckley.

Seven weeks later, a girl of three went missing from the Spring Lane halting site. Her parents told the Garda that she liked to play on the dump, and so the Dog Support Unit was sent to see if they could locate her.

The little girl was found safe and well, hiding at home because she had taken some sweets when she had been strictly told not to. But the Labrador from the dog support unit led its handler to the dome-topped fridge underneath the overhanging trees.

When the gardaí opened the fridge door, they found it hard to understand at first what they were looking at. Both bodies were locked together in a putrid embrace, their flesh swollen like pale green pillows, their leg bones protruding through their skin. Their faces were jammed close together, as if they were kissing, except that Mrs Buckley's face looked like a Hallowe'en turnip, carved into a mask, while Aidan had hardly any flesh on his face at all. He was a skull, with most of the skin and flesh ripped off his cheekbones, and his eyes nothing but empty sockets. Even his lips were gone, and half of his tongue.

It took a while for the gardaí to realise that Mrs Buckley had been eating Aidan's face in a futile attempt to stay alive.

Mrs Buckley was buried a week later at St Catherine's Cemetery. Over two hundred family and friends attended, and her grave was heaped with flowers. Sinead wore a black coat with a black velvet collar but didn't cry. She had cried enough already.

Aidan was buried at night in a cillín, an overgrown graveyard for unbaptised children and unrepentant sinners, in Glanmire. Although the practice of burying children in cilliní was obsolete, his mother had wanted him buried there to be close to his stillborn sister.

It was so dark when three Travellers buried him that the only glow came from her cigarette.

From the date of the funeral, Buckley's Stores in Ballyvolane no longer stocked cheese.

★

About the Authors

GRAHAM MASTERTON is best known as a writer of horror and thrillers, but his career as an author spans many genres, including historical epics and sex-advice books. His first horror novel, *The Manitou*, became a bestseller and was made into a film starring Tony Curtis. In 2019, Graham was given a Lifetime Achievement Award by the Horror Writers Association. He is also the author of the Katie Maguire series of crime thrillers, which have sold more than 1.5 million copies worldwide.

DAWN G HARRIS published her first full-length novel, *Diviner*, in 2018; a supernatural thriller with a compelling twist of psychology, which has now been released in a French language edition as *La Divinatrice*. She has written short horror stories together with Graham Masterton, based on her original ideas, and they have sold internationally. Widely praised for her innovative style, her writing has featured in US publication *The Horror Zine* and on the UK television show *This Time Next Year*. Dawn has also completed her next novel, a deeply psychological thriller with a ghostly edge.

Printed and bound by CPI Group (UK) Ltd, Croydon, CR0 4YY

01/02/2025

01829692-0001